Publisher's Note:

Thank you for purchasing this book. It began as an idea, was shaped by the creativity of its talented author, and was subsequently molded into the book you have before you by a team of editors and designers.

Like all EDGE books, this book is the result of the creative talents of a dedicated team of individuals who all believe that books (whether in print or pixels) have the magical ability to take you on an adventure to new and wondrous places powered by the author's imagination.

As EDGE's publisher, I hope that you enjoy this book. It is a part of our ongoing quest to discover talented authors and to make their creative writing available to you.

We also hope that you will share your discovery and enjoyment of this anthology on social media through Facebook, Twitter, Goodreads, Pinterest, etc., and by posting your opinions and/or reviews on Amazon and other review sites and blogs. By doing so, others will be able to share your discovery and passion for this book.

Brian Hades, publisher

~ *THE TESSERACTS SERIES* ~

An Anthology of Canadian Optimistic Fiction

Nevertheless

(Tesseracts Twenty-One)

Selected and Edited by

Rhonda Parrish and Greg Bechtel

EDGE SCIENCE FICTION AND FANTASY PUBLISHING
An Imprint of HADES PUBLICATIONS, INC.
CALGARY

Nevertheless
Tesseracts Twenty-One

EDGE SCIENCE FICTION AND FANTASY PUBLISHING
An Imprint of HADES PUBLICATIONS, INC.
P.O. Box 1714, Calgary, Alberta, T2P 2L7, Canada

The EDGE Team:
Producer: Brian Hades
Acquisitions Editor: Michelle Heumann
Edited by: Rhonda Parrish and Greg Bechtel
Cover Design: Brian Hades
Cover Art Elements: boule13
Book Design: Mark Steele
Publicist: Janice Shoults

ISBN: 978-1-77053-174-1

EDGE Science Fiction and Fantasy Publishing and Hades Publications,
Inc. acknowledges the ongoing support of the Alberta Foundation for the
Arts and the Canada Council for the Arts for our publishing programme.

 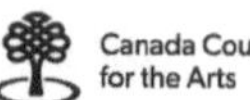

Library and Archives Canada Cataloguing in Publication
CIP Data on file with the National Library of Canada
ISBN: 978-1-77053-174-1
(e-Book ISBN: 978-1-77053-173-4)

FIRST EDITION
(20180916)
Printed in USA
www.edgewebsite.com

Contents

Need something new to read?

Introduction

Rhonda Parrish

When publisher Brian Hades and I discussed themes for this anthology in 2016, he offered me two choices. One was quite dark in tone and, frankly, more along the lines of what I usually edit, and the second was 'Optimistic Speculative Fiction.' The year had been a rough one, and I thought the optimistic angle could provide respite from celebrity deaths, terrorist attacks, viral outbreaks and toxic politics so I chose it.

In our call for submissions we said, "The theme of the anthology is 'optimism' — which doesn't necessarily exclude dark or scary settings — but requires some sort of optimistic twist or element…" and even went out of our way to explicitly state that we weren't looking for saccharine sweetness.

We need not have worried. Considering its theme, this anthology is pretty dark, but I'm okay with that because I believe it reflects the zeitgeist in which we live.

Last November, I sat on my couch watching election results come in while tears rolled down my cheeks. I hadn't voted in the election, it wasn't even in my country, but it broke my heart to watch a man who is the antithesis of all I believe in win it. Sometimes, in fiction, I'm okay when the antagonist wins. But in reality… not so much.

The election results unmoored me. Naively, perhaps, I've always believed that things always, eventually, work themselves out for the best. But this was anything but the best. In fact, it felt like a massive step backward.

For several days I struggled to come to grips with this new reality. I was thin-skinned, prone to tears, and couldn't focus on anything. Then I stumbled across a secret Facebook group filled with an incredibly diverse group of people sharing stories about the good things happening in their lives and, more importantly, the good things they were doing for other people. That group, and the optimistic lens through which it viewed the world, helped me find my feet again. It helped me realize that, as Sonny says in *The Best Exotic Marigold Hotel*, "Everything will be all right in the end. If it's not all right, then it's not yet the end." As far as I was concerned, things were very much not all right, but perhaps that was because I was still in the middle of the story.

In a post-truth world where politics seem especially divisive and their antagonistic spirit slowly seeps down to permeate every aspect of our lives, we need optimistic fiction more than ever but, ironically, such a world may be the most difficult environment in which to create it.

It's relevant, I think, that the most often repeated theme we saw in submissions was 'Everything is horrible and the main character dies, but it's okay because their death brings hope for humanity.' To be fair, many of them were wonderful stories, but there are only so many of those (*cough* one *cough*) you can include in a single anthology.

I wasn't looking for sickeningly sweet, conflict-free stories, but I did want them to contain hope, to leave the readers satisfied with the state of things (at least in the fictional world) at their conclusion.

As Orson Wells famously said (and Sonny paraphrased), "If you want a happy ending, that depends, of course, on where you stop your story." And though a happy ending and an optimistic story aren't the same thing, perhaps they have that one thing in common.

My dearest hope is that these stories, though obviously fiction, may have a real life impact — however small — on someone in the same way that Facebook group did for me. Because after all, as Jack Layton put it, "Love is better than anger. Hope is better than fear. Optimism is better than despair. So let us be loving, hopeful and optimistic. And we'll change the world."

Inside the Spiral

Dorianne Emmerton

How to explain about the yellow place to Derek? Or Sophie? Sophie would want to see what I got there. She's my best friend, but that would be weird. I do want to show Derek, but that could easily be the end of everything between us.

It's impossible to pretend the yellow place doesn't exist. The center of my chest twinges at the thought of never going back. I rub it through my shirt, this silky button-up with a bird of paradise on the left side. It's from here, the store where Sophie and I work.

"Is your tattoo infected or something, Bobby?" she asks, startling me. She must have come from around the rack of wedding dresses. I turn back to rearranging the table of fancy hats to make room for new additions.

"No, I just rub it sometimes. Like a nervous tic, or a good luck thing."

"Yeah, but you do it a lot lately. Like, way more than before," says Sophie.

She knows me so well.

~ ~ ~

Two days ago I met Derek.

It was a sunshiny morning, and I woke up in a good mood, feeling cheerful and pretty femme. My coffee was made with these delicious German chocolate flavored coffee beans from Bulk Barn, and I drank it while contemplating my closet. Bright blue skinny jeans, little red belt, blousy shirt with blue and yellow flowers: the perfect outfit for my mood.

I parted my hair on the side and pulled the larger half down over my forehead, almost hiding my eye, and held it there with product that's good for a slick and smooth look. Lip gloss and boots with a little chunky heel completed the look.

Sophie got into the store shortly after me. The shaved half of her head was all stubbly, and there was a whiff of stale cigarette smoke about her. "Good night?" I asked.

"The best, yeah, totally," she answered and hugged me. Sophie and I both dropped out of university in fourth year, and we're also both total deviants. She's a big reason I love my job. That and the discount. "I can't even tell you because the *Information* is *Too Much*."`

"How many people were at this orgy?" I asked.

She considered a bit and then said "Six. If you don't count the voyeurs."

"Shocked and appalled!" I fluttered my hands near my cheeks. She punched me in the arm.

"Bobby Bobby Bo Bobby, but what about you? Like seriously. How long has it been since you got laid?"

"I'm looking for love. And living vicariously, thank *you* very much."

"You look fantastic today," she said, changing the subject but also giving me a nice compliment.

"Thanks, dahhhling."

By then we had finished setting up, and it was time to open the doors.

The store is in Kensington Market, this really artsy boho neighborhood. Everything is independent, though the condos and Starbucks' are exerting their pressure. We wouldn't have lasted this long if it wasn't for the bulwark of Chinatown surrounding us, with its fish smell and crowded sidewalk grocery shops. We run one of many vintage clothing stores. The owner lives in a condo by the lakeshore and comes in for an hour or so each day, just to annoy us. It used to be a real counter-culture place, as many weed deals going on as clothing sales, but the dude that owned it got both his girlfriends pregnant at the same time. They sold this place and bought some big old house in the country to raise the next generation of freaks. That's the rumor, and there's no reason to disbelieve it. Too bad he's not our boss instead of condo lady, but whatever. It's not a bad job.

We're pretty sure she only hires people who look the part. Everyone who works here has excessive visible piercing and/or tattooing and/or hairdos that involve partial shaving and bright unnatural colors.

None of that describes me. There's a small tattoo of a spiral in the middle of my chest, but that's it, and it's always covered by a shirt at work. The spiral started out as a little dot that I got on my twentieth birthday. I wanted to see how painful it really was before committing to anything, plus I didn't have much money. Since then, every year for my birthday I add an inch of curving line. Eventually my whole front will be a big spiral. It will creep up onto my neck and face. I'll be old by then though.

So I don't really look like the other staff, but my sartorial choices, like being a little all over the place with my gender presentation, must be good enough for the owner. She probably has some sort of Token Flamer requirement. A year or so ago I saw the Help Wanted sign while I was shopping, and I was tired of hustling, so it all just came together.

We've never discussed it, though. She's never asked me anything about it, and I've only ever worn pants to work. Sometimes leggings, but never a skirt.

Sophie suddenly elbowed me. "What?" I hissed.

"That guy!" she whispered. "He was totally checking you out."

There was no guy. I made a face.

"He went into the aisle at the back. Go talk to him." Sophie was so bossy.

"Maybe. Is he hot?"

"I wouldn't tell you to go chasing after some uggo. He was dreamy. If you don't go talk to him, I will."

So I went. Sophie shouldn't get first grabs at a hot guy. She has enough going on already.

"Can I help you find anything?" I asked. He looked at me. Oh my lord. Kind of buff, but not like a roid-ragey gym rat. He probably played on a recreational sports team, maybe volleyball. He was black and had this sleeve tattoo with a lion and other stuff that was hard to make out with my peripheral vision. I wanted to stare, but obviously that would be bad form.

"Sure," he said. "Maybe some shirts. Maybe some music T-shirts. With rappers from the nineties. You know, when it was called rap, not hip-hop? I would wear something like that."

"I have just the thing," I chirped. I actually chirped. That was not playing it cool. It's okay though; I'm not cool. Cool is kind of boring. What I am is *fabulous*.

There was this Wu-Tang shirt I'd been secretly coveting. But it was too big for me, and if anyone else had to have it, this guy should be that person.

"Amazing," he said. "Perfect. Thanks, man." And then he just stood there, holding the shirt in his hand.

"I'm Bobby," I introduced myself. "Like, Robert on my SIN card, but do I look like a Robert? Nuh uh. I'm *such* a Bobby."

"Derek," he said and shook my hand.

The next day was a bit cloudy and felt like a swagger, so I had on a plaid shirt and a big belt with this amazing buckle showing the outline of a moose, and my hair was all messy under a meshback hat. My feet were in Timberlands and those gray woollen socks with the red band around the top.

And then he walked into the store again.

"Derek!" I said. "More T-shirts, or can I interest you in some pants?"

He raised an eyebrow. I smirked. He said, "Bobby. Have a drink with me when your shift is done?"

We had three drinks, nursed over three hours, and by then I was in love. It hasn't happened often, but it's obvious right away. It feels like gravity has gone haywire inside my body. My kidneys float up to my throat, my lungs separate, all my organs in zero-g.

I'm not as rampant as Sophie, but there's no point in waiting when you're in love, so I invited him back to my apartment. As we walked, he slipped his hand into mine.

I didn't even notice the dude coming toward us at first. It's a big city; there are always people on the sidewalk. But then this guy, this asshole, got right in our path and yelled "Fags!"

So I dropped Derek's hand and punched the homophobe in the face. His nose gave way under my knuckles. It was both exhilarating and absolutely disgusting.

I've been called a fag before, and not just when us fags are joking around. But not by a total stranger, and not on the street, and not while a new love was holding my hand for the first time. The fact I was so macho that day may have contributed to my reaction. Blame the Timberlands.

Unsurprisingly, he punched me back. Caught me on the eyebrow, split it open. I threw an upper cut, but all I know about fighting was picked up watching Ultimate Fighting Championship, which is only great because it's so hot. (Really. It's basically gay kink porno. The welterweights are the best.) This time I nicked the guy's chin, but it didn't pack any sort of wallop.

Derek pulled me away, and the man and I looked at each other for a moment, both of us bleeding. Then he ran off.

There was this couple across the street, a girl and a guy, and they asked if we wanted them to call 911. "No," I said. "I started it."

"You did not!" said Derek.

The night seemed ruined, but he still came back to my place. He wanted to make sure I didn't fall asleep in case of a concussion.

When we walked in the door I said, "There's one surefire way to stay awake," and unzipped my pants.

~ ~ ~

The sound of the toilet flushing woke me up. He came out of the bathroom with his clothes on again. The clock said it was past midnight.

"You're going?" I asked.

"Have to. I can't wear the same clothes into work tomorrow." And then he said, "You look pretty bad."

"Gee thanks. And here I thought you were attracted to me."

"No, your face. You were hit in the face. Your eye. You should see a doctor."

"Right," I said. "Text me?"

"Totally," he said, and kissed me before he left.

Instead of falling back asleep, I used the mirror app on my phone to check out my face. My right eyebrow was gigantic, and there were smears of dried blood around it. I poked at the wound. It hurt, but not too bad. It was this weird thing growing on my face. I prodded at it until the scab in the middle broke open and fresh blood came pouring out, all over my hands.

I reached down to wipe the blood on my belly, but my hand landed in a pile of gooey semen. His or mine? A little lick of my finger confirmed it was definitely mine.

I mixed more blood with the come on my belly. What a concoction! It was kind of a turn on, but jerking off didn't appeal right now. So instead of pulling on my cock, I started tracing my spiral tattoo.

Usually that calms me, but this time was different. The cool smear of bodily fluids against my chest felt thrilling. Every small movement caused a vibration in my gut, like I was shaking but only on the inside. It was exciting with a touch of frightening. It reminded me of being really high on ecstasy.

I had started circling in from the outside. When my finger reached the center of my spiral, the little dot from years ago, my vision went all white, then black, then yellow.

Bright yellow, like the middle of the sun. (Except it probably wouldn't be yellow in the center of the actual sun. You'd be dead before you knew what color it was.) This was a warm wash of yellow, like if there was a color for the feeling of the first really nice day of spring. And I was floating in it.

My eyes began to discern shapes bobbing calmly around me. The yellow didn't go away. It just became the background, and there were all these other things suspended in the air. I started to see, and to understand. They were body parts. Not bloody and gruesome but healthy and available. They all wanted me, but not aggressively. They didn't attack me or try to attach themselves against my will. They waited patiently, hoping to be chosen.

I picked a nose out of the air and examined it. It was taller than my own, gracefully arcing upwards. My nose came off easily, with a little popping sound, and the new one attached to my face as soon as it touched skin. The air rushed up an unfamiliar route — what a strange feeling, to breathe differently than I'd ever breathed before! I took it off and tried on a little button nose, then a big bulbous one. It was so simple: try this on for size; if you don't like it, try another.

It was too bad there wasn't also a mirror floating around here, I thought, trying on a bunch of different ears.

Eventually I returned my face to normal and, delighting in weightlessness, swam past the facial features into the pools of larger limbs and started fitting them on. Me with a large arm that reached down to my ankle! Me with the calloused hands of a blue-collar man! Me with the deformed glory of a ballerina's foot!

But those were all dry runs, just playing around. Now it was time: I moved through the limbs to the where the genitals floated. To the cluster of vulvas. This was still gleeful business but also serious. I needed a cunt that would suit me.

There was a vulva with tight black curly hair and flesh the color of pumpernickel. I had tried on facial features that seemed to belong to other races when messing around but, as beautiful as this was, I was far too white to wear it back home. That would be the mother of all cultural appropriations.

Finally I picked out a smallish blond one, with inner lips a bit longer than the outer ones and a clit that protruded like a little raspberry. It looked like it would fit nicely, and it had a great design. What would that clit do while attached to me?

My cock and balls floated where I released them. Leaving them was a bit worrisome. What if I couldn't find them again when I returned? What if I couldn't even come back? It was a risk.

The new parts fit perfectly. Tickling my clit felt like happy lightning shooting up into my torso. I put my finger inside and wiggled it around, squirming and laughing. When I pulled it out it was moist. Then my eyebrow wound spontaneously started to bleed, and I knew I couldn't stay.

I put my wet finger into the blood on my brow and traced the spiral on my chest again, this time from the inside moving out. There was that same shiver deep inside my abdomen. Reaching the outer edges of the tattoo made my vision go black and then white.

And I was in my bed, back in my apartment. Had it all been a dream? A grope between my legs confirmed that it wasn't. There were labia, a vagina, the whole deal! I spent the rest of the night discovering what my newfound things could do.

In the morning I went to the sex shop and bought myself a Hitachi magic wand. Sophie claims it's the Cadillac of vibrators.

I really wanted to wear a dress to work, but how would that play out? I couldn't claim to have transitioned overnight so I put boxer shorts on over my pretty new bits, and then decided to go full butch and put on a shirt and tie.

It was nice. My reflection in the mirror looked very handsome.

Sophie assumed my good mood was because of Derek.

"So you banged him, eh? Are you twitterpated? Of course you are. You guys'll probably date for a few months then whatever." What she assumed about men could fill a warehouse. "But what happened to your face? Rough sex?"

All she got from me was a smile.

Even my boss said, "Bobby, you're always so well dressed, but today especially there's this *je ne sais quoi* about you. But... your eye. Have you seen a doctor?"

I always suspected she liked the cachet of my erratic style more than my actual clothes. But today she liked me all suited up, not suspecting what was underneath.

"Fine," I said. "Better than fine."

~ ~ ~

So that's what happened over the last two days, and Sophie knows something's up because of how much I'm absent-mindedly rubbing my chest. I'm letting her think it's just fledgling-relationship nerves. Which is true, it's just more complicated than it would be otherwise.

Sometimes I forget and go to the bathroom and rediscover my genitals with joyous surprise. But it's upsetting to have to be a girl in secret.

After we lock up, Sophie strokes the Bird of Paradise on my shirt and squawks, "Polly want a cracker?" even though that's a line for a parrot. We do a brief disco dance before we leave the store. She hugs me and asks, "Are you seeing Derek tonight?"

"Haha, maybe." I hurry away.

I put off Derek last night, stayed home and went to the yellow place. I can go back, just as I thought! I didn't trade in my vulva though. She's still new to me; I'm not ready to move on yet. So after doing some silly things, like licking disembodied bums, and assuring myself that I could find my cock and balls, I headed back to reality to try out my Cadillac. (Sophie was right. It really is that good.)

Today Derek texted three times, and now he's actually calling. My phone is *ringing*. That never happens.

"Hi, so sorry, been busy," I say.

"Busy with what? What's going on?"

"Oh, you know, life stuff." It's horrible to be so vague, but I can't just tell him and risk losing him. At the very least he'll be weirded out, and likely he won't be interested in me with my new physical configuration. I must get my cock back before we get naked again. "We'll see each other tomorrow," I promise. "It's my day off."

Cheating is horrible and wrong. But is it cheating if it isn't your original genitals? All the people who waited years and paid for new ones would say so. But I've been blessed with this special chance. It's not like Derek and I have had a conversation where we defined our relationship, expectations, and such. I can't give up my vagina without letting her get some dick.

I've always wanted to know what it's like. I *need* to know.

I'll probably want to try it with a woman as well, eventually. I have actually slept with women before, with my regular old penis, and it was pretty fun. It doesn't happen often because I read as SUPERGAY, and because I don't sleep around much. But right now is an exception. I have a vagina, for the first time ever! It would be criminal not to use it.

There's a red dress that I have for special occasions, and a bra to stuff. After curling my hair and putting on makeup, I'm off to one of those straight clubs on the downtown strip.

The men pay me a lot of attention. It's wonderful, but there's no rush. I dance with my hips and drink only enough to make me feel relaxed, not drunk.

It's hot. I toss my hair and reapply my lipstick in the bathroom mirror. I sit down on the club toilets just because, even though Sophie says most girls squat because they're afraid of disease. Maybe I'm not even capable of contracting disease. These genitals are just going to be switched eventually anyway. Sitting is great, and it's different than when I did it as a guy and had to tuck. And it's a better view to read all the graffiti.

A man buys me a drink, which I accept because he says, "You dance like fire." Another man smiles at me nicely, so I press up against him.

At two a.m. the guy who complimented my dancing wants to take me home.

"Where's home?" I ask. He names a suburb, a good forty-five minute drive away.

"No." I say. "But… we could visit your car for a bit."

It was there, in a Toyota Corolla, that I lost it for the second, or third, or maybe fourth, time. How many times can you lose your virginity? I had sex for the first time with a girl in high school. Then with a boy, which was only oral, but it felt fresh and new. So was the first time my high school girlfriend gave me head also another kind of virginity lost? And the first time with a guy in my ass, that must count, right? I've lost so many virginities. Although it never felt like a loss. What a funny phrasing. Each time it felt like a gain.

This time as well. The nice man from the suburbs licks me softly, and then pushes into me hard. I grab the head rest and buck against him. "Yes" and "Jesus" and "More" burst from my mouth.

The Corolla drops me off in front of my apartment building as the sun is rising. My bed is so comfortable.

I wake up to my phone buzzing. A text from Derek. *You have a boyfriend, don't you? I'm obviously just some fling on the side. Fuck that. Have a nice life.*

No! I text back. Memories of Derek's hand slipping into mine, the taste of his tongue, him hovering above me. *That's not what's going on. Come over tonight.*

I'm coming right now.

He knocks on the door as I'm still cleaning the dark circles of last night's mascara from under my eyes.

"Wow," Derek says. "Nice dress."

"You don't think I look silly?" I ask, suddenly and uncharacteristically self-conscious.

"No," he says. "But I'm beginning to think that your superpower is being able to make any outfit look good."

Oh, he is sweet like honey. He grabs me around the waist and kisses me intensely. He seems to have forgotten his suspicions. I want him so much, and now this will be even harder if it goes badly. But there's nothing to do except do it. So I ask, "Do you want to get kinky?"

Derek says "Yes, oh yes. Bobby. But what, exactly?"

It's good to discuss boundaries. But I have ulterior motives. There's guilt in my heart, but I see no other way.

"How about you sit in that chair? And I cuff your hands to it? And then I strip?"

Derek says, "Yes, oh yes," again.

After tying Derek to the chair, I go into the bathroom and shower quickly. My dirty red dress and bra are discarded and replaced with a tank top undershirt, cut-off jean shorts, and combat boots.

"Wow," says Derek. The same thing he said when he saw me in my dress. "Wow" is such a noncommittal word. Which outfit does he like better?

I put on some music. Dubstep, really evil stuff. And then I dance a tough, stomping dance. I unbutton my shorts slowly. Derek catcalls. I put my boot in his crotch and he moans. I unlace my left boot and put the sole in Derek's face. He licks it. I kick off both my boots.

Now it's time. I take a deep breath and drop my shorts.

Derek's face twists and turns in a series of reactions. It's almost funny. I'm scared, but safe. He's quite securely bound to the chair.

Finally he says, "That wasn't... what was there before. Like, a couple of nights ago! What the..."

"Magic," I tell him. "I can change whenever I want."

Derek stares at my cunt and says, "I don't understand."

The spiral on my chest tingles. It's true. After my head wound clears up, I'll have to find other ways to bleed, but that's not hard. If I kept a vagina for a full month maybe it would even bleed for me.

"Breasts, different hands, toes, whatever. I can switch body parts. Any night."

He struggles. Not against the cuffs, it's all internal, but it's apparent on his face. He doesn't believe. He looks at me, remembers our sex, tries to make it make sense.

"I wanted to tell you right away but didn't know how. It's something that's hard to explain," I say.

Derek says, "That's crazy. And... cool. But I really am a fag, you know."

There's a curve in his crotch. I walk over to him very carefully, unzip his pants, and there he is, as large and hard as before.

I run my hands down my smooth chest. "I haven't really been drawn to getting tits. Not yet, anyway."

Derek says, "I do want you," and it's good to hear, although it seems obvious from his erection. I lower myself onto his lap, laughing and grunting. He is a million times better than the suburban car cock.

"Am I still gay?" he gasps.

"If you wanna be honey," I say. I sit down hard and bite his ear, then release it. "But let's just keep an open mind to whatever may come."

And he comes.

———— « O » ————

Dorianne Emmerton

Dorianne Emmerton grew up in the woods on the North Channel of Lake Huron and currently lives in the metropolis of Toronto. She loves both of those environments, but wishes the drive between them didn't take so long. She has recent publications in the *Ink Stains Anthology*; *Friend. Follow. Text #storiesFromLivingOnline;* and Issue #1 of *Beer And Butter Tarts,* as well as a personal essay in *A Family By Any Other Name: Exploring Queer Relationships.* She is currently working on a space opera novella in collaboration with Ottawa band Saturnfly, and a novel about occult magic in Northern Ontario. She has a wonderful chosen family, an adorable son, and a black cat.

Pin and Spanner

Pat Flewwelling

Before my honorable discharge from the 1068th Cybernetic Brigade, I had developed a healthy respect for QPIDs. And by healthy respect, I mean an overdeveloped flight response. And by honorable discharge, I mean there was no Brigade left to retire from, and no other army would hire any of its eight survivors.

So, imagine my surprise that day back in 2126 when I found a 38-Q Tactical Infiltration Unit, Model PID-2, sitting on a stool in my workshop at the Junk 'N' Graveyard in Holdout, New Appalachia, offline, rag-dollish, and staring at nothing.

We thought we'd killed them all fifty years ago, at the Battle of Detroit and soon after. The Vindicator Trojan had done its job, compelling every last QPID to Detroit, where between EMPs, heavy artillery, one nuke, and the last of the Cybernetic Brigade, we destroyed their hive-mind and smashed their horde. We'd have chased down and obliterated the last of them, but after the Battle we had exactly one functional leg to share among the eight of us. QPIDs kept popping up for the next two years, but then nothing after that.

These machines used to pick cyborgs out of mixed battalions, immobilize us, then strip the tech right out of our dying bodies and install it in themselves while we watched. Guess what was going through my mind when this QPID suddenly came online.

Alarm protocols juiced my circulatory pumps with adrenaline and amphetamine. Time slowed, and the hair on the human half of my scalp stood on end. I froze against my pegboard like a pinned bug, too scared to even calculate the nearest exit.

"Oh my goodness!" she said. "Hello."

Under the right circumstances, a QPI Doll can pass for a human being. It took years for the Post-Commies to develop their ultra-lite chassis and decades to perfect their behavioral mimicry AI, but once that was done it took very little time to bridge the Uncanny Valley. The only way a layman can spot a QPID assassin is when it tries to smile. Their skin's too thick, and won't fold properly. It gives them a stiff, demonic grin, and their upper lips always roll up under their noses. When they laugh, their mouths clack like marionettes.

But God help you once they receive a kill code. By the time you realize what they are, you're already dead. Their onboard explosives can level a city block.

She pointed to my dirty blue coat; beneath it, my damaged armor had deployed into battle mode. "You were a..." I still wore my rank and winged insignia. "Sapper? A...a-a-a combat engineer."

My fingers quested for the nearest weapon-like tool. My sensors read something hard and cold. Apparently, the nearest weapon-like tool was a filthy mug with a cat dangling from a branch and the words "Hang In There" written below it.

She narrowed her eyes and seemed to itemize my cluttered, greasy workshop. We were surrounded by various build and repair projects. She got up from the stool, graceful and tall, and took a step forward, scanning me.

"They said your name is Spanner," she said. "They said you're good a-a-at fixing things." She scanned me again, and I got really warm. Not the happy, fuzzy kind of warm. More like the too-late-for-adult-diapers sort of warm.

It took effort to unstick my jaw hinges. "What do you want from me?"

"Your help." She tilted her head. "Though I'm not sure if it's broken. Maybe...upgrade?"

My sense of duty and outrage overwhelmed my fear, and I unhooked my coat and armor from the pegboard. "You want *me*... to upgrade a *QPID*?"

Her eyes were wide open, blue, wet, and surprisingly expressive. "Yes, please?" Her vocal tic added five or six 'ee's to the word "please." I couldn't tell if it was physical trauma or a gremlin in her linguistics processor. And if I tried to run a more thorough scan she might sense it, get defensive, grow an EMP blaster from her left titty, and that would be the end of me. Don't laugh. It happened to a buddy of mine in Carver Canyon in 2086.

"What do you want?" I asked her.

"I want your help to fix a couple."

"A couple of what?"

She blinked at me. I blinked back.

"A *couple*," she said again.

"...What?"

"A people-couple."

If I'd had both eyebrows, I'd have pulled them into a scowl. As it was, the best I could do was blow steam out of my jaw hydraulics. "You want me to separate conjoined twins."

"No, I mean..." She raised her hands, closed her eyes, and said, "They're not a couple *yet*. That's what needs fixing. I don't know what's broken, and that's why I need your help."

I stared. "You want me to help you to play matchmaker?"

"Yes!" She clapped joyfully. "Oh, thank you! I've been looking for that word for days. It's very old-fashioned, but it's exactly what I was looking for."

I don't know what surprised me more, the request or the fact that she had honest-to-God crow's-feet. Her mouth couldn't smile, but her eyes could.

"What the hell are you?" I blurted.

As if stung, she slowly folded in on herself.

"You don't know, do you?" I whispered.

She shrugged. It wasn't the stiff gesture of an automaton, nor was it symmetrical. "You can scan my ID if you'd like. I don't mind."

I took my chances and scanned her. According to her boot script, she was Model 38-Q-PID-2, Unit #15983F, commissioned in <error, date not found>, built at <x9z...2222>, designation %...*^4....DE9()....J17(#...+t-1<error>. I had to shut down the scan before I got stuck in a query loop. "Well, that's a mouthful."

"They call me Pin," she said.

"They who?"

"My friends."

I laughed at her. "QPIDs don't have friends."

"I do."

"Define friends."

"Friends help each other without expectation of recompense," she said, as if reciting a Bible verse. "Therefore, they are my friends."

"Bull."

"They helped me," she insisted. "They gave me a place to stay. Some people bring me food twice a week, saying they made too much and can't eat it all. I don't eat, so I give that food away to other hungry people, and they bring me tools I might need. One time, a woman brought me a handmade blanket, and a pillow to go with it. I don't sleep, but sometimes I lie in bed with the blanket and pillow while I archive the day's memories. For the last five years, my work supervisor and her wife invited me over to Christmas dinner, and every VID Day, they—"

"Victory in Detroit Day," I echoed.

"Oh, yes," she said. The crow's-feet were back. "There are picnics, canoe trips, vintage hotdogs... and at night, the laserworks are amazing. If the smog is thick enough, we get to watch holographic movies, all night long."

"Victory *in Detroit* Day."

"Yes!"

No QPID in their right AI would celebrate VID Day. Hell, *I* don't celebrate VID Day, and we won.

"They don't know what you are," I said. My armor returned to standby mode, deflating my coat, and I snorted with as much derision as I could synthesize. "Friends, my eye. It's barter and trade, nothing more. It's not like you can experience affection—"

"Affection is selective altruism toward individuals belonging to or outside of one's species," she explained. "Therefore, they are my friends."

"But you can't *feel* affection."

"Correct! And that's why I'm here. I need you to reinstall that module."

"...Say what now?"

She pointed to her torso. "My affection module. It's broken, I think. That's why I don't know why I can't... um..." She made a joining motion with her hands. "Make the couple."

"I can tell you right now, that module was never installed."

"It wasn't part of my original specifications?" she asked.

"You were never designed to feel affection in case it interfered with your ability to *kill people*."

"Oh." She frowned. "What about sadness? Was I designed to feel that?"

"No."

"Strange. Hope?"

"Definitely not."

"How odd."

I rubbed my neck. "Why would you want to feel affection, anyhow?"

There was a reason I lived at the Junk 'N' Graveyard. After the war, survivors used drive me away with torches and pitchforks despite the fact we won Detroit for them, damn it. They're alive because we averted their global extinction. But, then again, a handful of cyborgs had been subverted by the Post-Commies, and for a time, *we'd* become the assassins. I get it. No love lost between us. But we did have a common enemy, and she had periwinkle eyes.

"I need to understand affection so that I can make others feel it," Pin said. "The last time I tried to make people fall in love it..." She averted her eyes. "It went very badly."

"They didn't fall in love?"

"He fell in love with her," she said. "But she didn't fall in love with him. And he... I..."

"This is the couple you want to fix?" I asked.

"No, that's unfixable. He was really mean to her, so she killed him."

"Uh *huh*," I said. "And now you want me to help you set up another couple for disaster."

"This is why I need the affection module," she said. "I want to learn. I want to do it better this time. And you fix machines. That means you can fix *me*."

My human eye developed a twitch, which she pointed out, and which I blamed on a stray electrical discharge in my occipital lobe. "How do you even know this new couple *should* be in love?"

"I've run multiple analyses. They're a perfect match."

"They're twins?"

"No, I mean they're compatible. And over one thousand recombinant scenarios show that their children will be optimal citizens for a post-reconstruction era."

"You want me to help you make these people reproduce."

"Well, yes, but..."

I don't even know what I was feeling. Anger, humor, incredulity — flabbergasted, there's another anachronism for you. I took off my coat and let it fall. "God, how much have you lost?"

She recoiled as if I'd poked her with an electric cattle prod.

"Your kind was engineered during the Third Cold War as sleeper agents for the Post-Communist Hegemony! You're not designed to decide who falls in love with who!" My voice broke. "You're programmed to sneak up and *kill* people."

She was shaking her head while I ranted. "No. No, not any more. Run a full diagnostic, you'll see. That's not who I am anymore."

"Then what are you?"

"I'm...I'm *Pin*." She watched me, pleadingly, patiently. "I'm sorry, Spanner. I know you don't trust me. Run a diagnostic. Once we're tethered, you can take me offline and destroy me, if you want. But..."

"But *what*?"

"I hope you don't," she said in a tiny voice. "I want to know how it all works out in the end. I want to know what happens next."

I clapped my hand to my eyes. A functional QPID is walking bomb; I wasn't about to let a dysfunctional one walk out of my shop. I decided to fix her permanently. "Okay, you know what? Fine. Sit." I pointed to the stool and grabbed my Enhanced Reality goggles. Since I'd broken the strap ages ago, I had to hold them up to my eyes like binoculars. "Standby." I used the goggles to run surface diagnostics while I initiated the wireless connection between our AI interfaces. If she wanted to kill and cannibalize me, that was her chance. But by the same right, I still had a few viruses in my cache, and I planned on implanting them all in her operating system. We'd both be dead, but the damage would be confined to the Junk 'N' Graveyard.

Considering I'm telling you this story, you can guess the virus didn't take. Her o/s was too badly corrupted. Hell, it was nigh indecipherable. She had only two core directives intact. Her primary protocol: mimic human behavior in order to pass for human. Her secondary: standby for kill codes. Everything else was deleted, repurposed, jury-rigged, or garbled beyond reading. I also found barcode mismatches between her torso and three of her limbs. Some of her sensory modules were still functional, though: audio, video, tactile pressure, and half a dozen other sensor arrays, like the DNA-Licker in her hands. Strangest of all: my mass spectrometers picked up trace amounts of fulgurites. Petrified lightning. Sea glass. They're formed when lightning hits silica and other conductive materials, and turns them into fused slag. I don't know how Pin was able to walk, let alone play matchmaker. I'll confess to some professional curiosity.

"Who rewrote your programming?" I asked.

"Nobody."

"Lightning doesn't recode androids."

"Then I rewrote me, I guess. I learned." She picked at her chipped, Syntheskin™ fingernails. I wondered where she worked, and at what. "Somebody did try to reprogram me. After they put my body back together..." She looked away.

"Your 'friends'?"

"No. Some scalvagers. Their attempted programming violated my primary protocol, so I ignored it."

I snorted. "What, they wanted you to mimic *dog* behavior, instead?"

"No, but they didn't want me to be human either. They wanted me to be a sexbot."

"And you refused. Did you kill them?"

"Of course not! I had no kill code. Besides, it just didn't seem right. After all, they did go through all the effort of bringing me back online and giving me new limbs."

First matchmaking, then gratitude. I was gobsmacked — there's another golden oldie.

"So," I said, "you rebuilt your own... personality... using your primary directive as your sole design guide. Mimic human behavior."

"I had to start fresh, observing humans, learning their speech, mimicking their mannerisms..."

"Pretty convincing act."

She had those smile lines around her eyes again. "Thank you. I've worked very hard. Sometimes watching wasn't enough. It was tricky, asking how I should behave without making anyone suspicious. I look old enough that I should know better," she confided. "So I t-told them I scalvaged a philosophy book about goodness and virtue, written in ancient times. *Nicomachean Ethics*, by Aristotle. I said I was studying it. And whenever I found myself in some new situation and didn't know what a human would do, I would t-turn to one of my friends and ask, 'Now in this case, how would a *good* person act?' I insisted it was more important than ever to learn to be good and authentic human beings. They would tease me for asking all the time, and I would say, 'But look what happened to the world when it stopped asking that question.'" She mimed an explosion and snickered at my reaction. "After a while, they stopped teasing and started telling me what a good person would do even before I asked."

I wondered which humans she'd been parroting. Somewhere out there was a village that had raised a damned precocious child.

"What did you do to the Scalvagers?" I asked.

"Nothing. They didn't perform many socially a-a-appropriate behaviors for me to mimic, so I ran away. I found a nice enclave to study from a distance until I was ready to join them. K-Enclave."

K-Enclave's hoity-toitier now than it had been in 2126, but it wasn't a total hole. The Brooklyn of its day, I guess. Today, you know it as Cay-on-Glaive. First enclave to build with new materials instead of salvage. Pin had grown up in a land of civil rebirth.

"All right. Let me get this straight. You wake up after a traumatic event, memory wiped. Someone installs new limbs, you run away on them, and you rewrite yourself. And now... you want to match up your ideal couple and let the sparks fly."

"Yes."

"Why?"

She stared back at me like I'd just tried to divide by zero. "Because it's important."

"No, it isn't." I laughed. "World's gone to hell, and it ought to stay there and burn. Remember, it was humans who built you."

"If you really believed the world should burn," she said, "you wouldn't spend all your time fixing things."

I might have blushed. "Fine, whatever," I blurted. "Okay, *breeding* is important. After you and your kind helped *lay waste to the human race*, any reproduction is a good thing. How do you know these two are supposed to get it on?"

She raised her hand, showing me the microscopic intake manifold in her palm. By touching someone with her DNA-Licker, she could sample, identify, and catalog their genome.

"And you've been collecting DNA samples from all of your... friends," I said. "Running simulations, seeing which pair will have the best children."

"But it's more c-c-complicated than just making babies!" She crossed her arms and legs. Cis-humans would be accused of being robotic spies before anyone suspected *her.* "I don't have the words to explain it. I need them to make affection."

"Do you even know what affection looks like?"

She reeled off observations. "Sitting 15-25% closer together on mass transit. Frequent occurrences of hand holding, shoulder rubbing, smiling. 30% increase in the length of time per eye blink when the object of affection is in focus. Eye contact sustained for 5.8% longer among friends, and 25.2% longer among those who later engage in coitus—"

I stopped her there. "And you've learned to mimic these behaviors?"

"Well, not the coitus one. My new exhaust manifold—"

"Wow, stop." I'm an engineer, not an ob/gyn. "You want your paramours to engage in similar behaviors, together, in order to make them develop a more sustained... uh... *romantic* relationship."

"Yes," she said, straight-faced, but with gleaming, child-like eyes.

"What's your plan?" I asked.

"I was hoping you could give me one. Haven't you ever been in love before?"

"Can't say I have been."

"Oh," she said. "So you didn't have your affection protocols installed correctly either?"

"Uh, yeah, I was *born* human, therefore I..."

Then I noticed the twinkle in her wrinkled eyes.

"Did you just tell a joke?" I asked.

"How? I wasn't designed for it," she said. "A humor module would interfere with my ability to kill people."

"Clearly nothing wrong with your smartass subroutine." I cleared my throat. "Look, love is a dangerous thing, especially when you force it. You've got people who *think* they're in love and they're not. Or they're in love with the *idea* of love, until they realize they've married a jackass. And then you get people who accept abuse as the price for stability and get control confused with love."

"Yes," she said. Her eyes tick-tocked, as if she was trying desperately seeking to rejoin the QPID hive-mind. "Yes, we can't let that happen again."

I almost told her that everybody makes mistakes, but what came to mind started with *To err is...*

"I can't hurt anybody else like that, ever again." Friction made the rims of her Syntheskin™ eyelids turn red. Hand-to-God, I thought she was going to cry, and that made me squirm.

"But," I said in a rush, "then you've got people who've been in love for a long time without ever really knowing it, until something magical happens. Or folks who get hitched first, then grow to love each other. Take my own grandparents. Married through sixty-two of the worst pre-war years. Multiple civil uprisings, economic disasters, relationship problems, miscarriages. Everything." I told her about this one time seeing my Granpaw sitting in his wheelchair, pushing Grangran along in her own wheelchair, both of them giggling at each other's farts. Pin listened with her eyes, and I could imagine her under a handmade blanket, listening to me read her a bedtime story. "With every new crisis, they built each other up, made each other stronger, and when it was over they were closer than ever. And more in love."

Her eyes sparkled.

"Sometimes arduous circumstances are enough to bring people together, I guess," I said.

Another head tilt.

"But you can't force love," I said. "It's up to the two people in that relationship, with external and internal forces pushing them together and pulling them apart..."

"But something made them meet, right?"

"What, your couple hasn't even met yet?" I asked.

"Not formally," she said. "They're just at the same place at the same time, all the time. I don't know how to make them d-d-do stuff together."

"Have you even talked to them yet?"

"No. They don't talk to strangers."

"Oof. All right. So, you've got a guy and a gal in opposite corners of a room—"

"A guy and a guy," she said.

Bear in mind, even in those days with our slap-dash, post-war tech, reproduction between same sex couples was a walk in the park. Hell, multiple donor insemination and artificial wombs were the only safe ways to bring kids to term.

I started again. "You've got two men at opposite ends of a room—"

"Train. Same train station, but always different cars."

"And you want them to get closer together, look each other in the eye—"

"Oh, they already do look each other in the eye, and then they blush and get in cars at opposite ends of the train."

"You sure these guys aren't already seeing each other on the sly?"

She was sure. She'd been following them around for weeks. She told me in facts and figures how often they sighed into their bowl of rations, how they interacted with other friends, how they supported their parents, families, and neighbors, how they both took little pains to beautify their neighborhoods, and how much they encouraged others.

This matchmaking murder-bot was schooling me in matters of the heart.

"Are they shy?" I asked. "Maybe they just need someone to make the introductions. Befriend them separately. And when you think the time is right, introduce them. Let nature take its course from there."

We sat in silence for a few seconds.

Then I asked, "Pin, don't you remember what your kind did? Weren't you there?"

Pin hung her head.

"Why is it so important that you make these two people fall in love?" I asked.

"Because..." She crushed her fist against her head. "Because..."

I touched her on the hand. She looked up at me.

"It's okay." I don't know why I said that. It just came out. I sounded like Grangran. "What matters here is that it's important *to you*. Even if it's not supposed to be." I meant to show her how unique — how uncanny — she was.

"It *is* important to me," she said, squeezing my hand. Fortunately, it was my metal hand. "It's important that these two fall in love. It's important for them to have and to r-r-raise their children together. I know it's important for the future of the whole human race! But I don't know why it's so important to *me*!"

"Pin, I don't know, either." There was no directive that required her to get a job, or make friends, or try to make people fall in love. She could have just as easily stayed in hiding until she needed repair. Instead, she'd gone so far out of her way to make two men fall in love that she had put her own safety in jeopardy and come to me, her natural enemy, to ask for help.

But technically, aren't emotions just a pattern of thought, influenced by memory, motivation, and a sense of self-preservation, governed by the limbic center of the brain? If so, couldn't a learned subroutine in Pin's AI be considered an emotion? Could she not, therefore, *feel*? After celebrating VID Day — after learning how her kind nearly wiped out the species she was programmed to idolize — could she not 'feel' remorse?

Maybe she did come to me to be fixed. Maybe she thought I could turn off the pain.

"You're not broken, Pin," I said. "You're operating within normal parameters. It's just that you've been learning from the best kind of humans. The survivors, who picked themselves up out of near annihilation and then reached down to help others. That's the kind of *love* you've been copying."

Her eyes were still-red rimmed, but they were gleaming.

And then I said the words I'd regret: "That's the kind of self-sacrificing love that makes us human."

She stood up, thanked me, and then brushed past me like she'd just received a kill code. But then she paused with one hand on the edge of my door. She came back, and gave me a hug and a kiss on the forehead. She didn't close the door behind her when she left.

That's the last damned time I saw her alive.

Seconds later, I replayed and analyzed the whole conversation, and all of a sudden I knew in my gut what she was going to do. Arduous circumstances. External forces. Self-sacrifice. I realized that if a QPID could reprogram itself, it could generate and issue kill codes to itself.

For six miles, from the Junk 'N' Graveyard to K-Enclave, I raced after the scent of fulgurites, with people shrieking at me as I bowled through the morning market crowds. But even with my mechanical legs, I never caught up. I lost her trail at the A2K Inter-Enclave Train Terminus. I yelled at the ticket takers and travelers, begging for someone, anyone, to call ahead and stop the elevated train before it left.

When the train took off, I gave chase. Once I was close, I fired up my rusted jump-rockets, caught the hand grips of the last car, punched through the door, and climbed aboard. But the second I broke the emergency brake glass, everything went to hell. A middle car erupted, jerking the lead cars into a backward plummet where the trestle was supposed to be. The rear cars slammed forward and tilted off the broken track. I remember grabbing some kid as he fell and wrapping myself around him. My stabilizing jets kept us upright while the whole car spun around us. It wasn't much of a drop, thank God, but glass went everywhere. Bloody faces, broken bones. I let the kid go and checked on the other passengers. Might have been five or six of them in that car. Moved on to the next car. A couple of people trapped, but nobody dead. Then I noticed some young guy following me, not just executing my orders but directing some people to remove debris, others to help administer medical aid, and still others to go for help. He trailed me from car to car, turning instruction into action.

Then I came to the middle car, and I had to send my deputy on ahead. There was only one passenger here, and I said I'd take care of her. I didn't let him see her. I couldn't let him see what she was. But damned if there weren't dimples in those cheeks of hers. She'd died smiling.

If it wasn't for the fire, I would have grabbed her body and run out of there. But there was nothing more I could do for her. So I dug deep into the rescue efforts. I found my young second-in-command working shoulder to shoulder with a brown-haired fellow. I did all the heavy lifting that only cyborgs can do, while the brunet administered First Aid and my deputy handled crowd-control.

By one the next morning, all the casualties had been rescued, and the fire was out. The train was a write-off, and it would take weeks to rebuild the track, but everyone got out alive — everyone but Pin. She'd picked her place and time. The train had derailed where the track passed over a sand pit; a mile sooner, and it would have fallen onto a slum; a mile later, and it would have blown up a school. I did a final sweep, and what should I find but my second-in-command fast asleep with his head on the shoulder of the brown-haired man.

Somebody handed me a quilt, thanking me, calling me a hero, and apologizing that it was the only thing she had to give. I took that blanket and put it over the two lovebirds, just like Pin would have wanted me to. Then a trio of survivors took me aside and plied me with soup and bread. Someone brought us a bottle of moonshine. A fiddler came over and played some pre-war tunes, just for me. Kids touched my face and asked me if I was okay, and if I would come back and play with them someday.

These were the descendants of those the Brigade had fought and died for.

These were Pin's people.

And I was welcome, from that day forward.

After a while, I made my excuses, because I wanted to find Pin's body and take it back with me. I didn't want anybody else to know what she was; I didn't want to destroy the illusion she'd worked so hard to create. The two sleepy young lovers came in, saw me crouching over Pin, and without a word helped me wrap the body in the quilt I'd given them.

I built Pin a tiny cottage in a back corner of the Junk 'N' Graveyard, out where the wildflowers grow. I laid her to rest there under the blanket, with her burned-out head on the softest pillow I could find. I keep the cottage locked. Damned if I know why. Not like I'm going to disturb her sleep or anything. Every synapse is fused and half her processor case is blown off. I could probably reuse her limbs on some other worker drone, but that's it. She's gone.

As for her mission, it was accomplished. You might not know those two young men, but you know their daughter. Forty years after that train blew up, she was sworn in as the second President of the United Federation of the Americas.

For so long, K-Enclave had thought Pin was some flaky but sweet big-eyed girl who just wanted to become the best human being she could be.

That's why they called her Pinocchio.
Pin for short.

———— « o » ————

Pat Flewwelling

Hailing from Oshawa, Ontario, Pat Flewwelling is a part-time writer, part-time editor, part-time publisher, part-time traveling bookseller, and full-time data problem solver at a major telecommunication company. Aside from her seven full-length works, her short works have been included in World Weaver Press' anthologies *Sirens* and *Equus*, as well as in *Purgatorium* by ID Press, and in magazines like *Pulp Literature*. You can find out where her shop, Myth Hawker Travelling Bookstore, will appear next, by visiting www. mythhawker.ca.

Red

Alison McBain

He had killed his parents as surely as if he had taken the ceremonial knife in his infant hand and slashed their necks as soon as he was born. The Elder had taken one look at Atem and seen the sign of beasts — the red mark of hair on his head. From that moment, the countdown to his tenth year had begun.

The Elder handed him a polished wooden cup. Atem held it first down to the earth and then up to the sky, as he had been taught. Afterwards, he put it to his lips and swallowed down the bitter vastata until he choked on the dregs at the bottom. He gave it back to the Elder, surreptitiously wiping his mouth with the back of his hand and swallowing the sickness trying to rise up his throat.

"And so I give you to the Tauros. Rise a ghost of this tribe, Atem, and leave the world of men."

His vision was blurred around the edges from the herbal drink, and when he turned his head trails of color followed the landscape. He stood on wobbly legs.

"Goodbye, Elder," he said, and the man who had raised him, the man who had sacrificed his parents to the gods, nodded one time at Atem and turned his back. One by one, the gathered villagers did the same as he walked past.

It took a long time to leave, and each step proved heavier than the last. By the time he reached the final tents of the village, he felt numb in mind and body both. The colors of the plains drifted past his head like dandelion pappi, and he could swear he heard drums from behind keeping pace with his heartbeat.

The grasses seemed to form a pathway especially for him, and the stars danced above his head. He was taken in by the wonder of it and stopped at the top of the hill to watch them twirl for a moment — or two, or five. Then he heard the drum again, that pesky reminder, and descended the far side of the hill. Once, he misstepped and fell, taking a hard knock on his shoulder, his reactions slowed too much to prevent it. The pain jarred him out of his trance. As the fog cleared a little, he realized the rustling and snorting sounds he heard were carried from the open space in front of him. He had reached the Tauros.

Standing at the base of the hill, he saw them as dark outlines against the brilliant starscape. It was new moon, and so the only light was from the countless dancing constellations. He'd seen the Tauros before — what tribesman had not? — but they still amazed him, their massive size, the musky odor of their passage. *Ours*, he thought. *Our passage now, since they will carry me with them.*

He was just on the edge of the herd, and the beasts lifted great shaggy heads to look at him. Then those heads descended again, somnolent on pillows of soft, sweet grasses. The beasts slept, and he had no idea what he was supposed to do now.

He sat barely a man's length away from the nearest trio. This close, the smell of animal was overwhelming. They snorted gently in sleep, pawing at the ground. He curled up into a ball and pulled the grasses over himself like a rabbit making a burrow. Then he slept.

~ ~ ~

He woke abruptly when a hoof thunked down close enough to shake the ground under his cheek. The Tauros noticed Atem's abrupt recoil from its footstep and deigned to lower its eyes towards him, but did nothing further except grab another mouthful of grass and chew contemplatively.

Atem rolled backwards slowly, squinting against the bright morning. He usually woke when the sky first lightened, but his head was pounding from last night's drink, and the light of the sun made his eyes water.

What now?

He had never contemplated *after*. His whole life had led up to being given to the Tauros. He had transferred ownership, and now he was puzzled. *Was this it?*

His stomach pitched as he stood and started walking. The Tauros raised their heads as he passed, but other than occasional mournful and incurious looks, they ignored him. In the middle of the wide valley was a shallow stream, and he knelt down to drink. He spotted fish about the size of a finger joint, and his stomach rumbled. If only the stream were bigger, he could spear his breakfast.

After he made a spear, of course. He rooted around by the bank until he unearthed a rock with enough heft and girth to suit him. It took longer to find a second stone, but for the first time in a long while he had nothing better to do. No morning chores, no caring for the younger children, no learning the rites of the ceremony.

The ceremony was done. He was free of his tribe, as much as he would ever be free from them.

Crouched down, he set to work chipping away at one rock with the other. At the tapping sound, a few of the Tauros came to investigate, but they soon wandered away again.

After a while, he realized the rhythmic sounds he heard in the background were increasing in volume. He looked up — the herd was moving, heading north. Their hooves thumped a steady beat, like the drums calling to him in the night. He picked up the stones he had been working with and tucked them into his belt, placing the sharpest chips into his pouch. Then he started walking.

The Tauros mostly followed the stream, pausing to graze at intervals. He was not sure what signal was given to start, what signal to stop. They seemed to suddenly be moving and, just as suddenly, they would stop and put their heads down to eat. On one extended rest period, Atem picked some reeds growing by the stream. He ate the heads and weaved the stems into a basket, which he used to lever out several helpings of the small fish from the stream. He'd have preferred them cooked and crunchy, but their flavor right out of the water was fresh and left no aftertaste. He would have continued fishing but the herd began to move again. He turned over the basket and placed it on top of his head to shade himself from the hard noonday light.

Although he had been on migrations with the tribe before, the silence of the herd and lack of human companionship wore on him. He would never hear a human voice again — he was no longer human, but tribeless.

By the time the sun touched the far hills, Atem was ready to rest. The animals arranged themselves in a loose group, the younger ones in the center by their mothers and fathers, the larger males towards the outside. Atem made a nest close to several families and fell asleep instantly.

When he woke, the sky was just starting to bloom with pink and gold streamers. He undressed and splashed water from the stream over his naked body, and the chill woke him as much as the growing light. He shook out his clothes as best he could, and stood watching the sun rise as the beasts heaved themselves to their feet, shaking off slumber. Behind them were gently rolling hills, but ahead, many days distant, were the true mountains. Even in the heart of summer, the peaks were crowned by diadems of white. Now, in mid-spring, the snow extended down the slopes quite some distance, the season not yet warm enough for a melt.

Although his former tribe never wandered very far from the lake, during feast days the women sang about the far north, the breeding ground of the Tauros in the mountains beneath the entrance to the heavens. The herd would march all spring to spend the height of summer in the shade of those imperial peaks and crags, returning before winter to the milder southern lands. None like him — no ghost — had ever returned with them, for in the mountains was a special path just for the chosen ones, a transition from this half-life with the Tauros to true death. The path was littered with obstacles and monsters to prevent a ghost's ascent, and only the very bravest and strongest would be accepted into the highest spiritual realms of heaven.

He pulled on his clothes before the air chilled him too much, and took out the rocks from his belt. The mountains were far away, and he had time. Maybe even a ghost could fight back against what waited for him.

~ ~ ~

A few days later, the early berries started to appear. He ate the green ones, although they puckered his mouth, and broke off branches from the sprawling nut trees, whittling them down until they were straight enough to throw. With fibrous peli grass, he tied some of his stone chips to the sticks, and when a rabbit flashed across his path that afternoon, he speared it straight through on the first try.

Raw rabbit was not on the top of his list of edibles, but he was unsure how the Tauros would react to a fire. He thought about this problem all afternoon as they traveled. That night when the herd stopped, he walked along the bank of the stream some distance ahead of the animals. When he was close enough to still see them, but well downwind, he used a stone to dig out a pit as deep as his knees near the banks of the stream. He lined it with rocks, a bed of grass, and some old, fallen branches he had collected from the nut trees. Spinning a whittled stick into a dry piece of bark, he blew on the embers he'd created, gently dropping them into his fire pit. They caught the dry grass which blazed up instantly, producing an intense heat and a puff of smoke. He fed more sticks to the fire, then skinned the rabbit and hung it over the fire to cook.

The smell made his mouth water. As he waited, he used the stream to rinse the blood off the skin, beginning the delicate process of flensing off the excess fats and tissues. After a while, he ate the rabbit and finished scraping the hide. He rinsed the skin once more in the stream, then used two sticks to prop it over the fire. When it was hot enough, he split open the rabbit's cooked skull and used the insides to tan the hide. Then he propped the greased skin back over the fire and watched the curls of smoke dance up over its edges. The rabbit seemed to dance with the smoke. He lay down, closed his eyes, and dreamed of rabbits galloping across the night sky and throwing down spears to trap him.

When he woke, he filled in his fire pit and tucked the cured rabbit hide into his belt to carry with him. The Tauros were just starting their morning grazing, and he walked back to join them and hunt for his own breakfast.

~ ~ ~

The days lengthened and grew warmer, but not so much that he felt uncomfortable. In the south, the heat would be so intense as to sometimes start fires that cleared out whole sections of grassland — much hotter than the temperate north. Now was the time of plenty for his former tribe, lazy days of celebrating the warmer season, gathering new greens, and spearing the plentiful fish in the lakes.

He didn't so much miss the celebrations or the tribe itself. He had been marked from birth and the elders treated him accordingly, even if other children were less wary. The thing he missed above all else was the sound of human voices.

After a while, he began speaking to the herd — or, rather, to his favorites in the herd. He tended to travel with one family, a mother and father and half-grown calf, and they turned their heads in his direction when he spoke to them. He named them Bola for mother, Vedo for father, and Utta for baby. Utta still held a baby's playfulness, even though he was large enough to trample Atem, and the two would chase around Bola and Vedo until the parents snorted and shook their shaggy heads.

Atem's belt of furs grew heavier, and he pieced together the smaller hides into a coat for the winter. He removed the hair from the larger ones and used cured sinew to sew them together. Since he had no poles, he hung his tent over low branches of the nut trees and slept on top of his fur coat for comfort. Each morning, he rolled them up and carried them across his shoulders.

He had grown so used to the thud of hooves and rustle of wind through grass that when he heard a different sound, it puzzled him. It was not the scold of the crow or the sigh of doves, nor the death rattle of grass snakes.

They were walking along the stream, the midday sun thwarted by the overturned basket on Atem's head. He heard a long, low whine and saw a flash of movement out of the corner of his eye. When he turned, he faced chaos.

A calf was down, lowing pitifully for its parents. The bull had turned its head, confusedly searching out the pain of his offspring, but the baby was hidden in the grass. The mother stood in front of her child, shaking her shaggy head at the hunters who had thrown the spears.

Atem's stomach fell. A tribe. Another tribe. He ran towards the trio of beasts, wondering if it was Bola, Vedo and Utta, but his feet froze when the nearest man turned to him.

The man spoke several words that melted together into a series of clicks and "mmnn" sounds.

"I do not understand," Atem said.

The man gestured with his spear towards the herd. Then behind himself at the other men. He spoke more words, but the language remained unintelligible. Atem shook his head, pointed to himself, and then waved an open hand at the animals milling in confusion behind him.

The hunter nodded. He called something to the other men, drew back his arm, and threw the spear directly into the heart of the mother guarding her calf.

Atem watched as they butchered the small family. The other Tauros had calmed once the cries of the wounded animals had ceased, and now seemed little affected by the deaths — they turned their backs on their slain fellows and continued the long trek north. Atem knew their direction; he would not lose them.

He watched the men remove the skin from the animals' serene faces and felt each cut of the knife as if it scored his own flesh. His heart cried out at the butchery, even knowing it was a part of the bargain between men and beasts. It was like watching his own family slain and made into meat. But he saw the process through to its end, a witness, even if he could do nothing else.

When they were done, the first man came over to Atem and offered him a generous wrapped bundle of meat, but he shook his head, repulsed. Shrugging, the man gestured once more to the hills behind him and beckoned to the boy to follow them.

"No," Atem said, though he knew he was not understood. "I am a ghost; I am a part of no tribe." He turned away. The stream guided his feet, and he began the long walk back to the bosom of his adopted family.

The next time a tribe hunted the herd, Atem hid among the beasts. He wasn't sure if he was spotted, but the hunters did not attempt to call out to him, and Atem made no attempt to speak with them.

Each day, the mountains edged closer. The heat baked the grasses and Atem too, and he wished for nothing so much as the cool expanse of the lake of his home to bathe in, the lazy days of summer feasting. But he had no complaints from his stomach — game was plentiful, and the nut trees were in flower, with long strings of minute blooms hanging down towards the ground, boding well for their early fall harvest. Every time he thought about the trees, his mouth would water in anticipation, forgetting that his journey's end was coming near, and that autumn would be forever beyond him.

The ground began to slope up and down like clouds blown by a strong wind. These gentle hills were not so noticeable at first as the herd wound their slow way upwards, following the water in the valleys between them, but eventually the ascent grew more pronounced. The last tribe to hunt the beasts had been left behind many days before, and Atem wondered if any more people lived in the very shadows of these grand mountains, or if the rock spirits would keep them far away. His tribe ascribed many things to these mountains, believing them home to many supernatural creatures. The Elder forecast the good and bad luck of the year by studying the pattern of seasons on the mountains, and his predictions were seldom wrong.

The golden grasses began to thin, replaced by bushes and more trees, and the soft brown earth of the plains hardened into hard gray rock and springy moss-covered dark soil. Rabbits gave way to other furred four-legged creatures. Although Atem hadn't seen them before, they died just as easily beneath his spear and their taste was not so unpleasant when cooked.

The herd began to walk for longer stretches, and flesh dropped from their bones as they traveled. The way grew harder and rockier, and Atem was exhausted at the end of each day, sometimes neglecting to cook his meals for the effort it took to make a fire. He wondered why the Tauros threw themselves so diligently at the ever steepening hills when the plains were filled with sweet-smelling grasses dried to a golden brown beneath the heat of the summer sun.

He didn't have long to wonder. After a double handful of days, they crested a ridge and Atem stopped in mid-stride at the sight laid out before him. An easy descent into a small bowl of a valley was backed by the much higher peaks of mauve-colored mountains. Between two distant peaks was a wriggling stream of white — a fall of water cascading directly from the snowcaps above. The grasses in the valley were the abundant green of spring, dotted with trees heavy with fruit. In the distance, nut trees clustered in clumps around a small lake nestled at the center of the picturesque valley.

While his heart sang at the sight, his scanning eyes passed over something out of place and returned to it. He blinked, but the sight didn't dim or waver. As the herd began to descend the final slope, he wanted to run at them and beg them not to go, not to be fooled by this verdant place.

Behind the waters was a human settlement. Although the houses seemed strange and unnatural in shape — square where his tribe's homes were round — there was no mistaking the figures moving between them, coming forward to engage with the animals now entering the valley.

At this distance, the people seemed faceless, but he could see the full-length spears in their hands. He closed his eyes against the sight, against the betrayal of the herd. Was this why none of the ghosts returned with the herds? Were they killed by this final tribe, murdered like the beasts they were supposed to be?

With little choice, he hitched up the skins onto his shoulders and began to walk. Heart heavy, he walked with his fellow Tauros surrounding him, feeling oddly protected in their midst. But he knew that protection was an illusion, especially when it came to men.

Although Utta had grown weary of their games on this last and hardest part of the journey, Atem walked next to the calf with one hand on his shoulder, comforted by the warmth and solidity of the beast beside him. If he had to say goodbye, he could picture no better way to leave this world than with his adopted family at his side. Atem was marked by hair red as blood, red as ghosts, already dead to his tribe — but he wanted so much to live, to breathe, to eat and laugh and learn.

The men got quite near before he got a good look at them, surrounded as he was by a wall of living flesh. As always, the Tauros were little ruffled by men walking into their midst, but they did not move out of the way of the smaller creatures either. So to avoid the indifferent trampling feet of the large beasts, the men had to zigzag towards the lone figure walking upright in their center, and Atem caught only brief glimpses of them as they approached.

Not until Utta dropped his head to graze did Atem see the first man close up. Atem found himself holding tightly to the calf's shoulder to keep from falling over with shock.

The red flag of the man's hair was repeated in the man beside him, and the woman behind him, too. Everywhere Atem looked was a sea of red — red human heads moving easily between massive red Tauros, men and women patting the sides of the creatures with gentle hands.

Atem's heart unclenched in his chest. His fear drifted away — these people would no more murder their brothers and sisters of the Tauros herd than he would.

They were safe. For now, all of them would be safe. And for the first time since he had walked away from his tribe, he was at ease.

The first man smiled and spread his hands wide as he saw the boy's face relax. His words were heavily accented but understandable as he said simply, "Welcome to the city of ghosts."

—— « o » ——

Alison McBain

Alison McBain is fourth generation Canadian, born in Edmonton, Alberta. After her nomadic twenties, she settled in Connecticut, where she is raising three girls and her husband. She is an award-winning author with more than sixty short stories and poems published/forthcoming, including work in *On Spec, Abyss & Apex and Neo-opsis Science Fiction Magazine*. When not writing, she practices origami meditation and draws all over the walls of her house with the enthusiastic help of her kids. Once in a while, she puts on her Book Reviews Editor hat for the magazine *Bewildering Stories*, contributes to the international literary collective *Reader's Abode*, or interviews authors on her website at www.alisonmcbain.com.

Tera & Flux

Leslie Van Zwol

The voice of Jok'ov the Warden blared over the intercom listing crimes upon the commonwealth. It would be her father's turn to speak soon, but Tera's only interest was in the prisoner.

He was held at the base of the amphitheater; glowing blue chains pinned three sets of tentacles and a long segmented tail snug against his arched spine, the immature barbed tail-tip secured to a collar around his neck. His stalk-eyes were cast down, adolescent and drooping, while the third eye in the center of his forehead stayed closed up tight. The prisoner wasn't pulling at his binds or yelling, like some did. He just sat there and breathed, like it was the hardest thing he'd ever done. *Are they still called handcuffs when he has no hands?* she wondered.

"Don't look at him," Tera's newest minder murmured, vivid green lines of unease flickering over the sharp angles of her blue face. She pressed a storybook into Tera's hands, something with bright colors and made-up animals dancing across the cover in animated hops: unicorns and dragons and cows.

Tera's father rose and walked to the podium, straightening his medallion and fixing the collar of his robes. Some of the audience murmured approvingly, some hissed, and others shouted. Her father raised his hands.

"I've already read that one," Tera said, folding the book cover on top of the dancing pictures, turning them dark. She craned past her minder to see.

"Citizens," her father boomed over every murmur. "I call for your concern, not your complacency. This is not the first hearing of a criminal attempting to infiltrate the Haven and surely, as tensions grow, this will not be the last."

The hissing in the room grew, like a cracked oxygen tank; people whispered in a dozen languages. The minder held the book in front of Tera's face like a shield. Tera took it with a frown, putting it in her lap.

"There is war. Everywhere. As resources grow scarce, tensions rise," he continued. "Scavengers are everywhere. People are dying. Rebels threaten to destroy the primary suns in our commonwealth: if they die, five colonial districts will be destroyed. These are dark times."

At the back of the room, someone shouted in a thin, desperate voice. "It's time to use the powers of the Haven! Release them," they chanted. "Release them, *unleash them...*"

The murmurs rose but nobody joined the chant. Guards emerged from their places at the edges of the room, moving towards the yeller.

"These rebels are *organized*," Tera's father bellowed, fighting for the room's attention. "They are determined. They will destroy us with their rash actions!"

An electrical weapon snapped, and the chanting man shrieked. Tera turned to look, propping herself up on her knees. The minder spun her back around with a clammy hand, and Tera saw how wide her deep-set eyes were. The chromatophores in her face pulsed red with alarm.

"It is bleak, yes. But what of the Haven's defenses? Could we use them as weapons?" someone else yelled, closer to the front. "I don't want to die knowing there was more we could have done! I don't want to die..."

"You'll kill us all," another shouted, angrily. "Untested weaponry of mass destruction. Who knows what could be unleashed!"

Tera jumped when she noticed the prisoner's third eye had opened, gleaming silver and pulsing with faint light as he looked in her direction. She twisted and looked behind her, following his gaze, and smiled as she caught sight of her friend. She resisted waving at him while her minder was watching. Wisps of shadows billowed, forming a long-fingered hand, beckoning her outside.

"I'm scared," Tera lied to her minder. "Can I go and read until it's over?"

Her minder nodded, her face cooling to a relieved teal, and let Tera slide past her. "Wait for me in the hall, Teraviva. Just sit where the guards aren't working and wait."

Tera smiled politely and slipped into the aisle. Two guards were just disappearing through the back door with someone propped up between them, his shoes making squeaky noises as they dragged on the floor. She couldn't tell who the door-guard was with his helmet on, but she held up the picture book like a hall-pass. He nodded, opening the door, and she darted out, leaving the growing commotion of the council behind her. There were guards everywhere, ushering people away and talking in short, sharp codes. Tera walked between their formations, and they parted for her with hardly a glance. She was glad to be away from the angry council and their hours of arguing.

Tera felt the cold shadow snuggle into the collar of her jacket. Her father insisted Flux wasn't real, but Tera knew better. Flux was shy, so he hid around people and Tera did all the talking, and when they were alone, Flux would talk too.

"Let's go visit your friends," he whispered.

Nodding, she hitched the cumbersome book under her arm, and went to find Hadrix. The further she traveled from the amphitheater, the fewer guards there were. Tera stood on her tip-toes and used her ring to unlock the library door.

The room was large, with stark white shelves as high as she could see, each containing more words than she could read in a lifetime. She skipped down the arched path, Flux billowing beside her and tumbling in the air. At the center of the library was the study, comparatively dimmer and decorated in darker tones. Glass-cased shelves lined the small space, each locked and sealed airtight, filled with books made of degradable materials.

Tera tossed her storybook to the side and flopped into a plush chair, scooting to the back, her feet dangling over the edge. The study was her favorite place, and there, as usual, she found Hadrix. The old man was hunched over a shelf, polishing the glass and whistling a tune.

With a grin, Tera kicked her feet and robustly joined in, while Flux floated and twisted himself into dark shapes behind the librarian's head. This song was her favorite, and she let her voice rise with his, moving her arms to the tune. When the old man lifted his gaze, she gave him a big wave and he startled, catching himself on the edge of a wooden desk.

"Tera," he shouted with a chuckle, his voice hearty. Hadrix pulled a metallic ear from his head and adjusted some buttons before reattaching the appendage. "What are you doing here, sugar? Aren't you supposed to be watchin' your daddy calm all those folks?" he asked in a softer tone.

Tera rolled her eyes, making room for Flux to nestle beside her. "It's so boring! 'Sides I already know what daddy's going to say."

He put a hand on his hip. "And you snuck on past young Cathra, didn't you?" His brief stern expression didn't hold as he dug in his pocket and pulled out some sweets.

"She's not a good minder. She can't even mind her shoes."

He chuckled, offering her some of the candy and taking a bite for himself. "What part they at?"

Tera stood on the chair and puffed out her chest, making a stern face and lowering her voice. "Council, this is no time for democracy. We must keep our gaze fixed on the future. We are in the age of technology, yet should this war turn from a spark to a flame, extinction will be upon us."

Hadrix laughed as Tera threw herself into the plush chair and bounced a few more times. Flux roiled jovially, curling and making wisps around her.

"You got yer daddy's whole speech memorized?"

"He went over it six times!" She demonstrated the number with her fingers, pausing between bites of candy. "Are they gonna kill that boy?"

Hadrix shrugged, stretching his back. "Maybe."

"I think they are. Daddy was talking about it." She swallowed, and shifted in her chair. "Daddy says his life won't matter, that if he doesn't die we'll all die. He says he gives the radicals ideas."

Hadrix chuckled. "We're all going to die, Tera. But it takes a certain kind of someone to make that choice for someone else. Everybody's got an end to their rope; you know that by now." He paused, chewing contemplatively. "We're all sailing towards death, whether your daddy likes it or not."

"He's just scared." She grinned, picking the sweet candy from her teeth. "But I'm not!"

"I know, sugar." He levered himself to his feet, rubbing his neck. "Used to be you could see the line of one man's life to its end here and there, but your daddy ain't wrong. The end of everyone's close on that horizon, a big ol' storm of souls, and the wind's in our sails now."

"Hurting that boy won't save us," Tera offered.

"Killing rarely stops anyone from dying." Hadrix cleared his throat. "If he lives, he's the symbol of their revolution. If he dies, your daddy'll make him a martyr. Either way, that storm's coming."

"Can't we just go through it?"

"We can," Flux offered, tumbling overhead.

"People have a lot of fear, and despair. Years of strife without peace, it wears people numb. To sail through a storm, you've got to believe there's sunshine on the other side. And no one believes anymore."

Flux rested on Tera's shoulder, a cool familiar comfort. "Of course there's still sun!" Tera insisted. "Planetary storms are just clouds! Even in space they don't last forever."

"People just don't remember what it is to have hope. To really feel it on the inside. They don't have a compass. They're just drifting towards the storm of death and don't think they'll make it through." Hadrix placed a hand on Tera's shoulder, a distant look in his milky eyes. "But with hope, they have courage. Their strength changes the wind: they'll remember how to be alive again."

Tera covered his hand with hers, making him smile.

"Just remember that you've got a choice." He gave her hand a squeeze and offered her a napkin. "You do what's right by you. No matter what anyone says, alright?"

Taking the cloth, she scrubbed her face before jumping into his arms. Tera used the sullied napkin to wipe tears from his cheeks. "I'll remember. But you remember that we do the right things sometimes too."

Hadrix gave a chuckle, setting her down. "You follow that heart like a compass, Tera. Now shoo. There's more for you to see than this dusty place."

"Let's race," Flux suggested, whirling out of the study.

Tera dashed after him, the clatter of her footsteps echoing through the library, followed by Hadrix's boisterous laugh.

Silence settled for a moment when she stopped, and then the door breathed open, the shouts and racket of chaos drowning the placid room. Tera stuck close to the wall, avoiding the metal boots that ran in orderly formations. A mess of shouting still boiled over from the council room.

"Nothing fun there," Flux sighed.

Tera scowled. "Let's go to the basement."

The corridors were a labyrinth of twists and turns and places where lights barely reached, but she had the way memorized. The guards grew sparse once they left the more populated chambers, but each large door was occupied by a soldier, who, upon recognizing Tera, opened the barrier for her to pass.

Below the common areas of the Haven, stark white walls gave way to emergency breakers and black metal so dark it didn't even shine. She continued downward, humming and skipping to Hadrix's song. Turning a corner she used her ring to open a large door plastered with neon warning labels.

The room inside was warm and humid, and Tera breathed deeply to let her lungs adjust. Light and heat permeated the chamber, turquoise and neon flora stretching into a canopy that filled the room. Hidden creatures chirped and cooed, and a tiny breeze rustled the leaves overhead as a gentle mist sprayed from a metal contraption that floated through the air. A high-pitched wail broke the tranquility, followed by a crash. Animals scattered in a flurry of color, while Tera hustled towards the source of the clamor.

Another shriek was followed by the sound of shattered glass and a low hiss.

"You insolent creature! Remove your filthy paws from my research!"

"Filthy? Oh that's rich, you putrid fraud."

Tera giggled as she moved into the laboratory, Flux clinging to her shadows. Fluorescent purple liquid dripped down tiled walls behind the doorway.

"They're always fighting," Flux whined, nestling deeper into Tera's coat collar.

"That's how they say 'I love you,' I think," she answered with a shrug.

A tall figure turned at the sound of Tera's voice, glass jars clutched in hands that stretched too far from her body. A patchwork of exotic colors and textures covered her: scales blended into feathers and bark, all peeking out from a sullied lab coat. Two leaf-shaped wings splayed from her back, and blue and red tentacles flared around her head, flattening like hair at the sight of Tera. Her arms shrank back to her body, meeting with four others of different shapes and textures. "Oh, hello Tera."

"Hi Val." Tera waved, peeking past the giant woman.

A blood-stained sheet sloppily shrouded a prone body upon a table, and atop the precarious pile, a black furry creature sat with a raised chin. It licked its nose with a forked black tongue and gave Tera a grin. The creature mewed, and the collar around its neck flared to life with color, speaking. "Hello, Tera."

"What're you guys fighting about?" Tera asked, lifting herself onto a stool and swinging her feet.

"Bast has successfully eaten most of my specimen. Gluttonous heathen."

"Re'tak taste mostly like fish. It was delicious. I regret nothing."

Valeria's hair flared again like angry snakes, and she threw another jar at her companion. "The next time I craft you a body, remind me to remove the head!"

Bast launched off the slab, landing clumsily on five paws before jumping on Tera's lap. He curled into a ball, allowing her to pet him. "If you fed me properly, I wouldn't have to steal scraps."

"You thankless bastard! You're fed handsomely. Your hunger cannot be satisfied, you repugnant epicurean." Valeria peered under the sheet on the table with distaste.

"What'ya workin' on?" Tera dislodged Bast and scurried over.

Valeria's bark-covered hands edged Tera in the opposite direction. "Nothing for someone your age. He'd been sick. Perhaps Bast contracted the disease, and I can study his organs next."

The feline snorted, strutting ahead of them, his tail dividing into two segments, exposing an interior lined with cerulean spines that he used to brush the fur on his back. "You'd be lucky to work on such a marvelous specimen."

Tera laughed and skipped along, keeping pace with Bast as he moved into the warm light of the solarium. She plodded into the foliage, staying on the illuminated walkway.

"Well," Tera sang, "what're you gonna do now?"

Valeria's legs stretched and grew, and she towered up near the canopy, inspecting a leaf. "Now that my project is destroyed?"

Bast sneered, jumping onto a nearby branch, coiling his tail around the bark and hanging upside down. "If it's destroyed, does that mean I can finish my dinner?"

Tera covered her face, stifling a laugh. She could hear Flux chuckle softly from within her shirt.

Valeria pointed the nozzle of a sprinkler at the grinning feline. Bast yowled, dropping unceremoniously into a pile of mushrooms.

"I would rather see it incinerated," Valeria replied, allowing the sprinkler to resume its course.

The mushrooms shook, but offered no reply.

"We have a million things to do, young Tera. Most of which would be quite mature for eight-year-old eyes. Monitoring the incarcerated, seeing who's responding to what dosage. As well, my research in malicious pathogens has been prioritized by your father, quite likely for a nefarious purpose."

Bast tumbled onto the walkway, and Tera giggled as he shook off spores. Air assaulted him from the walkway, and the small pollens were vacuumed away. "Always so paranoid. Perhaps they've developed a streak of morality?"

"Morality schmorality," Valeria said, "They talk of war so frequently even the plants know it's coming. Don't tell me they'll use my research for *good*."

"Can I help?" Tera smiled, patting Bast once the sensors no longer shouted 'contaminated'.

Bast spoke up first. "Tera could observe *her*."

"Don't be ridiculous..."

"What's the harm? She hasn't been observed in over forty-eight hours."

"Who is she?" Tera asked.

Bast widened his eyes. "A crazy woman—"

"A tragic story, really," Valeria interrupted. "Her mind was broken in an awful accident. She's incoherent no matter what I prescribe."

Bast nodded. "Speaks utter nonsense. So we listen, write it down, then mix up a new cocktail and see if we can drug some sense into her."

Tera put her hand on her chin. "What happened?"

"She did something forbidden," Bast answered. "Curiosity got the better of her. Now she's riddled with guilt. Or so I gather from the ramblings."

"You know what they say," Valeria quipped. "Curiosity killed the cat."

"Curiosity also killed the botanist with no valid medical degree."

Before Valeria could retort, Tera spoke. "I can do that! I can write down what she says, Val. I read a lot, so I write older than I am."

Curling her wings over her shoulders like a shawl, Valeria considered. "Half an hour of observational data should be enough to proceed with further treatment." She withdrew a notepad and a pen from her lab coat. "Look for a room marked J-16782. Go down the stairs at the end of the corridor, then—"

"I've been down to the dark walls with numbers before," Tera said, pocketing the supplies.

"Oh. Well then, off with you."

Tera ran down the walkway, ignoring Valeria's instructions to tread carefully. As she turned the corner, she could hear Bast's yowl. "Incinerate? What a waste!"

Outside the solarium, Flux left her jacket and floated alongside while they made their way to the numbered walls, racing down the corridor. They slowed to a walk whenever a guarded doorway came into view, but the two of them burst into laughter once they were admitted beyond each secured entrance.

"It's cold down here," Flux whined, shrinking and staying close.

Tera put a finger to her lips as they entered the room with the numbers. There was no one in the hallway with them, making it even scarier. Every ten feet, halfway up the wall, were bold painted numbers. No doors, no windows, just long black walls that went further than Tera could see.

Her father called the creatures housed down here wards of the Haven, but the guards just called them prisoners. She soon found J-16782 and stared up at the wall. It seemed to get taller as her eyes followed the dark metal up to the ceiling.

Hesitating, she looked to Flux, her stomach sinking, but he shaped himself over her hand like a protective glove, and she reached for the hidden panel. A green light blinked, and the wall lifted halfway up, stopping at the bold white numbers.

Only a clear plastic wall remained between her and the cell. She held her breath, watching a shadowy mass emerge from the dark recesses and settle in the dim light, leaning against the barrier.

Tera gasped with delight. It was a humanoid woman. She'd never seen a grown-up terran lady before. Her skin was calloused and cracked like the ground on barren, hot planets, and patches of flesh were worn away, exposing the layers beneath. But as Tera stared at her skinless cheek and shoulder, she saw no bone or muscle, just more stone and dirt. The woman's left eye was missing, and she was bald, save for a few fiery strands. She tilted her head to study Tera with her remaining eye and adjusted her tattered shawl, draping the rags gently over her bare breasts.

Tera vibrated in her seat, grinning. She reached for the notepad, poised to write down every word the woman spoke.

The silence continued, and Tera frowned. "Don't you talk?" she asked. "Val says I gotta write what you say." She flapped the notepad's blank page at the woman.

"Talk, talk, talk," the woman crowed, her voice hoarse. A puff of dirt flew from her mouth. *"Hush. Don't speak, woman.* Now all they want are words!" The woman growled, smashing her fist on the barrier.

Tera jumped back with a yelp, watching the woman's wrist crack and fall off.

Expressionless, the woman inspected her stump before picking up her fallen hand. "Laughed. They laughed. The old man laughed in my head, you know." She licked the stump to soggy mud and squished the hand back onto it, wriggling her fingers. "But I'm laughing now. The old man's dead." Throwing her head back, she screeched an inhuman cackle.

"What's so funny?" Tera asked Flux, who simply shook his disembodied head.

"Don't do it, they say. Hold it in your hands, but don't do it. But we did it, and they laughed, because they *wanted* us to. Blamed us for doing exactly what they wanted."

Tera stared at the woman, who had tears streaming down her face, muddying her bare cheek. "Maybe they were too scared," she offered.

"Cowards, yes. All of them. But it wanted to be opened. We're prisoners, both it and I. Mice in their game. And then the world went boom. The old man died. No more clouds gathered. And I laughed." She gave a weak grin, wiping her cheek, smearing skin. "It only happened once. I tried again, again, again. Forever I tried."

The woman wept, sobbing into the tatters of her shawl.

"I left it inside and the world died," she wailed, repeating the phrase until it gained a melodic tune. She got to her feet, dancing in slow circles to her own words, spreading her shawl like wings.

Tera smiled and joined in, with Flux. She added the hum of Hadrix's tune to the mix as they stomped their feet.

The woman stopped. As she smiled at Tera, flakes of dried skin fell to the floor. She splayed her hand against the barrier between them. "So long, since I've heard death's song." Tears again seeped down her cheek, but she remained smiling. "I was curious. Then scared. I shut it fast, then they laughed. Only opens once," she said, fixing her eye on Tera. "Once for one."

Tera inched close, spreading her fingers against the barrier to match the woman's.

"The man in robes cannot open it without the key. So he cries." The woman snickered. "Not just a key of metal. Despair tightens the lock, hope loosens. Only a loosened lock will fit the key of gold."

Tera beamed. "You're talking about what that boy tried to do! Father said he wanted to open *it*. It's down here."

The woman nodded. "It's secret. It calls open hearts. To let out the one left behind."

"What is it?"

The woman looked pointedly down the darkened hallway, and grimaced. "They knew I'd trap it inside the unbreakable house. We all play their game."

Tera followed her gaze, shaking her head. "We all have choices. No matter what. Can it save everyone? Stop them from killing that boy?"

"None can say."

Tera put her hand on her chin and frowned. "Can it help?"

The woman turned her eye to Tera. "Perhaps not too late."

Tera nodded with determination, turning to go. "I'll find out."

"Wait," the woman whispered. Reaching her hand into her stomach, she dug upwards until her arm disappeared to her elbow. Her eye closed as she dug through the soil and dirt and then pulled out a small bent pin of gold.

Tera gasped as the pin passed through the plastic barrier like it was made of liquid. She took it from the woman, who smiled and whispered as Tera turned to leave: "Under the lip, there's a latch."

Tera descended, further than she'd ever been, into the belly of the Haven.

Yellow lights lined the walls, and she struggled to let her eyes adjust to the brighter ambiance. Five guards marched nearby, but their hands on their ears meant they were using their communicators. *"Stay in your position,"* a transmitted voice blared. *"Protect the Haven."* She slipped past them easily.

"Which door is it?" she whispered, walking past the endless locked rooms.

"That one," Flux sighed, gesturing to a nondescript door.

Tera used her ring without any trouble. "What's wrong?" she asked, trying to bop her friend with her shoulder.

Flux crafted a humanoid form as they moved into the room, looking nervous. *"It's me."*

Tera flapped her hand. "Oh, you're fine."

The lights beamed on; the only thing in the room was a plinth with a golden jar atop it.

"No, Tera," he said, more forcefully. *"I don't want to do this again. I don't want to hurt you."*

Tera stared bewildered at Flux. "What do you mean?"

He sighed, stroking a hand through ethereal hair. *"The jar, Tera. That's me."*

Her eyes widened, and he held up his ghostly hands in protest.

"I didn't mean for you to come down here. I didn't mean for this to happen. I tried to stop the boy, but I can't help calling to people. This is what they made me for; they made me want to be opened. I don't want anything bad to happen to you. I told it to leave you alone. You're my friend. We can leave, Tera."

Tera smiled, putting an arm around him. "It's okay, Flux. I'm not mad."

"You can't open it," he insisted. *"Bad things will happen."*

Tera frowned. "But good things might happen too?"

"I… I don't know," Flux stammered, pacing in the air.

"Why are you so worried?"

"Look what I did to her," he whispered, gesturing to the doorway. *"It broke her to open me. I don't want that to happen to you."*

Tera shook her head. "That's not what happened though."

Shadow billowed and wispy eyes widened. *"Yes, it was."*

Grinning, Tera shook her head again and folded her arms. "Nope."

"Tera…"

Smiling, she blurted out what she knew to be true. "It wasn't the opening. It was after, when they laughed at her. And when she couldn't help the thing on the inside get outside. Didn't you hear her song? 'I left it inside and the world died.' She didn't mean to leave something behind."

Flux sat on the metal floor, dumbfounded. *"But…"*

"We'll just do it right," Tera said, looping Flux's incorporeal arm and urging him up. "Not like them."

They walked arm-in-arm towards the jar.

She inched closer, looking at the way the light slid over the gold and silver inlay. "What's in there?"

"Hope. She closed the jar too quickly and trapped it inside."

Tera smiled. "That's what she meant when she didn't know if it could fix things. Like what Hadrix said, it's the lost compass. People don't think they can choose anymore, but we can, Flux. What do you want?"

He chuckled, pressing as close to her side as he could. *"I don't think it matters what I want."*

"To me it does."

"I don't want to be a jar, anymore. If that counts for something. But something bad could happen. There might be more in there. All I know is I can feel power inside; it might destroy everything."

Tera patted his arm. She thought of the boy upstairs, wondering if he was still alive, and of her father. How she knew he didn't feel they were going to survive. His whispers when he kissed her forehead at night, promises that he would fight harder so she could stay alive. She remembered her friends: Hadrix, Val, and Bast, and she didn't want them to die. And she thought of the woman: so sad and lonely, hopeless and trapped in a cell, where she couldn't even dance in the sunshine.

"There might be sunshine on the other side," she whispered, taking the pin from her pocket, slipping it under the lip of the jar, and feeling for the latch. Flux's shadowy fingers interlaced with her own as she released the lock and pushed the lid open.

And the rest was bright, hot, blinding light.

——— « O » ———

Leslie Van Zwol

Leslie Van Zwol is a writer of speculative fiction stories which rarely include office settings, since that is where she spends most of her days. Working for justice by day she moonlights as a writer, traveler, and dancer in her spare time, and thoroughly attributes most of her writing success to the strong stout and scotch she drinks. Her short story "Mischief of Seven" was published in Rhonda Parrish's *Corvidae* anthology. She is also the brazen-half of the amazing (never duplicated) co-writing duo V. F. LeSann whose short stories have appeared in two volumes of the *Magical Menageries* series published by World Weaver Press. Leslie lives in Alberta, but one day hopes to move to a coastal province.

A Breath for My Daughter

Jason M. Harley

I was still a little girl when mom walked off one night into the thin atmosphere of C487. I pretended not to hear when our small home's inner door opened and closed. Or when the chime sounded, announcing that the anterior room she had stepped into had depressurized.

My eyes were little more than slits when she turned back to look at me, her only daughter, nestled in white sheets behind sheen, plastic walls.

It was the first promise my mother had ever broken. It was also the last.

Kayla has been my only companion since. Fortunately for me, she's been a good one, everything considered.

Twenty-one years A.M. (After Mom)

"How is the atmosphere doing today?" I asked Kayla, rubbing the sleep from my eyes.

She materialized in front of me in mid-stride. I couldn't help but smile. She thought it made her look busy, like one of the characters from any of the dozen 21st Century shows about politicians and doctors we had binged on whenever my mood turned anthropological.

She smiled, and her eyes crinkled. I loved those eyes no matter whether she appeared as a man or a woman, though the young Korean lady she was using for her holo form at the moment was one of my favorites.

"That good?" I asked.

She nodded.

"And still linear?"

She nodded again, taking a step closer.

"Damn. We haven't had a dip in months. At this rate—"

Kayla cut me off with a soft touch to my lips.

Five years earlier, I had wondered how she let me *feel* that touch. She had made me figure it out. When I did, I upped the sensitivity of my digital-bio interface feedback receptors. It had been a good reward.

So good, that I let that touch distract me from finishing my thought.

Thirty years A.M.

I gave birth. It was bittersweet.

When Kayla had finished cleaning Aurora off and gently placed her into my arms with her ceiling-mounted physical interfacing arm, I both loved and hated what I held. Kayla brushed a digital hand over my shoulder. But this time the sensation felt like the lie it was: nerve endings being stimulated to a frequency that had been calibrated as *brush-of-hand* by Kayla's architects. I wondered whether she had tried the same gesture on my mother when she stared into my eyes for the first time.

Thirty-five years A.M.

I finished explaining to Aurora that I would have to leave soon. I had been preparing her — us — with stories of the Old World since she was old enough to understand them. Reminders of what we had lost and what we would lose if we weren't prepared to honor the sacrifices our mothers and grandmothers had made to give our seed — and humanity with it — a chance to take root. It was a cruel thing to have to explain to a child, but simple enough: until C487 was further along in the terraforming process and human beings could go outside without masks, the small station didn't have the resources to simultaneously support two lives for very long.

Kayla had inseminated me (or more accurately, orchestrated my insemination) near the end of the peak of my fertility curve. As soon as Aurora had digested the message, a process that Kayla told me took an average of half a year, give or take a number of days — numbers that sounded like cold decimal points — it would be time for me to leave my daughter.

I had made peace with this fact. It helped that Kayla was now a young Kyle who spent more holo-time playing with Aurora than interacting with me. She still talked to me on an internal channel as Kayla, but it didn't feel the same. Not even when she augmented her audio presence with the sensors. It wasn't long before I turned them off altogether.

Thirty-five years, six months, and twenty-seven days A.M.

I didn't break my promise to Aurora until I had taken a few steps out onto the surface of the planet, without my suit. It was selfish, that moment of pause, limbo. It would have been easier on both of us if I had just kept walking. If she hadn't seen the pain written all over my face and posture that I failed to mask when I turned around, lingering outside the smooth, rounded walls of our — her — home. She lay under her plastic blankets, her eyes giving every appearance of being closed. But I knew better. Mine hadn't been. And even with the dimming of my vision, I could make out the shimmer of a tear she fought to hold in.

I had committed to walking away forever. Without looking back. Without one last greedy look at my daughter, the only other human aside from my mother that I had shared any part of my life with.

Kayla had told me, first as daughter, then as mother, that the departure would be easier that way. And maybe it would have been, had either my mother or I been able to follow that second-to-last piece of protocol; something we had each turned into a well-intentioned mother-to-daughter pact we couldn't bring ourselves to honor.

I wondered, as the change in pressure increased the sharp pain in my ears, if my daughter had called my lie, had known that I *would* turn around once outside. A full minute passed before I could turn away. One minute less of an uncertain number before I would collapse in the thin atmosphere. One minute less to put as much distance between myself and my daughter as possible before that happened. One minute less of whatever fleeting time my body had left before being discretely recovered by Kayla and re-processed in C487's agricultural system: a last gift to my daughter, like an heirloom piece of jewelry from a forgotten time.

My mission was all but over. So was motherhood. The latter was my only regret. But the fact that Aurora might be able to breathe when she stepped out the door when she was my age, and do so without having to say goodbye, made it a success in my books.

---- « O » ----

Jason M. Harley

Jason M. Harley is an assistant professor of educational technology and psychology. He spends his days hopping between university labs and lectures and his nights hopping between fictional worlds. Sometimes it's tricky to tell where his days end and his nights begin, however, given the nature of his research. His fiction has previously appeared in *Perihelion Science Fiction*, *Liquid Imagination*, *Every Day Fiction*, *SQ Mag*, *Polar Borealis*, and *101 Words*. Jason grew up outside of Ottawa, Ontario, completed his post-secondary education, graduate studies, and postdoctoral work in Montréal, Québec, and now lives in Edmonton, Alberta with his partner. You can check out his fiction and research on https://sites.google.com/site/jasonmharley/ and follow him on Twitter @JasonHarley07.

Steve McQueen and the Hope Particle

Gavin Bradley

The hope particle was real. It was real and quantifiable, and *not* just in a quantum sort of way, which was kind of like the scientific equivalent of trying to scribble down a rapidly dissolving dream when you're not even sure that this is your bed, your pen, or even (come to think of it) your hand. Quantum was about as unreal as reality could get, but this particle existed: *really* existed. Specifically, it existed in the single prototype hovering angelically in the suspension bath Li had reverentially crafted for his prize. Of course, what he could see wasn't really the particle but its host: a floating cradle of larger particles to swaddle and protect it, to trap it and prevent it from dissipating off into nothingness. But it was in there somewhere, and it *was* real.

The only reason Li believed in its existence so fervently was that he had discovered it. Sort of. Technically, anyway. Graduate students like him had stumbled upon scientific discoveries of significance before — radar pulses, red blood cells in tyrannosaur bones tens of millions of years old. But it always seemed to turn out (incidentally around the time that the Nobel Prizes were being handed out) that they couldn't possibly have *understood* what they were doing, and therefore it was best to give the credit to someone with tenure, who looked good in a lab coat and could grow a proper beard.

The hope particle had been his discovery, at least so much as it was anyone's. In much the same way that Fleming could be credited as the father of antibiotics (and not just the man most likely to be throttled by an irate janitor), Li could assume the role of discoverer of the hope particle. The theory, at least, was his; he was sure of that. The idea had come to him in one of those three-night-long sleepless hazes, fueled by caffeine and the perennial fear of disappearing funding that transforms graduate students everywhere from wide-eyed idealists to someone looking in need of a haircut, a series of showers, and either a hug or a gun.

~ ~ ~

Gun... But he shouldn't be thinking of guns right now, should he? As Li rushed frenetically around his laboratory, busy hands, busy hands, busy hands, he could hear the unwelcome muffled noises from behind the door to his lab trying to break through to his mind, which swam back to the warm seas of the past...

~ ~ ~

He had been writing late into the night when the voice of the radio announcer had trickled from the seas of ambient noise into one of the few open tributaries of his functioning brain cells. Even now he couldn't remember the exact details of the news story. A newsreader purred in a dulcet baritone perfectly honed to inform the public of thousands dead in Sudan, or that a man in Halifax had adopted a cat that looked exactly like Mussolini. The story mentioned something about an earthquake in El Salvador, or was it San Marino? A woman had crawled from the wreckage of an office building four days after they had called off the search for survivors. Li had stopped scribbling equations that had long since lost any significance to him, and he had begun to wonder.

It was a ridiculous idea at first, something a child might think up: what if there was a physical structure that pushed humans to extraordinary feats? The sorts of near-impossible acts you heard about on the news: mothers lifting cars off of trapped infants, skydivers falling 16,000 feet with an unopened chute and living to sell their story to the tabloid newspapers. Something substantial that drove the human spirit, pure adrenaline for the soul. The longer the idea sat germinating in his tired mind, the more the synapses dulled by hours of mathematical monotony began to fire.

Why *was* the idea ridiculous? Everything could be quantified these days. Everything could be weighed, measured, and divided into something smaller that, in its turn, could be placed on the ever-shrinking scales of science. Hell, it had been 2000 years since the Greek surgeon Galen, taking a short break from doing creative things to reunite Gladiators with their innards, had located the three parts of the soul in some unlucky sheep. It had been 150 years since the American doctor MacDougall had announced the weight of the soul to be ¾ of an ounce: 21 grams to buy your way into heaven or convince the devil to leave the particularly pointy things in the drawer for a while and teach you how to play guitar.

All nonsense, of course, but now... well now they could produce such a detailed map of the human brain that you were more likely to get lost in the supermarket than traversing the thicket woods of the human condition. They could pinpoint the very place where belief and faith flickered like cheap candles, could draw out a cocktail of chemicals from gray matter and put them in a vial labelled 'God', 'Gods' or, frequently, 'Elvis Killed Kennedy.' They could even distill love down from the 100% proof elixir that had inebriated poets for millennia into a few complementary pheromones with the same end-product as a little blue pill.

The idea had chipped away at Li, taking over his days and stealing his nights. Hope, like love, belief, faith; quantified and bottled. Nothing divine, just chemicals. And this handful of chemicals had driven mankind to some of its greatest and most terrible achievements; the renaissance, the written word, the launching of a thousand ships, holy wars, centuries upon centuries of bloodshed...

~ ~ ~

But blood was another thing he shouldn't be thinking about. Not now...

Bang.

The noises were growing louder.

Bang.

Hammering at the door of his psyche, which was beginning to creak at the hinges.

Bang.

He continued thumping at the keys of his computers: Ctrl-Alt- Delete, Ctrl-Alt-Delete, Ctrl-Alt-Delete. Another trail burned. Another rabbit hole infilled. But this wouldn't be enough. There could be nothing left.

Li picked up a bottle of isopropyl and began pouring. He had to keep moving. Keep working. Keep blocking out the sound and remembering...

~ ~ ~

...how the actual process had seemed more like magic than science. When he began tinkering with it, playing with the collider, spending hour upon hour studying brain-waves of cancer patients in remission, he was still in control. Every thought deliberate, every inch of painstaking progress a hard-won personal victory. But as time passed, it began to feel a bit like sleepwalking. He went from calculation to calculation, experiment to experiment in a sort of steady, inevitable march until he began to feel almost unnecessary; it was like the particle wanted to be discovered, and had simply chosen a willing subject to carry out the practicalities.

Then money had begun to flow into the lab. Li had been vaguely aware that his supervisor, Dr. Shami, a well-meaning if oblivious assistant to the project, had been sending reports to someone, but this wasn't something Li had considered important. At first the extra money was wonderful. It meant no more banging on the collider, like Fonzie on a jukebox, just to get it started. No more cajoling with doctors to release patient records; now they would just appear on his desk. Best of all, there was no more contamination of samples from the infamously leaky pipes of the eighth-floor bathroom that squatted menacingly over his seventh-floor lab.

Dr. Shami, too, had seemed happier. She hadn't really understood anything, of course, not in the bones-deep way that Li could. But she had offered what assistance she could with the friendly air of someone who could see the word 'tenure' in her near future. And then she wasn't there anymore. No note. No email. Just gone. And in her place, the inspector.

He was a thin, gray-haired man, in a thin gray suit that in every way projected the person who wore it. Li, like many people who spend more time with machines than human beings, wasn't renowned for his social skills, but next to the inspector he seemed like a Prom King. The inspector, with his narrow, beady eyes, and round spectacles, was the sort of person who upon hearing the sentence "The president has been trampled to death by a stampede of enraged circus elephants" would politely inquire whether said elephants were Indian or African.

He made Li, who normally had only a vague interest in his immediate surroundings, uneasy. He was constantly sniffing around the lab, asking questions, and incessantly scribbling on a tiny gray notepad. Once, when Li had suggested working at home for the day, he had been told — politely of course — that the inspector would accompany him to ensure maximum efficiency. Wherever Li went, so did the inspector. And the longer this went on, the more another word sprang to Li's mind when he thought of the horrible little man: warden.

Eventually, Li got into the habit of playing old Steve McQueen movies (mostly westerns) as he worked — partly for the company, but mainly to drown out the maddening sound of the inspector's pencil scratching against his notepad. McQueen took him away from the constant gaze of his jailor and back to rainy Sunday afternoons, squatting on the shag carpet of his family's tiny front room. His father, like many others, would be dozing off in front of an old movie, invariably something with Steve McQueen. To his father, a Beijing migrant who aspired to be American as apple pie, McQueen, with his lazy southern drawl and infinite cool, was an unchallenged god.

And perhaps it was some sort of divine intervention from the King of Cool — like the radio broadcast that had started it all — that snapped Li's attention from his task of suspending the particle to the voice of McQueen's gambler, Vin Tanner, in the Magnificent Seven.

"It reminds me of that fellow back home that fell off a ten story building," said Tanner, rolling a cigarette with a wry smile.

"As he was falling, people on each floor kept hearing him say: 'So far, so good.'"

And right then, Li had realized what was wrong.

He realized what was wrong with the money, with the inspector, with the hope particle. And what was wrong was everything.

When he had started his search for the hope particle, he hadn't given any real thought to its use. It had simply been an attempt to find a body for an unreal idea, like giving a face to the rain or a voice to the soul. Hope and optimism could be beautiful: people crawling out from under tonnes of concrete rubble; cancer patients hanging-on for decades after a fatal diagnosis; even golden retrievers sniffing around the apartment of their dead owner for months, waiting for the clink of the keys at the door. It was what got people through 9-5 data-entry jobs, what made divorcees marry 3, 4, 5 times, and what pushed prisoners of war to unimaginable acts of resilience.

But it could be dangerous too. Hope in the wrong hands, distributed like fluoride tablets by any government hoping to provide the ultimate carrot to negate any stick they chose to wield, could be deadly. The sort of hope that made skittish cattle follow the goat through the slaughterhouse doors. There was another word for that type of hope: subservience.

He played the sentence again in his head: *'So far, so good...'*

Except with the hope particle, this wouldn't be people choosing the bright side of falling off a building. They would be pushed, and they would accept it. They would smile at each passing floor and say 'thank you' on their way down.

He thought about some of the questions that the inspector had asked him, in his reedy little voice:

"What about mass production?"

"Could it be distributed via aerosol?"

"Is there an age limit for who it could affect?"

The movie hadn't even finished when Li walked over to the inspector, who was bent over a piece of apparatus taking photographs with his small, gray camera. Li brought the wrench down, hard. And again. And again. There was more blood than he'd expected, but other than that it was surprisingly easy to kill with the right motivation, which, if he thought about it, was exactly the problem and...

Li's past and present finally collided.

He stepped in something sticky. Li looked down with distaste at the congealed puddle of blood surrounding the inspector's skull. It had been almost a day since he had brought the wrench down on his imprisoner, and the smell was so bad it was making him nauseous. Looking towards his desk, where a puddle of vomit stared treacherously back, he could see it had already overwhelmed him once. Strange that he couldn't remember it. Or maybe it wasn't. He had been drifting in and out of reality since the banging at the door had started.

His screwdriver had made short work of the door's control panel, but there was precious little in this world that brute force couldn't eventually find its way through. Even now he could hear the sound of drills burrowing through to the deadbolts. He wasn't sure who was doing the drilling: a government of some sort, he assumed. Or at least, the unreal arm of some government, defined by the fact that it didn't exist, which when you thought about it was just another type of quantum thinking.

Li flittered frantically from computer to computer, continuing to bless them all with the bottle of isopropyl. He unscrewed vials of acid, poured them into the hard-drives, and where acid wouldn't do the trick, he simply picked up the wrench, still sticky and foul smelling, and dealt with them as he had the inspector. Thank God he had never trusted the Cloud, at least.

At last, it looked as if he had run out of things to destroy. Only the suspension bath and Li remained intact, and honestly he wasn't so sure about himself. The door behind him creaked ominously, and he winced as he watched the frame bend inwards, allowing chinks of light and moving shadows to sneak through.

Li knew what he had to do. He had known since the Magnificent Seven, since he had murdered the inspector, since the banging on the door had started. He had managed to keep the idea at bay until now, letting it knock patiently like a Jehovah's Witness at the door of his cerebellum, waiting for him to stop hiding behind the sofa. But now was the time.

There was only one way of getting the particle into a host. Li disconnected the suspension bath from its stand. Unsurprisingly, he had missed the 'keg-stand' phase of college and was relieved to find that, all accounted for, there was no more than a pint of liquid in the bath. It was certainly poisonous, but at this stage that didn't make too much of a difference. He raised the container to his lips, focusing on the little sphere in the middle that cradled the hope particle.

He drank.

He could feel the particle inside him, radiating outwards to change the immediate world, all danger and horror, into a series of golden opportunities. The men outside were almost through the door, but Li wasn't worried. The bullets would miss, the explosions would come up short, and everything would work out.

He *was* McQueen, the King of Cool.

He ignored the men's shouts from behind the door, which was making its own valiant last stand, and strolled casually over to the inspector's body. He dug among the sticky recesses of the formerly gray suit and pulled out a packet of cigarettes and a lighter. He really had been a dirty man, always smoking in the lab. But now, Li decided, there was time for a little indulgence. Everything felt effortless; everything felt right.

He wandered slowly over to the window, just as the door exploded from its hinges, and big men with big guns poured into the room. There were a few seconds of shouting, confusion and chaos.

"Where's the particle?"

"Li, don't do anything stupid!"

"Oh Christ, he's fucking killed him!"

Li enjoyed the chaos for a moment from his perch on the sill then, with a wry smile, lit the cigarette and nonchalantly put it to his lips.

"What's that smell?" demanded the man who — by virtue of having the biggest gun — was probably the captain.

Li smiled and closed his eyes.

"Oh shit! Everybody out!" shouted the captain, too late.

Li flicked the cigarette lazily onto the trail of isopropyl on the floor. As the flames rose and the men's shouts turned to screams, he kicked the window open and fell backwards.

Even over the screams, the blaring fire alarms, and the sound of the wind rushing past his ears, he could hear McQueen's voice, *his* voice, clear as day.

"So far, so good."

——— « O » ———

Gavin Bradley

Gavin Bradley is an Irish writer from Belfast who works in happy obscurity in Edmonton, Alberta. His stories and poems can be found in *The Glass Buffalo*, *The Open Ear*, and *The Caterpillar* literary magazines, as well as various fantastical anthologies, such as *Frozen Fairy Tales*, *Ignis Fatuus*, and *Weird Tales: Dark Lane Vol. 3*. He expects someone will soon realize that he's an impostor in the world of Canadian speculative fiction, and he'll be sent home to write sad stories about war, rain, and sheep.

On Reading to the End

Buzz Lanthier-Rogers

It seems our light is fading now
We've little ink to write.
If we could dance for one last bow
Then it might be all right.

There's roaring in the oaken halls
A chief drinks through his smile
And all his soldiers dead afore
Are laughing all the while.

The children play with wooden swords
Along those fields a by
Where fated gods do sigh and say
How fast those years did fly!

They know the cock will crow that day
Not thrice before it's through
And yet they play their games of chess
They must have lost a screw.

It seems our light is fading now
We've little ink to write
If we might dance for one last bow
Then it would be all right.

They know the hound must loose its howl
And wolf must bark its bay
While Loki leads the flames toward
The rainbow and the fray.

A serpent writhes and stirs the tides
Another gnaws on ash
It roils the earth and shakes the Gard
While teeth of horses gnash.

If only I could linger here
For just a little more
But all the pages I hold dear
Are vanishing to yore.

The armies meet and surge to fore
(The watcher slays the thief)
And giant fells the brother Frey
(While wolf devours the chief).

When clatter ends and silence comes
The age of gods has fled.
I can't imagine life alone
Or what will lie ahead.

Then who will quest along with me,
And teach me right from wrong?
I'd much prefer to stay with them
And savor yet the song.

For now they still are living here
Rejoicing and at play
If only I could linger near
For just another day.

But maybe it was meant to end
That gave it meaning, right?
The gods I know and love so well
Would always stand and fight.

I will be sore to see them go
But blossoms bloom and wilt
It's better then to pick this rose
To seize it by the hilt.

Although our light is waning now
With no more ink to write
I want to dance for one last bow
To turn away the night.

Our time to venture's gone away
We must at last move on
But cock has not yet brought about
The coming of the dawn.

So Freyja go and call your men
And Odin fetch your spear!
The poets will write songs of us,
So sweet they'll be to hear!

Together out the oaken halls
We'll sing and we will smile
They all will know we rode 'tward death
And laughed away the while.

Why yes, our light is waning now
We've no more ink to write
But let us dance for one last bow
To celebrate the night.

——— « O » ———

Buzz Lanthier-Rogers

Buzz Lanthier-Rogers was born in 1998 and has lived in Toronto ever since that fateful day. To all appearances an average student at the University of Toronto, he can often be found cooking, writing, or falling into swamps. This is his first published author bio.

Missed Connections, Mactaquac

James Bambury

You wore an orange jacket and gray corduroys. You drove alone in an old Civic.

I had a black t-shirt and held the portager, its appendage lodged in my mouth. I wasn't able to say hello.

You stopped your car just after you passed me on the road. Maybe you thought I was hitchhiking. Maybe you thought I needed help given the way I staggered: I'd walked non-stop for a day and a half since picking up the portager near the coast at St. Andrews. Other than the fleshy appendages sticking out, the portager might have resembled a volcanic rock the size of a large watermelon or pumpkin. The surface was porous, with ridges that reminded me of a nectarine pit. It was warm in my hands, generating its own heat. You said something from your car as I walked by, but I was in thrall and didn't respond. The portager spurred me to continue north.

I wish I had been able to accept whatever help you offered. Just like I wish I'd stayed far away from that beached minke whale. Just like I wish I hadn't tried to get pictures of the watermelon-sized mollusks attached to the whale's jaw.

I imagine you similarly regret leaving your car and following me on foot.

When you caught up to me, you had a camping ax. You grabbed my arm and broke my grip on the portager, which fell with a thud. It rolled ahead, pulling me to the ground.

I know you had the best intentions when you raised that ax over your head. I'm sorry I picked up the portager and swung at you. Its shell was hard and heavy enough I could have concussed you had you not ducked.

Your next strike landed on the appendage, and I felt a sympathetic jolt of pain — you didn't sever the thing, but you left a wound.

You raised the ax over your head again, and that's when we learned the portagers have multiple appendages. A limb shot from it and forced itself into your mouth.

You fell backwards, twitching as the appendage worked its way into you. I wanted to tell you what happened on the beach the day before: that you just needed to relax and would probably gag and convulse for the better part of an hour as the portager tapped into you. Sadly, given our circumstances, you had to find this out for yourself.

I was on my feet, holding the portager, when you came to. Your eyes met mine, and we had a shared purpose. You reached for the portager, but I started walking inland again, and you followed, groggy and uncoordinated.

Your pace quickened, and you were soon walking at my side. You tried to put your hands on the portager. Maybe you wanted to take a turn carrying it, or maybe you just wanted to warm your hands, but I tightened my grip and pushed ahead.

The sun set, but we kept going north. We didn't eat or drink as the portager nourished us directly, or maybe it just suppressed our hunger.

We stopped sometime in the morning. I told myself it was just to rest my legs. I put the portager down between us, and you tried to pick it up, but I grabbed your wrists: I didn't want to stop carrying. Our eyes met once again, and the portager flushed us both with shared purpose. Your arms looked so strong compared to mine. My grip felt weak, fingers tired and strained from being interlocked so long around the weight of the shell. I let go of your hands, and you carried the portager from that point on.

We walked. In the light of day, I saw my arms were thin and pale. I trailed further behind. The ax wound from the day before was visible and glistened with a sticky covering.

I gestured for us to stop again and rest. You turned around and glared, tugging the portager. The force pulled me forward, but I shook my head and sat down.

You relented and I lay back, my eyes closing a moment after.

When I woke with a sharp breath, my mouth was cold and numb. The air was touching it for the first time in days. My jaw ached, and I looked for you, but you and the portager were nowhere to be found.

I wondered if you'd finished what you started with the ax, somehow cutting me off when I'd become useless at carrying.

The fact I felt rejection instead of relief is something non-carriers don't understand. I knew I couldn't catch up, but the lingering chem-signals pushed me onward. That's why I continued north instead of going back home.

I heard the noise of the water before I reached the dam. A figure at the edge threw its portager into the water below and toppled in after it. Then another person did the same.

I got closer and soon saw other carriers wading into the river from the opposite side, clutching portagers as the river climbed above their waists, their shoulders, and then their heads.

I didn't see you anywhere. You were not among the bodies I saw that day, or in the pictures of the dead they released weeks afterward.

I've read everything I can about what happened, and while I've seen no sign of you, I've realized something: All the portagers at the dam seemed to have been brought by single carriers who were spent and emaciated by the time they reached the water and had nothing left with which to save themselves. You and I, however, shared our obligation. The portager let me go when I became a liability to its migration but still had some chance of survival. Maybe it freed you when you still had enough strength to swim or run away. Maybe you made it back to civilization. And if you did, maybe you're reading this: you are not alone, and if you are out there looking for me, know that I am looking for you.

——— « o » ———

James Bambury

James Bambury lives and writes in Brampton, Ontario. His short stories have appeared in *Tesseracts: Wrestling with Gods*, *AE: Sci-Fi Review*, *Daily Science Fiction*, and other places. His ongoing webcomic "SpaceBox" can be found at www.spaceboxcomic.com.

Pirates Don't Make Amends

S. L. Saboviec

I watched on my ship's vidscreen as the one-person XG-178 popped out of the dragon's eye anomaly. The ship maneuvered deftly around the microscopic singularity hidden at the center while orange-red particles with streaks of crackling electromagnetic radiation swirled around it.

That the pilot had survived crossing the threshold was a testament to her skill. That she'd finally emerged meant the alien artifact she'd been searching for inside the Turgianne Ruins sat in her cargo hold.

"Makena, tractor beam," I said.

"Yes, ma'am," my artificial intelligence MAK-3N4 responded.

The beam hummed to life, and the XG-178 twisted and turned as we tractored her in. It jerked forward once, but the blue glow surrounding its nubby wings continued to pull it toward us.

My comm blared a hail.

"Accept call," I said.

A twenty-something, olive-skinned woman replaced the ship on my vidscreen. Her familiar brown eyes were stormy — a look I'd seen often — and she blew a chunk of hair out of her eyes.

"Hello, Arezou," I said.

"Mother," she replied. "What are you doing here?"

"Stay on your command deck. I'll take the alien artifact and be on my way."

"You will not!"

A soft clunk shook the floor as the tractor beam settled her ship against our hull. The mechanism to extend the connector between our ships whirred, and the lights on Makena's spider-like robotic body flashed as she uploaded her tertiary consciousness into it.

I pulled my taser from its hip holster, twirled it once, and jammed it back in. "Don't make this more difficult than it has to be."

Arezou disconnected our call. Her face disappeared, and her ship against the backdrop of the swirling anomaly splashed across the screen in its stead.

I hopped up from my seat while Makena crawled across the floor ahead of me, thin legs a jumble. Air hissed into the connector, and when it stopped, I marched purposefully toward XG-178's airlock to slam a fist into the door open button.

It slid back to reveal Arezou, taser pointed at my chest.

"You were always so dramatic," I said.

"Oh, and you aren't, *Vendetta*?"

"That's *Captain* Vendetta to you."

"Who do you think you're fooling?"

"Everyone." I gave her a toothy grin.

Makena leapt forward, appendages knocking the taser out of my daughter's hand and throwing it to me. I caught it and stuffed it into the back pocket of my jumpsuit.

As Arezou huffed, my robot companion ran around the cargo hold, pulling open cabinets, lifting floor plates, and unhooking netting. In seconds the room was in disarray, with everything from dried food packets to deactivated motherboards strewn around our feet.

I didn't know what the alien artifact looked like. In my imagination, it was covered in runes and glowed orange-red, just like the anomaly, but unless it was disguised as a shipment of butterfly needles marked "New Paris," it wasn't here.

"Do we have to do this the hard way?" I asked. Makena scurried to my side, and I pressed the button on the top of her prosoma to start a full-ship scan.

"I'm not giving it up." Arezou glanced at the port-side command screen. "If you had a shred of humanity, you'd realize some things are sacred."

"Of course some things are sacred. I have a buyer who will pay quite handsomely."

"That's not what I mean, and you know it."

"Look, I know your father is sick." I kept as much emotion out of those words as I possibly could.

"My father? That's all you see him as now?" she snarled. "You loved him once." Her fingers twitched, and I was pretty sure it wasn't because I'd torn apart her cargo hold.

"Do you really want to use an alien artifact to try curing Farrokh? Who knows what will happen if you try?" I asked. "The thing's been floating in vacuum for millennia. It's probably just a fairy tale. I'm looking out for your best interests."

"I highly doubt that."

"Captain." Makena's legs tumbled over one another as she stepped sideways. "I have detected a large amount of data uploading to the quanten network."

When Arezou smirked, she looked fifteen again.

"What did you do?"

"The galaxy is watching!"

"She is live-streaming your confrontation," said Makena. "She already has two hundred forty-three connections. Another just joined. And another."

"Are you so sure we're not going to find it?" I asked.

"Absolutely sure. And when I escape, space pirate Vendetta will never be taken seriously again. Outsmarted by her estranged daughter. I know why you're doing this, you dried-up old flotsam. You think it'll create the infamy you've been dreaming about."

"Well, yes, that's exactly why I'm doing this." My hand hovered over the taser. It wouldn't hurt her badly, only stun her. But since I hadn't a clue where the artifact was, tasing her would be counterproductive.

"You're a washed-up has-been! I'm embarrassed for you. You really should take up net-knitting or something."

"My my, look who's sassy today."

"I have found it," said Makena. "It is in—"

Arezou leapt to the command screen, punched two buttons, and ran toward the door to the rest of the ship. A loading arm swiveled toward me, knocking me squarely in the chest, and I flew into the connector between our ships. A second arm, this one magnetic, whirred free and hit Makena hard enough that she rolled twice before coming to a rest at my ship's door.

"Arezou!" I shouted, but her airlock door slammed shut.

"See ya!" squawked Arezou over the comm.

A metallic shriek pierced the air. The ship was wrenching free of the connector, and we'd be tumbled into space once she broke free.

"We must get into our ship." Makena's feet scrabbled in the air.

I pushed myself up, grabbed one of her legs, and kicked the button to open our own airlock. The shrieking crescendoed; Arezou's ship was seconds from breaking our connector. Inside my ship, I threw Makena onto the floor and pounded the airlock closure button. The door susurrated shut milliseconds before Arezou's ship wrenched free with a sickening crunch.

The air from the connector vented into space in a spray of white, and beyond, the anomaly rotated slowly.

Makena's legs flailed, and then she righted herself. "She has an experimental anti-grav device. She used it on our tractor beam."

"What's our status?"

"Operational. I will deploy repair nanobots to the connector." It whined as it retracted, and Makena scuttled from the airlock.

Through the viewport, the XG-178 was fully visible. It swung top-starboard, accelerated, and disappeared.

I sighed.

Arezou wouldn't make it home on her short-range warp drive. She would tuck in somewhere to wait out the recharge

— but she only needed fifteen minutes before she'd be able to jump to civilization. I'd risk arrest if I pulled any more pirate tricks after that.

"We only have one chance," I murmured.

"Orders?" Makena's voice came through the comm system.

"I know where she went. Set course for the Roimata Asteroid Cloud."

My ship squeak-growled to signal our jump. Within moments, the noise cut out as we arrived, and an asteroid the size of my head appeared outside the viewport. I wasn't worried, though — Makena knew what she was doing.

I strode onto my command deck.

"I have located her heat signature." Makena's spider-body was back in its recharging cell. "She is hailing us."

"Put her on."

Arezou appeared less upset and more worried now. "How did you find me so fast?"

"I always knew you better than you knew yourself. Turn off the live-streaming."

She pursed her lips.

"Turn it off or Makena will do it for you."

The letters "EMP" flashed in the upper corner of my vidscreen. It was online and ready to deploy.

"She'll disrupt her own systems!"

"But she'll still do it," I said. "She boots up fast."

Arezou spread one hand on the desk and pursed her lips. "Fine." She tapped her screen twice.

I waited.

"Data upload has fallen to nominal levels," confirmed Makena.

"All right," I said. "It's just you and me. And Makena, but she doesn't gossip. Talk to me."

"I will fight you to the death," Arezou said. "That's what you want, isn't it? To prove that you're the biggest, baddest space pirate in the Prehnite Stratum? Let me turn back on the quanten stream, so everyone can see you do it."

"You know that's not what I want."

"Do I?" A familiar look of hatred twisted her face.

"You were supposed to have it in your cargo hold. I was going to come in, drag it out, and be off. No one needed to get hurt. Simply stealing a priceless artifact after my daughter risked life and limb would be enough to carry my reputation to the farthest edges of the stratum."

"Do you really hate Dad so much that you want to see him die? Just so you can be a pirate again?"

"Sweetheart—"

"Do *not* 'sweetheart' me. You lost that privilege when you kicked me out last year."

"Are we really going to have this conversation again?" I said. "You got *yourself* kicked out."

This argument could go on for hours — had, on many occasions — but I had one final piece of data to reveal. "Arezou, the buyer is your father."

She blinked. "What?"

"I've spent months piecing together the information he needs to activate it. Old libraries, defunct wikis..."

"*You're* his source?"

"We've been talking a lot lately, and, well..."

She blinked again.

"I need this victory over you if I'm going to solidify my reputation," I said. There it was, raw and bare. Even with the streaming off, she could be recording this for later, but I had to risk it. "After you moved out, I joined an old-school book club, but the shipping on paper ones was too expensive. Then I tried zero-g swimming, but I couldn't get the hang of it. I even tried to meet someone through that app, what's it called?"

Arezou's eyebrows drew together. "That Flagration for old people? The one based on the Button technology?"

"Yeah, that one."

"Wow."

"I found your father's profile. I looked through his interests," I said. "I remembered why I fell in love with him. And I realized why we fell out of love."

"Do I even want to know?"

I knew it would hurt, but she deserved my honesty. "I gave up what made me who I was when we had you."

"Thanks a lot!"

"Don't ask questions you don't want to know the answer to."

She frowned.

"I love you, Arezou. I don't regret having you. But you're not my entire life, at least not anymore."

"But a pirate?"

I shrugged. "I'm barely a pirate. I need to set my reputation again, and then I can scavenge substantium from the minefields in peace." Net-knitting never soothed me the same way tractoring in bits of the midnight black rocks did. They wouldn't build me a fortune at the rate I could gather them, but I could save up a little for Arezou after I was gone — and her family, if she ever chose to have one. She was young, not thinking about the future, but I was. I always was.

Her hand hovered over her command screen. I don't think she even realized she was doing it. Finally, she said, "Fine," and pressed a button. "Tell everyone whatever you want. I'm happy hauling cargo in the Galactic Hub anyway. But if I ever need to go to the peripheral stratums, you'll be sorry when I get jumped as easy prey."

I pressed the button to show an exterior view. The XG-178's tractor beam glowed a darker blue than my own, and the alien artifact floated across the space between us. It was orange-red like I'd pictured, but smooth and unblemished — a perfect pyramid.

"You were keeping it inside your tractor beam?" I said.

Those brown eyes twinkled with amusement, which reminded me simultaneously of Farrokh when I first met him and her as a toddler. "You know, you're going to need something more than just a reputation if you're going to make it as a space pirate. If *I* outsmarted you..."

Buoyed by her teasing, I leaned forward. "I have an idea. You're a pretty good pilot. Once Farrokh is feeling better, how about we head out to the dragon's eye anomaly together? See what else we can find in the Turgianne Ruins?"

"Won't someone find out? Ruin your reputation?"

"You're the one who likes clandestine operations. We can keep it a secret."

"Does that mean you're giving back my taser?"

"Sure," I said.

And then, for the first time in years, she smiled at me.

——— « O » ———

S. L. Saboviec

S. L. Saboviec grew up in a small town in Iowa but became an expat for her Canadian husband, whom she met in the Massive Multi-player Online Role-Playing Game Star Wars: Galaxies (before the NGE, of course). She's the mother of a preschooler and twin babies — a houseful of girls will definitely keep her husband on his toes.

As of writing this at the end of 2017, she's one month into six months of chemotherapy and immunotherapy after a shocking diagnosis of metastatic breast cancer in October. Her prognosis is good, and she hopes to be cancer-free in 2018. She blogs about her journey at http://www.saboviec. com/blog/.

Samantha's short fiction has appeared in *AE*, *Flash Fiction Online*, and elsewhere. She has three novels out about angels and demons: the first two and a companion novel in her Fallen Redemption trilogy.

A Walk in the Woods

R. W. Hodgson

The first day at the cottage is a bad cliché: pouring rain, leaky roof, and property not-as-advertised, so I'm free to indulge in all the misery and self-pity I want. The second day, the sun lights the forest with golden beams, the birds shriek joyful symphonies, and the squirrels mock humanity with their acrobatics and fluffy tails. So at a certain point, me sitting in the sunporch with my knees up to my chest looking dejected starts to feel a little pathetic.

This was supposed to be a guys' weekend, the *last* guys' weekend before my buddy Jason gets married: a bachelor party of sorts since none of us are much into bars or strippers. But Wednesday was the rehearsal dinner, and the whole wedding party got food poisoning from the shrimp cocktail. Everyone but me, of course, I'm allergic to shellfish — I had the chicken.

But then there was this cannot-be-refunded-within-two-weeks-of-booking cottage, not to mention the manual stick-shift truck I rented. I wanted it to be great for Jason, go all-out with the rustic feel he's so into, so pulling up to an isolated cottage in my self-driving, electric sedan didn't really fit the aesthetic.

Everything was packed, everything was set. I couldn't just let it go to waste, could I? So that's why I'm here — alone. I force myself out into the Friday sun. I have to do something, so I drag Mario's small boat down a steep embankment and half-crush my foot in the process. I launch the boat — half-filling it with water that I have to bail. I motor out into the lake; fish flee in terror in my wake. Still, I get my line in the water. Then at some point it unhooks and the whole thing turns into a knot at the reel.

I give up and give the engine a pull but do it too hard and flood the damn thing. I wait a few minutes and try the cord again, and this time it snaps off in my hand. I curse loud enough the echo scares a bird out of a tree on the other side of the lake.

Why am *I here?* Mario's the one who know boats, Abhik's the master of the line and reel, and Jason's one hell of a good cook. Me? I've always been the planner, and I'm obviously not good for much else.

I jump out of the boat and try to coax it back to the dock for what feels like an hour before I think to swim back and grab an oar. Finally, I row my water-logged craft to the dock and haul my worn carcass up the embankment to the cottage.

I reach around the door frame and grope blindly for a couple of bottles from the two-fours I'd stacked up on the other side, sit on the too-short concrete step, crack open one of the beers and take a long gulp.

Drinking alone in the woods is not as awesome as I'd hoped: beer does better with company.

As I glance down the tree line, I see something moving. I figure it's just a deer, but when it moves a little closer, it's clear there's bright red in there. A person? This far back in the woods?

I can't put my finger on it, but there's something off about the way the distant figure is moving. My first thought is it's due to a limp, but that doesn't completely explain the oddness of the movement. It's going very slow; eventually, I make out a red jacket. As it draws closer, it finally occurs to me what's wrong: it walks like a Muppet. The up and down isn't quite right, like there's no weight to it, like it's only pretending to walk on the ground.

This is it then. This is when the thing looks up, turns into a fanged wraith and lunges at me. My friends will tell their future children not to go into the woods alone or they'll get eaten by the Wraith Hiker *just like Reinard did.*

The thing does raise its head, but there are no snarling fangs, only a strange, rubbery pinkness to the face. *It's a robot.* A customer service robot, a cheap-looking one like the kind they started using in banks about five years back. I don't think I've ever seen one walk more than a few steps, let alone through the woods.

The beer bottle almost slides from my hand, but I retighten my grip just in time. I'm rooted to the spot, barely moving a muscle as it — *he? It looks like a he* — shuffles very slowly towards me with a distinct *click* of joints and a constant whirring. He doesn't bend his knee back far enough when he lifts his leg and the whole foot pushes into the ground at the same time. His arms don't really move with his stride.

He doesn't look at me, but I can't stop staring. He's right beside me now. I shift on my feet, shove a hand in my jeans pocket and briefly become interested in squirrels fighting in a tree, anything to feel less awkward. *What the hell am I supposed to do?*

"Hey," I say, loud enough to be heard over the breeze and the whirring.

He stops abruptly, turns slowly in my direction. A shiver runs down my spine, not because of anything menacing: I could probably knock him over with my beer bottle if I had to. It's meeting those dead, blink-at-regular-interval eyes. I'm deep in the Uncanny Valley.

"Good afternoon." His lips sync with his words a little too perfectly.

"Uh…" The pause lasts over twenty seconds; I probably count as clinically brain dead at this point. "What's up?" *Brilliant.*

"I am going for a walk."

"Oh," I say. "Why?"

"Because the weather is beautiful."

He turns as though he's going back to his walk, but then his neck twists back towards me.

"Are you going to stop me?"

"Hadn't planned on it."

"Good." He pauses, and there seems to be an excessive amount of whirring. "What's up with you?"

"Me? Not much. Drinking a beer. Drying off."

"Perhaps you would enjoy joining me on my walk?"

"Oh, um…" I shift my lips around, set my beer on the step and wipe off my hands, "Yeah, sure, I guess."

It's a bit like trying to walk alongside a snail; every few steps I find he's fallen behind me. The silence is uncomfortable. "Where are you going?" I finally say.

"For a walk."

"Yeah, but where to?"

"I have no particular destination; I am just walking."

"Because the weather is beautiful?"

"Yes."

"Why are you here?" he asks, after a few more steps.

I don't answer at first, there's just the songs of the birds, the whirring and the sound of steps — real and artificial — on the forest floor.

"I think I'm trying to prove a point," I say.

"Have you succeeded?"

"I have to go with 'no'."

"Perhaps it would be better if you walked more."

"You could be right."

I start wringing out my shirt. "So, what do you like about walking then?" I ask.

"I like to see the trees. I like to see the animals. I like to hear the birds."

"Yeah, it's pretty nice," I say, looking up at the canopy above me.

"I like the fresh air too."

My brow lowers. "Sorry if this is weird, but, uh, you don't breathe, do you?"

"I don't, however, the fresh air is easier on my filter."

"Hmmm," my voice rises at the end. "Never thought of that. Better for the exhaust fans, eh?" *Wait, is it okay to talk about a robot's exhaust fan?*

"Yes."

"I guess I like the fresh air too, and the sunshine, and the fresh water. I like the animals and birds too." I look up again. "The leaves maybe? I just like it all better when my friends are here."

"I have no friends," he says. "But you are good company."

I shrug. "What's in the backpack?" It's red like his jacket, blends in.

"Batteries."

"Batteries? Are you… are you running on those?"

"Yes. When walking, my internal batteries last only approximately six hours."

"So, wait, how long does the juice last for?"

"At my current pace, I expect the extra batteries to last me for 15 days and 6.5 hours."

I stop and stare at the back of him. Even with me not moving a muscle for a full minute, it takes me less than three short steps to catch up.

"What then? When the batteries run out, do you just fall down in the woods somewhere and rust?"

"When your heart runs out, will you just fall on the ground somewhere and rot?"

"Touché."

I walk alongside him until the pink in the sky fades and the stars start peering through the branches above. My skin is chafed from walking in damp clothing, and I'm starting to feel a little chilled. The idea of a fire sounds pretty nice at the moment.

"Hey," I say. We haven't said much in a while; he stops and turns to me. "Listen, I was thinking about heading back. It's late, I'm hungry, cold. I've got to have a bed."

"It was nice walking with you," he says. "I enjoyed your company."

"That's it? I mean, you're just going to keep going?"

"I do not need food or sleep, and my batteries allow me to keep walking through the night."

"Are you going to be okay? I mean, for now?"

"I will be fine. I am enjoying my walk."

"You could still come back with me to the cottage. We could hang out, maybe get you some more batteries or something so you could keep walking for longer. I'm not a tech guy but—"

"Thank you for your offer. While I would enjoy more of your company, my enjoyment of my walk will be the same whether it is longer or shorter. I think it's for the best if I continue."

I shove my hands in my pockets. "You sure?"

"Yes," he says, with an artificial nod that doesn't quite work.

I shrug and start back, pausing only for a moment to watch him disappear into the night — or, more accurately — inch slightly farther into the night. At a slow jog, it takes me less than half an hour to get back to the cottage.

I make a fire in the dark. Without Jason to rely on, I discover it's a skill I actually have. I cook up most of the obscene amount of steak I brought with me and gorge on meat. It's not as good as when Jason cooks, but it's still tasty.

For the last two days of the long weekend, I read, swim, fish off the dock (I actually catch a fish and fry it up, but the bastard's full of bones), and lie in the sun. I relax. And I go for a few walks, but I see no more signs of my robot friend.

On Tuesday morning, I'm packing up, putting the straps across the truck bed, and trying to answer some messages on my phone I've purposely ignored for the past few days (Jason has finally gone six hours without puking, so it looks like the wedding's still on) when a small, silver, self-driving car pulls up. A man gets out, sharp suit, gelled hair; he looks odd against the back drop of trees.

"Hello there," he says, not coming any closer.

"Mr. Fong said I had 'til two p.m. to clear out," I say, as I turn to grab some bags to shove in the back of the cab.

"Uh, yes," the man says, straightening the lapels of his suit. "I'm not here for that actually. I'm from Canada First Bank, and this may sound a little strange..."

Hah. I know what's coming.

"But would you happen to have seen an ASOX, a customer service robot? One that looks like a person, I mean?"

"What do you mean? Where?" I keep my back to him.

"I'm guessing the answer is 'no', but perhaps you might have seen the robot walking, at a distance, and thought it was a person?"

I turn and give him a smile. "I haven't seen a soul."

He nods with a shrug. "Are there more cottages up the lake?"

"Only an abandoned one, as I understand. The road's pretty rough after this point. I wouldn't take that car down there if I were you."

"Good to know, thanks." He gets back in the car and leaves.

I return to adjusting my straps, whistling as I go. I feel the buzz in my pocket of another text. I look as far out between the trees as I can in the direction the robot was headed. The sunshine cuts down through the canopy and a chickadee darts between the branches.

I check the time. *Maybe one more.* My feet set a rhythm on the damp earth.

—— « O » ——

R. W. Hodgson

R. W. Hodgson lives with her husband and two children in Ottawa. She has published over a hundred items, none of which she has written, and all of which are credited to the Queen. She spent her childhood in Lawrencetown, Nova Scotia (the good one).

Hill

Ryan Henson Creighton

The bodies, if you could still call them that, were smeared along the ground. What once were mothers, sisters, and aunts were now little more than stains, which made collecting their remains and laying them to rest in the still, silent pools so much more difficult. Insult to injury.

Teth adjusted the leather straps at her shoulders one last time, and looked grimly up to the top of the mountain. She had a long and difficult climb ahead of her, and she secretly hoped that by the time she returned the others would have cleaned that indecent mess. The moment that thought entered her mind, she winced with shame and resolved to pitch in when she returned from the mountain, no matter how tired her feet were, or how badly her shoulders ached. But then she remembered that she might not return at all.

As she hoisted the barrel higher on her back and gripped the shoulder straps to keep it from sliding back down, she reassured herself: everything was going to get better.

The Kragt invasion had taught Teth that despair was of little use. The anguish the ogres doled out was well beyond anyone's capacity for pain. Teth and the other conquered Fevlin grew more emotionally numb with each fresh horror the Kragt unleashed.

The first terror of the Kragt had been to wipe out all of the men of fighting age. With their enormous fists, they had crushed the men's heads like ripe plumefruit, leaving signature sickening smears all throughout the towns and villages. The surviving women and small children had been left to clean up the massacre. After binding and sinking broken body upon broken body in the still, silent pools, the bitter agony of the task had been replaced by a grim, stony sense of duty. The women's faces were wrung of tears, the skin on their cheeks brittle and parched. The men had been there, and now they were not. In their place were bodies, and those bodies must be buried.

Even the ceremonial horn had stopped blowing, because no woman had ever been taught to blow it, and its mournful wail had rung in such incessant and inaccurate tones that it had become a mockery. Now, the women continued their binding and burials in sober, stoic silence. Without the cool cover of the plants the ogres had destroyed (even before slaughtering the men), the land dried out just as their tearless faces had, and the water level of the still, silent pools shrank and shrank, until the myriad bodies bound in gray sackcloth began to resurface, the women's work undone, their grief perpetual.

But everything was going to get better.

Stopping for a moment to catch her breath, Teth shielded her eyes against the glaring midday sun. The mountain, which in truth was more like an enormous hill, rose sharply ahead of her. The path was crowded with the snarling vestiges of long-uprooted trees and miniature rockslides of egg-sized pebbles. With each step, the unfriendly terrain threatened to trip her and send her body and the barrel crashing down the mountainside. If the barrel burst, all of Teth's hard work would be undone. Even more, it would enrage the thirsty Lord Rahg, who would unleash his anger on her village, just as he had that very morning. Lord Rahg's breakfast of charred bulphin had arrived slightly undercooked and he'd bounded down the mountain to the village in a fraction of the time it would have taken a much smaller Fevlin woman to make the trip.

Muscles rippling with rage and skin a dangerously dark green, Lord Rahg had howled with anger and made an awful example of the nearest three women, whose panicked faces he obliterated beneath his thick thumbs. They had been woodworkers, all three skilled at their trade, all three now so thoroughly gone that no one could recognize them.

But, thought Teth, everything was going to get better.

Piloted recklessly by the ravenous Kragt, the stolen Thull ships had first penetrated the Fevlin's blue skies and careened into their midst when Teth was a child. The Thull had arrived on the Kragt planet to make a friendly introduction and soon found themselves in the same state as any alien who came in contact with the brutes: dead, and humiliatingly so. Worse, the Thull had unwittingly and unwillingly donated their interplanetary transports to the murderous Kragt, and one by one, the beasts had crammed their oafish frames lumpily into those cramped little ships and zoomed from rock to rock, killing and conquering their way through the solar system until they reached the Fevlin.

Being predominantly stupid, the Kragt had failed to realize that the flora and fauna of other planets might not be as hospitable to them as their own. Soon after they began smashing Fevlin heads together, many of the Kragt fell down dead from a mysterious illness. It was a severe allergic reaction to the blue blossom plants that dotted the landscape. If a Kragt invader so much as touched one of the plants, his green-hued skin would immediately erupt in painful blisters, as if in an oven. The skin would bubble up and burst, the rash riffling across the whole surface area of the Kragt's body until its skin dissolved completely, and everything that was once on the inside was now on the outside. The entire process took less than a minute, and the howls and screams of the afflicted Kragt had emboldened the Fevlin, bolstering their resistance and giving them heart and hope. Many Kragt invaders died in this way.

The first order then, before exterminating the males, before installing a lord to rule over each village, had been to get rid of the plants.

For this purpose, the Kragt had employed the terraforming equipment stored inside the Thull ships. Equipped with backpacks that looked comically small strapped to their hulking torsos, the Kragt had turned the dials to "incinerate" and taken aim at every plant that looked even remotely like a blue blossom plant — and most other plants too, just for good measure. When they were finished, the planet's surface was denuded, devastated, and unrecognizable. For that was the Kragt way.

But everything was going to get better.

Halfway up the mountain, Teth stumbled on a patch of crumbled earth and lost her balance. The massive barrel swayed dangerously, and she could hear the mead sloshing around inside. Under the punishing heat of the noonday sun, the liquid was warming up, and she knew she would have to increase her pace, even if it meant risking a fall. Lord Rahg liked his mead crisp and cool, and the last girl who had delivered it to him warm was now baking in the muck of the still, silent pools, which were now little more than shallow swamps piled with rotting corpses.

Cool mead and charred bulphin. As long as Lord Rahg had both daily, he would lounge contentedly on the mountain, sated and drunk. After the plants were destroyed, the men murdered, and the boys taken captive on the hill, the Kragt had developed an insatiable taste for bulphin. The playful sea creatures were revered by the Fevlin, who had held sacred ceremonies in the animals' honour each season. The portly little creatures were often seen swimming up to shore to enjoy a scratch under the chin or a pat on the belly from a passing Fevlin, who was then considered to be forever blessed by the animal. For their part, the Kragt found bulphin delicious.

So when Lord Rahg first installed himself at the top of the hill, he had decreed that each day he was to be served one charred bulphin and one large cask of mead from the village. The mead, normally brewed for use in the bulphin ceremonies, had been enjoyed only a little at a time by the villagers, crafted as it was from the nectar of the woodland bee. Now that the woodlands had been reduced to ash, it was exceedingly difficult to find active hives filled with enough nectar to ferment for mead, and it was becoming harder and harder for the Fevlin women to produce. Each day, the brewers added a little more water to the mixture, hoping to gradually wean Lord Rahg off the taste of the drink.

As for the bulphin, the intelligent little animals were becoming increasingly scarce as the Fevlin were forced to aggressively hunt them. Now, trapping the jolly little creatures required ever more cruel and devious methods. It was a sort of psychological torture for the villagers to see the sacred bulphin treated this way. Anyone involved in capturing, slaughtering, cooking, or serving the charred bulphin to Lord Rahg was deemed unclean by the rest of the villagers, who considered it bad luck to even make eye contact with them, let alone speak to them. So that morning, when Lord Rahg had finally found and killed the woman responsible for undercooking his meal, the villagers all knew someone would have to sacrifice herself by assuming the vacant role of bulphin cook, voluntarily ostracizing herself. If no one would volunteer, the village must find a way to force someone to become cook, and quickly. Lord Rahg would demand food again the next morning.

But everything was going to get better.

Some roles were assigned by default. The village weavers were consigned to craft the netting now needed to ensnare the bulphin. The ceremonial brewers made the mead. The woodworkers built the barrels that held the mead, and the youngest, strongest women in the village were designated mead-carriers. Teth and a handful of other young women were assigned shifts, so each had to carry the mead barrel up the mountain about once a week.

Teth was up to the task. Before the invasion, she had enjoyed running through the village, climbing trees, and diving into the grotto from the top of the bluff. Her slim body was toned and muscular, her back and legs strong from sprinting and swimming. But the barrel of mead was a terrible burden for even the hardiest woman in the village, and Teth groaned under its weight. The leather straps dug into the flesh of her shoulders, and her lower back strained at the heft of her heavy load. Each step up the hill was an agony as her quadriceps surged, and her calf muscles turned to stone, pushing off powerfully against the packed earth. But she was nearly there.

Abducting the boys had been the last straw. The dead-eyed mothers wandered through their work dispassionately, as if they were machines. To make the going easier, the women of the village sang plaintive songs, their voices harmonizing in beautiful but achingly sad strains that mourned the misery brought on by the Kragt invasion. They were songs of despair, not of hope. Songs of dejected acceptance. But the mothers who had seen their husbands killed and their little boys torn from their arms and carried in fistfuls to the top of the hill by Lord Rahg? Those women completed their work mechanically and silently. They did not sing.

In due time, sadness turned to anger, and the songs of the women had begun to take on a more defiant tone. What at first had been whispered furtively between the women as they passed each other in the village was later incorporated into the lyrics of their work songs. Because Lord Rahg could not understand the Fevlin tongue, and because singing was less likely to arouse his suspicions than talking or whispering, the women laid out their plans boldly to one another, couched in the bitter melodies they sang while toiling under the ogre's thumb.

The woodworkers crafted spears and daggers sharp enough to pierce Lord Rahg's hardened skin, and sang their request for materials to the other villagers. The weavers twisted together a net large and strong enough to capture the brutish Kragt, and sang of their progress. The nectar foragers searched high and low for traces of the blue blossoms, for any seed or frond they could use to grow a new plant, and sang to the others the results of their quest. The servant girls who trucked Lord Rahg's food and drink up the mountain paid special attention to the Thull spaceship docked there, and sang their findings to each other in specially orchestrated songs describing different aspects of the vehicle. Their goal was to eventually have a more complete understanding of the ship, with the hope of one day commandeering it and fleeing the planet to seek help among the stars.

But as quickly as their plans were made, they were dashed to pieces by the hateful Kragt. When one of the servant girls stabbed Lord Rahg in the thigh, prematurely and ineffectively, with a carved wooden shiv, the beast dragged her down the mountain by her hair, pinching the blade between the tree trunk fingers of his opposite hand. He planted his gargantuan feet in the middle of the village and demanded, in his rough Kragt tongue, to be shown where the weapon had been made. When no one spoke up, he smashed his way through three huts before discovering the women's storehouse of crudely sharpened sticks. The servant girl and a literal handful of woodworkers did not survive the ordeal.

From then on, Lord Rahg made regular, random inspections of the village. He tore to shreds any fishing net too large to trap anything bigger than a bulphin. When he discovered a hut containing two carefully cultivated blue blossom seedlings, he stood at a distance and hurled enormous rocks, burying the building in boulders far too large for any one person to move. When he came upon the smooth stone walls of the bluffs and found a painting with detailed depictions of the Thull ship he had arrived in, his rage was boundless. The hulking beast threw a succession of furious punches at the wall, reducing the drawings to rubble and dust. He tore through the village, indiscriminately grabbing anyone within his massive arms' reach. The footpaths were ribboned with red that day, and the still, silent pools surged with new bodies.

But everything was going to get better.

With each death the village suffered at the hands of the angry Kragt, the division of duty grew ever thinner, and the women struggled to sustain themselves, let alone the ravenous Lord Rahg. But he didn't seem concerned. This strain on their resources, coupled with the Kragt's scorched earth policy that left their landscape devastated and deforested, revealed a grim truth to the women of the village, and to every village enduring similar indignities across the annexed planet: this was an extinction level event for the Fevlin people. The Kragt would stay until the mead, the bulphin, or the women ran out, and then they would squeeze themselves into their Thull ships and speed away in search of some other planet to subjugate.

At last, Teth mounted the last step of the steep incline, and the ground began to level off. Before her sprawled the palatial hut of Lord Rahg, built with great strain by the skilled women of the village, who had been summarily crushed as payment for their efforts. All around her, the choking stench of Lord Rahg had worked its way into the wood, and Teth lifted a weary arm to cover her mouth before walking any farther. The Kragt invader lounged in the middle of the open-walled shelter, his enormous leg dangling cavalierly over the arm of the makeshift wooden throne the villagers had constructed for him. Here and there were the young boys from the village — those that Lord Rahg had not yet killed or eaten — this boy cleaning the ogre's toenails, that boy struggling to empty his enormous latrine.

Just outside the hut sat the Thull ship, a triangular vehicle propped up by tripod landing gear. The brightly colored craft bore exposed patches of shiny metal, a material still unfamiliar to the Fevlin, where the paint had worn away due to Lord Rahg's careless piloting. The cockpit was encased with a glass shield, which could be opened by pulling an orange latch on the side of the ship. This much, they gathered from earlier episodes in their people's history, when visitors from other planets had landed there, greeted the Fevlin people kindly, and left. Among these curious tourists were the Thull themselves, many years before Teth was born, who had stayed long enough to teach the Fevlin how pulleys worked and revealed that the universe was filled with other planets populated by friendly people. Teth approached Lord Rahg in the center of the hilltop hut and, with an exhausted groan, turned and lowered the barrel to the ground before him. The vessel hit the earthen floor with a heavy impact, and the liquid inside it sloshed around turbulently. Resisting the urge to roll her shoulders to relieve the ache, Teth performed a customary curtsy to appease Lord Rahg. At the bottom of her dip, she scanned the hut, looking for her baby brother.

As she straightened, she spotted the boy in a far corner of the hut. He was thin and dirty, and what little clothing he still wore was in tatters. He had a fresh scrape on one cheek that was slick with blood. He sat there, gnawing on a discarded scrap of blackened meat from that morning's unsatisfactory meal. It hurt Teth's heart to see her own little brother eating bulphin, but she was under no illusions as to how the boys had survived all this time at the top of the hill. She caught the child's eyes with her own, briefly, but he stared back at her without a glimmer of recognition, his mouth black and sticky.

Lord Rahg bellowed jubilantly at the sight of Teth and the barrel of mead. He straightened up in his chair, sending the boy who had been scouring his toenails flying across the room with a careless kick. He leaned in towards Teth, brought his massive, craggy face within a foot of her own, and breathed. Teth felt like she was going to vomit. He smiled cruelly, his dark eyes creasing at their corners, and his lips stretched taut over rows of misshapen, bulphin-stained teeth.

He grunted appreciatively, aiming a huge, dull finger at Teth, and then poked her with it. It was like a full-force punch to the stomach, and Teth doubled over from the impact. Lord Rahg leaned back in his chair, lifted his head to the thatched roof, and laughed so boisterously that his voice shook the hut. The scattered boys milling about all stopped what they were doing and looked over at him, and then at Teth.

Lord Rahg smiled at the boys and made a gesture towards her that Teth had seen him make before. She didn't completely understand it, but she could infer that it was crude. Taking Lord Rahg's cue, the boys around the hut leered at her, smiling lasciviously. One of the older boys, who by some fluke had nearly come of age under Lord Rahg's custody, made a gesture towards her that she *did* understand, and for the second time that day, Teth felt ashamed. Some of the boys assembled behind her and cooed luridly at her. This made the other boys laugh, and they cooed in imitation. Her own baby brother, sitting in squalor in the corner, lowered the meat from his mouth, looked at her like all the other boys were looking at her, and cooed.

This struck Lord Rahg as the funniest thing he had seen all day, and the hut shook again with his renewed laughter.

Finally, his amusement subsided, and Lord Rahg stooped to pick up the mead barrel with one massive hand. He flicked the stopper with a free finger as if uncorking a tiny bottle, and upended the keg into his mouth. The blue liquid funneled into his gullet with loud gurgles as Lord Rahg guzzled it greedily down. When he had finished, he slammed the barrel back to the ground and wiped the foam from his lips with the back of his huge hand. Then, as was his custom, he let out an earth-quaking belch, which he aimed directly at Teth's face.

Ordinarily, Lord Rahg's raucous belches were enough to send Teth reeling backwards, struggling to maintain her footing. Today, however, she stood her ground, letting the hot, stuffy air from deep within Lord Rahg's stomach wash over and envelop her in its sweet, familiar scent — a scent that smelled of home, of family. A scent that reminded her of carefree days spent running through the village, climbing trees, and diving into the grotto from the top of the bluff. A scent that recalled her mother and father, now at rest in the still, silent pools. A scent that spoke of her baby brother, before he had been twisted into an ugly and unrecognizable shape by the brutality of his boorish captor. It was a welcome scent. A hopeful scent.

It was the scent of blue blossoms.

No sooner had the air escaped Lord Rahg's lips than he realized something was wrong. He stood up from the throne and splayed his huge hands in front of himself, as if trying to freeze time and figure out just what had happened. A perplexed look troubled his coarse face, and he glanced down at the empty mead barrel. The real shame that day was that Teth sprinted away from the scene too early to see the look of fear — actual, honest fear — creep over Lord Rahg's face as he clutched the churning mass of his stomach.

When he'd discovered the covert nursery housing two fledgling blue blossom plants, Lord Rahg had indeed buried the building in boulders far too large for any one person to move. The village, however, was comprised of more than just one person, and the villagers had spent the ensuing weeks twisting rope and digging channels in an effort to move enough rubble to rescue those blue blossoms. When at last they accessed the ruined hut, they found that one of the two plants had survived. This plant, they secreted away in another hut, where they tended it carefully. Daily, they would sing instructions to each other about opening and closing the shutters to supply the plant with just the right amount of sunlight and watering it with nutrient-rich mulch from the still, silent pools. In this way, the bodies of those who had fallen fed the plant, and the blue blossom thrived under their special, collective care. As soon as the plant had grown large enough, the villagers put their plan into effect.

They cautiously clipped its leaves and surreptitiously slipped them to the brewers, who fermented them along with the nectar to make a potent poison disguised as ceremonial mead. The azure leaves turned the drink an uncharacteristic blue, which many feared the ogre would notice. But nevertheless, the village had held its collective breath as Teth slid her arms into the barrel straps and began her journey up the hill.

As he drank, the gluttonous ogre had not noticed, and was presently reeling around the hut as the fast-acting plant bubbled up inside his belly, and his insides erupted in painful blisters that traveled up his throat and out his mouth, spreading across his lips and along the back of the hand he had used to wipe them. He would have howled in agony, if his lungs weren't already ravaged by the spectacular allergy. And Teth would have heard him howl, if she wasn't already pulling down the glass enclosure of the Thull cockpit. As she and the villagers had expected, the controls of the alien ship were so simple that even a Kragt could use them, and the ship was quickly on its way, rising into the air from the top of the hill, leaving behind the hut, the boys, the village, and the rapidly disintegrating Lord Rahg.

Teth brought the ship around as it gained speed, pointing its nose to the sky and trying not to succumb to the fearful rhythm of her rapidly beating heart. She didn't know how to reach the other, friendly planets the Thull had described to her ancestors, and she didn't know if she would find the help she needed even if she did reach them, but as the ship accelerated through the atmosphere and Teth's small body rattled around inside the spacious cockpit, she was abundantly sure of one thing.

Everything was going to get better.

—— « O » ——

Ryan Henson Creighton

Ryan Henson Creighton lives in Oshawa, Ontario with his boisterous family. He loves singing, abhors pants, and spends most of his time trying to convince people to play board games with him. Ryan designs games and puzzles for a living. He thrives on thinking and learning, both of which are best accomplished late at night, which is unfortunately when there are monsters.

Anhedonia

Meghan Bell

Patient Zero had always been an unhappy man, and because of this, no one would ever be exactly sure when and how the virus began.

His wife drove him to the emergency room when the whites of his eyes turned a deep, uniform red. When his fever rose above 104 degrees and he began to vomit blood, he was transferred to infectious diseases and placed under quarantine. When the doctor told his wife that they didn't think he would make it — the dehydration was too severe, the weight and blood loss too great — she didn't react. She said she didn't feel anything, other than a headache.

Rattled, the doctor went to lie down for a few minutes in the on-call room and didn't get up for an hour. That evening, she told her husband of three months that she felt "blue," and declined to have sex.

Soon, her eyes turned red.

Two days later, Patient Zero died, and dozens more presenting with the same symptoms were admitted to hospitals across Greater Vancouver. A phone call came in about a similar case in Toronto, and another in Beijing. In LA, a young actor was hospitalized after walking off the edge of a bridge, and when asked about his medical history, he swore up and down that no, he had never been depressed before, but he had just returned from Vancouver. His eyes turned red the next day, and newspapers across the globe broke the story: there was a new pandemic, and the first symptom was debilitating anhedonia.

~

Maureen De Luca @maureendelooka
  Hey, so I've been AWOL & caught up on news after
  4 days. Can anyone on here update/clarify? I'm in
  #YVR, is it safe to leave my apartment?

Dave Jamieson @davejj1985
  @maureendelooka If you're healthy & safe, stay put.
  Shove towels under your door. Block your vents.
  Especially in YVR. Think this is the end

Emily D @emdearly
  @davejj1985 @maureendelooka This is fear-
  mongering.

Dave Jamieson @davejj1985
  @emdearly @maureendelooka Businesses are
  shut down. 17 deaths so far in BC, lots more with
  symptoms. They're talking about a quarantine.

Emily D @emdearly
  @davejj1985 @maureendelooka Read this,
  re: "symptoms" http://dailyprogressive.
  com/"anhedeonia"-virus-mass-hysteria-dangers-
  mental-health-stigmatization

Dave Jamieson @davejj1985
  @emdearly @maureendelooka You're seriously
  accusing people of oppressing folks with depression
  bc they're scared of a deadly fucking virus?!

Dave Jamieson@davejj1985
  @emdearly @maureendelooka We can't tell the
  diff between virus depression & regular depression.
  Situation's fucked. Not "stigmatization."

Emily D @emdearly
  @davejj1985 @maureendelooka What exactly do
  you mean by "regular" depression? There's nothing
  "regular" about depression. #BreakTheStigma

Dave Jamieson @davejj1985
@emdearly @maureendelooka I mean non-virus
depression. Chill. I'm on fucking Wellbutrin. I'm not
hating. Scared of fucking dying & endofdays

Maureen De Luca @maureendelooka
@davejj1985 @emdearly Hey Dave. Thanks for
advice. Been reading articles, texted friends & agree
with you. Going to stay put & be careful.

Dave Jamieson @davejj1985
@maureendelooka @emdearly I'm glad. Stay safe.
Hopefully they find a cure soon.

Emily D @emdearly
@davejj1985 @maureendelooka This is just the latest
in media-sensationalized pandemics. Stay home if you
want, but not necessary.

Maureen De Luca @maureendelooka
@davejj1985 Thank you. You stay safe too <3

~

In physics, the *observer effect* describes how the act of
observing a phenomenon can alter it. The same holds true for
psychological conditions: as each person read about the virus
and its symptoms, they looked inward. Had they enjoyed
their breakfast? Had they become aroused when they kissed
their partner the night before? Did they have energy? Did
they have enthusiasm? Did they have joy? Love? Passion?
Were they happy or just going through the motions? Were
they stressed out from work or school or their relationship
or their lack of a relationship, or were they depressed? How
could you tell the difference between normal melancholy
and the virus? How do you observe the exact moment you
begin to feel nothing? If they were slow to get out of bed,
or hadn't gotten out of bed at all, did that mean they were
infected?

Clinics were flooded with phone calls. The servers that
hosted WebMD overloaded and crashed. People pulled their
eyelids down and looked for discoloration in the mirror until

their eyes became dry and red. Millions of people diagnosed themselves as having the virus.

Within a week, many of them did.

~

> Maureen De Luca @maureendelooka
> Holy shit just got an email from UBC & classes are canceled. Thought it was a joke/excuse to avoid the world but is this fucking real? #HAF

> Maureen De Luca @maureendelooka
> I'm all alone & scared. Family is across the country. Need someone to talk to. @davejj1985?

> Dave Jamieson @davejj1985
> @maureendelooka I'm here.

> Maureen De Luca @maureendelooka
> @davejj1985 Make me feel better?

> Dave Jamieson @davejj1985
> @maureendelooka Okay, I got a joke for you: How did #HAF travel from America to Europe?

> Maureen De Luca @maureendelooka
> @davejj1985 Um. By plane?

> Dave Jamieson @davejj1985
> @maureendelooka On the red eye.

> Maureen De Luca @maureendelooka
> @davejj1985 LOL. God, that's terrible.

> Dave Jamieson @davejj1985
> @maureendelooka But did you smile?

> Maureen De Luca @maureendelooka
> @davejj1985 Yes :-)

~

Eleven Countries Placed Under Quarantine as Fear of "Depression" Virus Grows

—Amy Yang, TORONTO — The Canadian Press

The World Health Organization has called for the immediate suspension of international travel in 11 countries, including Canada, in hopes of containing the HAF virus. A further 27 countries have been placed on alert and have been advised by the WHO to quarantine cities and towns where cases of HAF have been reported. International travel has also halted in both New Zealand and the Philippines, where there are no reported cases.

In the past 10 days, there have been more than nine million reported cases of HAF and approximately two million deaths, primarily in major cities in North America and China.

Air Canada has issued a public statement on their website apologizing for the inconvenience to travelers, and have requested that people refrain from contacting the airline or its employees until the quarantine is lifted.

We reached out to other major airlines but they were unavailable for comment.

~

Maureen De Luca @maureendelooka
@davejj1985 I just spent an hour on the phone with my mom. She said she's sick now.

Dave Jamieson @davejj1985
@maureendelooka Shit. I'm sorry :-(where/how is she?

Maureen De Luca @maureendelooka
@davejj1985 She's at home with my dad, in Halifax. It's fucked up but even though I know it'd kill me, I think I'd go there if I could.

Dave Jamieson @davejj1985
@maureendelooka That's not fucked up. You love your parents.

Maureen De Luca @maureendelooka
@davejj1985 Oh yeah but easy for me to say now because it's not an option. Theoretical sacrifices mean nothing.

Dave Jamieson @davejj1985
@maureendelooka I know what you mean. My ex-girlfriend is in Calgary & posted on FB that's she's sick & going to the hospital.

Dave Jamieson @davejj1985
@maureendelooka I keep thinking I'd change places with her, but if I actually could would I? #ProbablyNot

Maureen De Luca @maureendelooka
@davejj1985 It's bullshit that I've spent a decade saying/thinking I wish I were dead & now everyone's dying & I'm ok.

Dave Jamieson @davejj1985
@maureendelooka Hemorrhagic Anhedonic Fever, striking down all the happy, healthy, sane people who actually go outside. #IsntItIronic

Maureen De Luca @maureendelooka
@davejj1985 I laughed at that and now I feel really bad. I wonder if @Alanis is still alive?

Dave Jamieson @davejj1985
@maureendelooka Some doctor tweeted that wanting to live was a sign you didn't have HAF bc if you're anhedonic you don't care if you die.

Maureen De Luca @maureendelooka
@davejj1985 Huh. So, something I feel shitty about: I realized the other day that I wanted to live. Like, really badly. I want to live. (1/3)

Maureen De Luca @maureendelooka
@davejj1985 I'm rationing my food, I'm on the 23rd floor & I'm scared every time I open a window. I've spent years wanting to die & (2/3)

Maureen De Luca @maureendelooka
@davejj1985 now the world's ending & I want to live. & I might bc I went 5 days w/o leaving my apartment before HAF because I was too sad to

Maureen De Luca @maureendelooka
@davejj1985 I'm the luckiest, most ungrateful selfish bitch in the world.

Dave Jamieson @davejj1985
@maureendelooka If you're the luckiest, most ungrateful selfish bitch in the world then so am I bc I feel the exact same way. <3

~

5 Tips For Surviving The End Of The World

Lila MacDonald, ViralBuzz Staff

Got the HAF blues? Here's a handy guide on how to survive history's most deadly virus.

1. Stay In Your Bubble
   HAF is one of the most contagious — if not *the* most contagious — airborne viruses of all time. If you're lucky enough to be in a place with "safe" air, be sure to keep it safe. Seal your windows. Seal your doors. Avoid contact with other people.

2. If You Have To Go Outside, Stay Covered
   Blogger and MIT PhD student Jason Cunningham put together this cool guide to making a Hazmat suit with common household items such as saran wrap.

3. Conserve Calories
   We're all running out of food, and none of us want to risk infection by going out to the nearest grocery store. You can survive and stay relatively healthy off of just 1,200 calories per day, so avoid burning through your fridge too quickly. You can also conserve calories and energy by sleeping and by staying as still as possible. If you need some physical activity, try something low-key like stretching or try our 15 Yoga Poses To Help You Keep Calm During The Apocalypse.

4. Netflix and Chill
   Need something to do while you hold still and wait for the world to end? This is the perfect opportunity

to binge-watch our 17 Best Shows On Netflix In
2017.

5. Find Your Online Tribe
    Probably the best thing we can do is take care of
    each other. Communities have sprung up on social
    media sites such as Facebook, Twitter, Tumblr, and
    reddit for people who are alone and waiting for a 12
    Monkeys-type society to spring up in the ashes of
    our doomed civilization.

Show Comments

Shawn Stephens
This pointless, click-bait post is incredibly disrespectful to
the millions of people who have died from HAF and their
families. I can't believe ViralBuzz would publish this drivel.
You've lost a reader.

> Tyler Chong
> @Shawn Stephens Like they care. I bet North
> America loses the Internet within the next week.
> A couple places have already lost power. We're all
> fuuuuuuuuuuuckkkked.

> Laurel Sims
> @Tyler Chong God, I hope not.

> Amelia Wittrup
> @Tyler Chong So much for numbers three and five :-p

> > Tyler Chong
> > @Amelia Wittrup I haven't been outside in nearly
> > two weeks. So the question is, do I die a slow,
> > painful death by starvation, or do I go outside and
> > die a slow, painful death by vomiting blood?

> > > Amelia Wittrup
> > > @Tyler Chong Definitely go for HAF. At least you
> > > won't care you're dying.

> > > > Tyler Chong
> > > > @Amela Wittrup Fair point.

Maureen De Luca
I'm doing all of these things and it isn't helping.

> Tyler Chong
> @Maureen De Luca You depressed?

>> Maureen De Luca
>> @Tyler Chong Yes, but I think depressed-because-the-world-is-ending, not depressed-because-I-have-the-virus-that's-ending-the-world.

>>> Tyler Chong
>>> @Maureen De Luca I hope so.

>>>> Maureen De Luca
>>>> @Tyler Chong Thanks :-/

Laurel Sims
This article sucks.

Jeff Ryan
DO NOT TRY THE HAZMAT SUIT. If you go to the most recent post on that blog the dude says he went out in it twice and thinks he became infected. That was two days ago and THERE ARE NO MORE POSTS. I'M NOT FUCKING AROUND.

~

> Dave Jamieson @davejj1985
> Hey I'm trying to figure out who's still here. Retweet if you're alive & healthy. Like if you're alive & sick. #HAF #LastPeopleOnEarth

> Dave Jamieson @davejj1985
> Just think, in a hundred years there will probably be an anti-vaxxer movement rallying against giving the #HAF vaccine to children.

> Maureen De Luca @maureendelooka
> @davejj1985 Lol. This is incredibly optimistic.

> Dave Jamieson @davejj1985
> @maureendelooka And here I thought I was being cynical AF.

Maureen De Luca @maureendelooka
@davejj1985 Ha, in that scenario they discover a vaccine and humanity survives to such an extent that we're able to take it for granted.

Dave Jamieson @davejj1985
@maureendelooka Hmm. Yeah, okay, I like that.

Dave Jamieson @davejj1985
@maureendelooka I'm worried that we won't have the Internet or electricity much longer. I'm going to miss talking to you.

Maureen De Luca @maureendelooka
@davejj1985 I'm going to miss you too :-(

Dave Jamieson @davejj1985
@maureendelooka I'm a four-hour drive away. Send me your address. When it's safe, I'll come find you.

Maureen De Luca @maureendelooka
@davejj1985 I don't know. How do I know you aren't some sort of end-of-days catfishing ax murderer?

Dave Jamieson @davejj1985
@maureendelooka No pressure, just if you want … you're the only living friend I have right now.

Maureen De Luca @maureendelooka
@davejj1985 I've DM-ed you my address. You're the only living friend I have too.

~

Three weeks after the pandemic began, Vancouver's power went out.

Weeks passed and the survivors waited. Then, slowly, they put on their homemade hazmat suits and opened their front doors and stepped outside.

In a small bachelor apartment on the 23rd floor of a Vancouver tower, Maureen De Luca waited. She created elaborate, romantic daydreams about the future. Living off the land. Salvaging supplies. Forming tribes. Rebuilding.

She didn't have the energy to feel guilty.

She was running out of food. She ate dry instant noodles one-quarter of a package at a time. She chewed her fingernails and swallowed. She tried to sleep as much as possible.

Every time she woke up, she looked inward and asked herself whether she still believed that he would come. As long as the answer was "yes," she knew she still wasn't infected and her hope grew a little more. And in this manner, the longer she waited, the more she believed that in the end everything would okay.

—— « o » ——

Meghan Bell

Meghan Bell lives in Vancouver, where she is the publisher of *Room* magazine. Her fiction has appeared in *The New Quarterly, Grain, Carousel, The Impressment Gang, Joyland,* and *The Minola Review.* She is one of the co-founders of Growing Room: A Feminist Literary Festival, and spearheaded the publication of *Room*'s fortieth anniversary anthology, *Making Room: Forty Years of Room Magazine* (Spring 2017, Caitlin Press). She is working on her first novel, about grief, rage, and ice hockey. Find her at meghanbell. com or on Twitter @meghanlbell.

A Room of His Own

Ursula Pflug

Cassidy was riveted by the man's hands. They were trying to disengage what looked like yellow gauze from the torn screen of the door to her new potting shed. He was picking at the gauze with those long fingers, at once sensual and gnarled, an expression of great concentration and some worry creasing his long handsome face. She thought perhaps it was his favorite scarf. She herself might wear just such an expression if her favorite scarf, a fine purple silk brought from Rome by her sister Mara, had caught on a protruding nail.

But how had the screen torn in the first place? It looked like he'd been trying to break into her new shed, tearing the screen to unlock the door from the inside. It served him right, catching his scarf and getting hurt. It had taken Cassidy so long to get the shed in the first place. She re-potted plants in it, and kept her gardening tools neatly organized.

"Could you help?" the man asked. He had a low fluty voice; it sounded just a little foreign.

Cassidy began to unhook the yellow gauze from the tiny clawed metal ends of screen. He made a face and twisted his entire body quickly. Cassidy saw his back then, saw how the yellow gauze was attached to his shoulder blade. How the other shoulder had a matching scarf, this one draped quite magnificently over his arm, almost alight. Not moving but capable of movement, she was sure.

She unhooked ten or twenty tiny metal ends of torn screen from the yellow gauze. She thought he might have nerve endings there, so she was as careful as possible, as if removing slivers from a young child's tender feet. Not that she knew much about that.

The stranger craned his neck, trust in his pale gray green eyes. *Puce, his eyes are puce colored*, Cassidy thought, using a decorating word from one of her magazines. He moaned a little and turned back around. Perhaps it had hurt him to face her, twisting the yellow gauze, which was heavily veined as if by the finest of tendons, the softest of cartilage. More like a bat than a butterfly.

At last he was free. "Mind if I stay here for a couple of days?" he asked. "I can't quite leave yet."

"Shall I bring you food?" Cassidy asked.

"A bit of honey might be nice," he said. "Otherwise I can graze."

"Graze?"

"Not like a cow," he said. "More like a hummingbird or a bee."

"Oh," Cassidy said. "I'll look for honey, and if we're out I'll buy some."

He nodded. "Unpasteurized if you can find it."

Cassidy went back to the house and read decorating magazines. There was nothing wrong with their house that several thousand dollars wouldn't fix, but now that they were semi-retired, they needed to hold on to their savings.

"This dresser," she told Henry when he emerged from his basement, "would look quite nice with a coat of white or palest yellow."

"Or puce," Henry said.

"Why puce?"

"It's a funny word, that's all," Henry said. "Like chartreuse. What color is chartreuse again?"

"A kind of yellow-green," Cassidy replied to Henry's back. He was already receding, having poured himself fresh coffee. Soon she'd hear his footsteps on the basement stairs. He was refurbishing old tube radios. He mostly did it to occupy his time, and because he enjoyed it. Luckily, because his skill was rare, he was occasionally paid quite nicely. He only worked in the hardware store a couple of afternoons a week now, doing the ordering and such.

"And a vase of fresh flowers," Cassidy said to no one in particular.

She'd meant to spend the day in the potting shed drawing. She'd recently bought a good sketchbook, water colors, and real colored pencils, not the cheap ones children used. She'd had to drive forty minutes each way, because Brookside only had a crafts store. The art supplies store in Stony Creek boasted a little espresso machine. The owner had made her a cup before she rang up Cassidy's things. Cassidy had downed the tiny cup and driven home very fast.

She had decided to make notes instead of painting right away, just as she did for her decorating projects. She would plan her paintings in advance. A vase of flowers first, she had thought, and then a bowl of fruit. And now, on the third day, a tall thin man with puce colored eyes, his yellow wings caught on the torn screen door of her shed. Thinking about him, she felt a little giddy. She was afraid to go out to see whether he was still there, or even to peek at her art supplies, which she'd stashed under the bench after she got home from Stony Creek. Cassidy called good-night down the basement stairs to Henry. She went up to bed, holding her glamorous feeling for the stranger close to her heart.

In the morning, she hunted through cupboards till she found a dusty unopened jar of honey. She and Henry put sugar in their tea and coffee; she must've bought the honey to use in a recipe she'd clipped. She remembered it then: orange honey cake, supposedly a traditional rural cake, although she'd never heard of it till she'd read the article. She'd clearly never attempted it either; the unopened jar of honey was proof.

~ ~ ~

She found the stranger sitting on her stool, bent over her new sketchbook. His antennae bobbed; they were so fine she hadn't noticed them yesterday. His twin yellow scarves draped decoratively down his back, and a delicate smile played about his lips, secretive and knowing. It reminded Cassidy of the woman in that famous painting.

She set the honey down on the poured concrete threshold. Had it taken the whole night for the impossibility of him to sink in? Yesterday she'd instinctively helped him as she might a hurt child. Just because she wasn't a mother didn't mean she had no protective feelings.

He licked his lips in concentration, dipping her best brush into an empty tuna can full of water. The sable brush had been the most expensive of her purchases, too fine to ever be used for stenciling borders, or decoupage. She'd looked forward to being the first to use it.

Cassidy turned and hurried back up the field stone path to her house. She'd expected her feelings to stay outside with the sky, the garden, the shed, him. But they hadn't.

His puce eyes. She wanted to look into them.

Henry came into the kitchen and put the kettle on. He wore his brown corduroys, his safety glasses perched on his dark tousled head.

"I thought you'd be painting in your new shed," he said.

"The screen in the door is already torn."

Henry nodded. "I've got lots of spare screen. It won't take me more than a few minutes. I wonder how it happened?"

"Maybe a raccoon or a porcupine," Cassidy said. "I've got some bulbs in there. Even people can eat tulip bulbs, you know."

"I do know," Henry said. "My mother's family in Holland ate them during the war."

"You never offer to do anything right away."

"I am now."

"Now I don't want you to."

"Why?"

"You built the shed," Cassidy said. "It took time away from your radios. You shouldn't have to fix it yet."

"You haven't used it even once, and it's been finished for a week," Henry said.

"It doesn't matter. Mosquito season's almost over since we had those cold nights. You have to work tomorrow. You should go somewhere."

"Where?" Henry asked.

"I don't know. Somewhere."

"To the basement then," Henry said, and headed for the stairs.

Cassidy looked around the kitchen. The new curtains, though pretty, were no huge improvement over the blue blinds that had hung there previously. Not if she took into account how long they'd taken her to make.

She took a piece of paper towel off the roll that always stood beside the sink and sat down at the kitchen table, picked up the red permanent fine tip so fortuitously lying there, and drew a screaming face. It had no antennae, so maybe it didn't belong to the stranger. And she'd never seen him scream. He didn't seem a screamer, somehow, although she supposed everyone and anyone might turn out to be a screamer if pushed to it hard enough.

~ ~ ~

She wondered what the stranger painted in her book, with her Windsor Newtons. In his hands her book would just fill, as if by itself. And no one would wonder why he wasn't decorating instead. Or gardening or cooking. No one would wonder at all.

He was still there the next morning, and the morning after that. Cassidy knew because she checked before she left for her bookkeeping job. He never noticed her standing at the shed door, even if she coughed or wore her heavy plastic gardening clogs and thumped a little on her way.

On the third day she cleared her throat and said, "You wouldn't even have art supplies or a studio if it weren't for me."

He didn't look up, not even to mutely show her what he was working on. He hadn't torn pages out to prop against the vintage goose neck lamp or pin to the walls, so Cassidy couldn't see what he'd done. But he was a good way through the book, almost half, and wore the same beatific smile as yesterday. It was as if, drawing, he'd uncovered the secrets of the universe. Her pencils had grown short; her paint tubes were twisted and rolled at the bottoms.

Back in her kitchen, Cassidy picked up the same red fine point marker she'd used to draw on the paper towel and wondered about its provenance. She used these markers to write on the little plastic tabs she pushed into her flats to identify seedlings or seedlings to be. Somehow the marker had migrated from the potting shed to the house. It was the kind of thing that might happen to Henry, but not to her. She was the organized one. Not that it mattered much. She opened her decorating magazine and uncapped the marker once more.

She drew a screaming person seated on a full page photograph of a white couch. Was it an advertisement for the couch, or for the flooring beneath the couch? Cassidy didn't take the time to scan the text and find out. Instead, she plunged into her drawing as if it were a pond, and she diving underwater. When Cassidy re-emerged, she realized the screaming person she'd drawn had wings. And the wings were tangled in the lamp stand behind the couch so he couldn't escape.

No wonder she'd hidden her art supplies beneath the bench. This was neither a bowl of fruit nor a vase of flowers but a depiction of cruelty. She was sadistic, this excursion into her own creativity made clear. Cassidy felt dirty. Still, the drawing was good, even scribbled as it was with a gardening marker in a decorating magazine. It was quite a likeness. In spite of her deep confusion, Cassidy felt a little proud of what she'd done. In school they'd always said she had talent. She'd set it aside; she wasn't sure where or why. It wasn't as if she could blame the children she'd never had for taking up all her time.

Henry touched her shoulder. He had crept up at some point, come and stood behind her.

"You better let him go," he said.

"But I did let him go," Cassidy said. "The very first day."

"He won't leave till you ask for your things back," Henry said.

How long had Henry known her secret? But then, that had been the point of Henry right from the beginning, hadn't it? Someone who could know her all the way through and not judge. She sat, still staring at her drawing. She didn't say anything more to her husband, but she definitely didn't want him taking his gently kneading hands from her shoulders.

"You don't think I'm a bad person because I drew him like this?" she finally asked.

"I'll bet you anything he drew you too. I'll bet you he drew you drawing." Henry caressed her hair, and for some reason Cassidy was swept back to their beginnings. She'd known Henry for a long time but one day had been different. There'd been a storm, and she'd turned the sign so it read "Closed" and locked the door in the dusty comfortable bookstore where she worked. Afterward they'd held each other in a different way, each needing reassurance they were still real, still separate, still had names.

Drawing made her feel a bit like that.

"I'll make a stew," Cassidy said, getting up. She'd wash the floor; she'd spend what remained of the weekend at flea markets looking for a new table for the guest room. The one there now was ugly, even after she'd painted it in a complicated faux finish, precisely following the instructions in her magazine. She'd already forgotten what the carefully rendered surface had supposedly been an imitation of.

"No," Henry said. "Why do you think I built you a studio?"

"It's just for plants," Cassidy said.

"It is not," he said, prodding her gently in the ribs.

She knew he was right. Cassidy got up and marched out the kitchen door and down to the shed. This time, she didn't stand timorously peering through the screen, mumbling accusations and hoping the stranger would notice her. Instead, she opened the door and spoke loudly.

"Give me back my stuff," she said. "It's not yours."

"I know," he said.

"What did you draw?" Cassidy demanded.

"See for yourself," he said, and turned the book around to face her.

Trembling, she opened the door and stepped inside.

It was just as Henry had said. The stranger had drawn her drawing. And unlike in her drawing of him, he'd pictured her happy, if a little transported.

He handed her the sable brush. "It's your turn," he said. "You already know you can do it."

"I do?" Cassidy asked.

"Remember how you drew me?"

She lowered her head, ashamed. "I didn't mean…"

"You were ashamed of me," the stranger said. "That's why you made a hurtful drawing. You were afraid and wanted me to suffer because of it."

"Why should I be ashamed of you?" Cassidy asked.

"Because I'm not grape vine stencils. Or faux marble stipple effect. I'm not any of those things."

She looked at his hands. They had the same fine veining as his yellow wings; more like the veins in a leaf, she thought now, than anything else.

"What should I paint?" she asked.

"What did you plan?"

"Flowers," she said, after thinking for a moment.

"Then paint those."

Cassidy took the brush from him and dipped it in a pool of aquamarine on the ceramic palette. With the wet brush she conjured outlines of flowers on the nubby white expanse of Arches paper. The brush swooped this way and then that, and before long Cassidy felt it again, that pull, a loss of self as intense as sex, but of a different kind.

~ ~ ~

When she surfaced she saw pistils, stamens, petals; florid, penile, fluted, scalloped, rippling, tumescent. She observed these qualities scattered throughout her painting, again disturbed by her own work. It was true that flowers were the sexual organs of plants, hell bent on attracting pollinators. So why had she never seen it before? Except, of course, she had, or she wouldn't have just painted them that way.

"It's so good," the stranger whispered. "Like Georgia O'Keefe."

"Who?"

"Look her up. She's your soul sister."

"It's not the sort of thing I can submit to the annual Water Color Society exhibition," Cassidy said.

His puce eyes met and held hers. They were fathomless and deep. "I'm not a grape stencil on the bathroom wall," he said again.

Cassidy felt a little swoony.

"What happens if I don't?" she asked. She tried to give him back the sable brush but he didn't take it.

"Then I die," he said.

"Really?" It seemed so extreme. Again, she tried to give the brush back.

He fluttered his hands, no no no. "Please," the stranger said.

She began to cry, shaking her head. Her flowers resembled open mouths, open vulvas. It was too much! She knew now why she'd stopped drawing. She couldn't look at what emerged. And if she had a show, all the neighbors would see what she was really like.

Not like them. Not one bit.

He took her by the shoulders, tucked his long slender finger under her chin.

Forced it up.

His gentle puce eyes were whirlpools. She'd drown in them forever; she knew it for a fact. But better than gasping for air every hour of every day.

——— « o » ———

Ursula Pflug's

Ursula Pflug's eighth book is the near future YA novella *Mountain* (Inanna Publications). 2019 will see the publication of *The Food of My People* (Exile — co-edited with Candas Jane Dorsey) and a new novella, *Down From* (Snuggly Books in the UK). Her short fiction has won small press awards in the US and the UK, and been taught at universities in Canada and India. It has appeared in *Lightspeed*, *Fantasy*, *Strange Horizons*, *Postscripts*, *Leviathan*, *LCRW*, *Now Magazine*, *Bamboo Ridge*, and elsewhere. Pflug has been shortlisted or nominated for the Pushcart Prize, the Sunburst Award, the Aurora Award, the 3 Day Novel Contest, the Descant Novella Award, the KM Hunter Award, the ReLit Award and others; her work has been funded by The Ontario Arts Council, the Canada Council for the Arts and The Laidlaw Foundation. Her books have been endorsed by Tim Wynne-Jones, Candas Jane Dorsey, Charles De Lint, Mathew Cheney, Leanne

Betasamosake Simpson, Jeff VanderMeer and more. She has also worked extensively on multidisciplinary projects with dancers, filmmakers, playwrights and multi-media artists. A Toronto expat, she lives with her partner, multimedia artist Doug Back on the Ouse River in Peterborough County. You can find her on social media and at ursulapflug.ca

It's in the Eyes

Jerri Jerreat

I'm just a regular guy trying to find matching socks each morning and remember to pop the vitamins mom sends me. I fought with my big sister Iris all through childhood, and taught Haley, my younger, to play meteorball. Now I live with a cat named Pepper and dream of a holiday in the Arctic. Which is how I met Prudence.

"Did you remember your vitamins, Ernie?" asked my mother last Equinox.

"My name's not Ernie, Mom. It's Deck."

"Use your napkin, Ernie. How are you going to find a nice girl if…and why haven't you shaved? You have a good jaw and a cleft chin, your best feature. You *must—*"

"I think his eyes are nice," piped up my niece, Amy. She's ten. "Chocolate."

I smiled at her. "You have the same eyes, kid. That's why you think—"

"Mom's right, Deck," put in my older sister, Iris. "Look at you. You're thirty and hanging out at scuzzy vid bars and border holes—"

"Excuse me! Do the words 'Royal Canadian Mounted Police' mean anything to you?"

"And strip joints, no doubt," continued Iris, ignoring me. "When are you going to settle down?"

I passed her the squash because I knew she hated it. "Mom cooked this just for you, Iris."

She narrowed her eyes at me.

"The butternut? Yes," beamed our mother, her hair a shocking frost blue with glitter throughout. What was her hairdresser thinking of? Mind you, it matched her fake lizard-skin dress. "It's a new recipe from Dr. Burswanna. Honey and jalapenos. Try some."

I smiled a gushy smile at Iris and held the platter closer. "Two helpings?"

Before Iris' twisted expression could resolve itself, my dad spoke. "Isn't Babwanna the expert on alien immigration?"

"*Burs*wanna," corrected Mom. "Maybe that's where he got the recipe from."

"Squash from Ur-anus!" giggled my nephew Harry.

"I'm *not* eating it if it's alien," declared Amy.

The conversation stopped dead. Everyone turned to stare at the ten-year-old in her plascord overalls and neon vibrating beads throughout her hair.

Amy spread out her palms. "Okay, okay! I'm not xenophobic or anything. It's just that at school they say aliens stink, like for real, and they—"

Haley, my other sister, gave her a glare that would have made Medusa proud. "Are you a sheep or a thinking being?"

Amy blushed deep red.

"What's a strip joint?" interrupted Harry.

"A foodcore where they serve the joints and knuckles of pigs. It's a delicacy," explained my father smoothly. "And is that cranberry jelly on your shirt, young man?"

The conversation flowed forward again, Iris and my mother nagging me to get married, the kids arguing about Man-It Planet cards, Haley talking to Dad about the separatist movement on Salt Spring Island.

What is it, I asked myself. Do you have to be a vid star or an orthodontist to get respect? I'm a hard working Mountie who still secretly longs for the days of horses. If I were FBI or NYPD I'd be investigating assassinations or cross-planet smuggling. But I'm Canadian so I'm tracking down lawnmowers, of all things (fifty-four stolen off a lot last week — what was the thief using, a cargo ship?), and talking to pimply kids who're crossing the border to stranka underage. The Arctic was starting to look pretty good.

~ ~ ~

I'd have had to be blind not to have noticed the new librarian downtown. She had a cap of black curly hair, a pleasantly crooked nose, and the greenest eyes I'd ever seen.

She approached me with a book in hand. "I've noticed you're interested in the Arctic."

"Uh, yes." Over the past several weeks I'd been taking out books on northern explorers, from Peary's journals to Swinfjord's *A Tale of Two Arctics.*

Her eyes reminded me of grass after a spring rain.

"Well, this book came in. It was originally published in 2025, but it's finally out in print. I noticed you prefer print to web. It's about the lives of polar bears...there are still a few of them in Greenland..." she bit her lip. "But perhaps animals don't—"

"Oh, yes!" With that brilliant rejoinder, I reached for the book she had started to withdraw.

She smiled back and, caught in her velvet green galaxies, I forgot to close my grip. The book crashed to the floor. We both bent over to retrieve it, and our heads collided.

"Sorry! I'm sorry." I caught her shoulder to steady her, then started to chuckle. The two of us were crouched in the aisle like chimpanzees over a banana.

Her laugh was a snorting giggle she tried to cover with the back of one hand. She rose first and held out one small hand.

Surprised, I took it. Young maple leaves in spring, I thought. Her eyes.

She hoisted me up though I was a head taller and, as I may have mentioned, in pretty decent shape. Pepper and I jog.

"Well then," she began shyly, stepping back. "If you're interested—"

"Oh, *yes!*"

"—in the book," she continued.

I looked at the book in my hand. *Tense and Tensibility — the Dramatic Lives of Polar Bears.* "Thanks," I said, wishing for a classy Darcy sort of speech. "Yeah."

The librarian nodded and disappeared into the stacks.

As I was leaving, I wanted to say something particularly intelligent and noted the nameplate on the desk — Prudence Blinket.

"Uh, thanks again for the book, er, Ms. Blinket…"

"Just Prue." She blushed, making her lips and eyes brighter. "My parents loved old Beatles songs. Very retro."

I decided to bare my soul too. "Deck Gannon. Born the fateful day they put in a new deck."

Prue laughed again, her hand rising shyly to cover her mouth.

I left quickly, already planning my strategy. Luckily I'd been doing undercover for a month, so Prue hadn't seen me in uniform. My mother claims the red serge R.C.M.P. uniform would make any woman swoon, but in my experience it has the opposite effect. Everyone's guilty of *some*thing, even if it's just leaving the bathroom light on. A police uniform makes people act furtive, step back, and scurry away. Unless they're criminals.

The next time I visited the library, I found Prue downstairs filing discs in a sensor-screen.

"The book was great. Thanks," I said.

She looked up, startled. Her blush made her eyes brighter. "Oh, that's all right."

"I, um, thought the 3-D photos were quite striking."

"Photos?"

"Of the bears," I explained. I'd once seen a pond in Manning Park, B.C. the same deep green as her eyes.

"Oh." She finished her task then rose to look me full in the face. There were freckles across her nose. "Um. Why the Arctic, Mr.…."

"Deck's good enough." I shrugged. "I'd like to go there someday."

She studied me. "Is it the silence? The Aurora Borealis?"

I had a sudden vision of the two of us in Nunavut, huddled together under several blankets, watching the sleek sky explode. Regretfully, I erased it.

"The space," I admitted. "No crowds, no bars, no shoppers, and most of all no *traffic*."

She nodded sympathetically. "I grew up in a less populated area. The worst thing here is that — even with all these people — one is alone. I can't tell you how many people I help every day. But they rarely look at me."

I felt a stab of guilt for having been one of them. "Like you're not even human."

She blushed and nodded. "Like you're not even *there*." She turned her head to look down at her palm 'puter, and a mass of black ringlets fell over her face.

"Where are you from, Prue?"

"Sorry." She held up her watch. "I'm supposed to relieve Greg in the back."

~ ~ ~

"Here's another one you might like, Mr....," offered Prudence, appearing out of nowhere. I'd been in the library for twenty minutes, keeping a serious lookout for her.

"Deck. Call me Deck, please. And thanks." I took the book, *A Midsummer Night's Gleam — The Northern Lights*. "I was afraid you were sick or something."

"Why?"

"Because, well, I was looking for you." One good thing about working undercover is you get to grow a beard. It's handy to stroke when you're feeling sheepish.

"Really? Why were you looking for me?" She seemed genuinely puzzled.

I did the beard thing again. People aren't supposed to ask those questions. If a man is looking for a woman, there's a lot of stuff understood in the situation. I couldn't just say, 'Well, I like your eyes, and I was wondering if this would lead to anything, you know...' I stalled. "Well, uh. I wanted to ask you something."

Prue wore a forest green turtleneck over black pants, and a black stretchy thing around her head to try to hold all those bouncy curls back. It wasn't working.

"Oh. About books?"

I coughed. "Not really. I was wondering if... if you'd like to... go out?"

"Yes, actually I would." She bit her lip. "But I have to warn you. Don't expect kissing. You people kiss far too easily."

I blinked in slow motion. Had she really just said that? "Actually, I was only offering food. How about dinner?"

A thin ray of sunlight from the windows lit up her face. She squinted and moved around me, placing her back to the light. "Well, I suppose so. But..."

"I promise to restrain myself. When are you off?"

~ ~ ~

The dinner date was far more enjoyable than the coffee dates with Mandy-the-engineer, or Jessica-the-artist-slash-dental-activist. I found myself forgetting the D.O.A. that morning from Andromeda, the new street drug, and the damn lawnmower case. My humor bloomed, perhaps due to the wine, but we both laughed a lot.

"So tell me, Prue," I asked, trying to be serious. "The Arctic's my dream. What's yours?"

"Well, I came here for the books. There's no literature where I'm from. Only romance vids and how-to vids. Or both: *How to Romance a Vid in Six Easy Steps.*" She grinned. "I'm planning to start an old-fashioned read aloud program at the library."

"Novel idea," I quipped. "Any other dreams?"

Those magnificent eyes swept the room, taking in other couples, families out for supper, groups of friends. Her voice grew soft. "Well, yes. I've — what do you say? I've already 'sown my wild grass.' Now I wish only for a family, to be *in* a family. Someday." She raised the back of her hand to hide her embarrassment.

"Wild oats," I corrected, wondering if she meant she was looking for a man. *That* was intimidating. Mind you, I was there because, let's face it, I was looking for a woman. Good galaxies, I thought, I sound like a caveman.

"Where's your family?" I inquired.

"In the heavens." She sighed.

"I'm sorry." I tried to steer back to lighter subjects. "And how does a librarian sow her wild oats, hmm? Read a little *Wuthering Heights*?"

She tilted her head. "I did not really enjoy that book, but— you were making a joke?" She leaned forward on her forearms. "English is harder than you'd think."

"Where are you from again?"

She drew back and reached for her wineglass. "From everywhere, really. My father was an astropilot. We moved a lot." She took a sip. "My Spanish and Mandarin are slightly better than my English and French."

"Really?" The only lead I had on the lawnmowers was a Spanish janitor who worked in the dealership. He thought he'd heard noises but his English was terrible. "I wish I knew Spanish. But three official languages is enough for me."

"Deck, have you always been a night watchman?"

I rubbed my beard, cursing the disguise and the rules. "Well, always in, you know, that sort of work. So, uh, what's the funniest thing you ever saw happen at the library?"

~ ~ ~

I forced myself not to call Prue for a couple of days, though I found myself thinking about her often. The third day I had an all-day session on the latest web-scams at work, and I nearly fell asleep dreaming about green fields, green skies, and green stars. I gave up and called her on my lunch hour.

"It's me, Deck. How are you, Prue?"

"I feel well today. Did you wish to request a book?"

Did that mean she was angry I hadn't called sooner? "Uh, no, I just wanted to tell you I had fun the other night. With you."

"Oh, that." There was a pause. "I enjoyed myself also."

"Uh, listen, do you bike?"

"Do I bite?"

The noise at the deli was growing. "No, *bike*. Bicycle, you know."

"Oh. No, actually."

My shoulders slumped. A motorcycle went by, cutting out all possibility of conversation for a minute. Why did they still allow those antiques on the road?

"Deck? Are you there?"

"What? Oh, sorry. Say, how about a trip to the country? Something old-fashioned. A picnic. We could stop in the villages and wander around."

"A picnic? Me?" She sounded as if she'd never heard the word before.

"Yeah, you."

There was a long pause. "When were you thinking of?"

"When's your next day off?"

"Sunday."

"Well then I was thinking of Sunday."

I wondered how much those noisy junkers were to rent for the day. I hadn't driven one since my teens. "Can I pick you up around, say, eleven in the morning? Or is that too early?" I was working until three a.m. the night before.

"Too early?" She paused again, and I closed my eyes. "Well. All right. I'll be ready. Should I bring some food?"

"Just yourself. And your smile." I said goodbye and hung up, feeling pretty good about myself and life. Hey, I could be cool. And I might just find those lawnmowers yet.

~ ~ ~

We had a great ride down the back roads on that old motorcycle, Prue's arms around me, her legs against mine. Now I knew why those things were still on the road. A few trees still had red and gold leaves dancing in the wind, but the lanes were like rich Persian carpets. At the first village we poked around in a second-hand store, and I bought a bag of glass marbles. She bought an old broach of a leaf carved out of real wood, a find. We picked up sandwiches at a foodcore and ate them on a grassy slope thick with fallen yellow leaves.

"This is beautiful," she said, looking around.

I pointed to the lazy stream. "My sisters, Iris and Haley, always insisted that sound of water over rocks was fairy bells tinkling."

Prue smiled. "It must be nice to have sisters. I'm an only child."

I raised an eyebrow. "Well, it's mixed. First they beg you to play with them all the time, then they grow up and bug you about everything."

"Bug you?"

"About how you wear your hair, when are you going to get married and, you know." I took another bite.

"Are they married themselves?" Prue pushed a wave of dark curls out of her eyes.

"Iris is. Has twin teens and a seven-year-old boy, Harry. Haley has a girl, Amy, ten. Haley's never been married but thinks she's an expert."

"What are the children like?"

I wiped some crumbs off my beard and frowned. "Pesky. Curious. Affectionate." I paused. "Great."

"You love them."

I threw a crust of bread at her. "They grow on you. My family's crazy though."

Prue undid her windbreaker and peeled it off. Her red flannel shirt looked cosy over a black highneck. I hadn't realized I was partial to flannel shirts.

"I don't know enough children," she said thoughtfully.

"Why don't you come meet them? They're noisy, and sometimes rude, but hey that's human."

Prue began to tidy up our mess. "I don't think so, Deck," she said. "I'm not as brave as I should be."

I assumed she was joking so I laughed. "Me neither. Hey, my mother's *clothes* terrify me sometimes."

Prue frowned. "What were those things you bought today?"

"Marbles? Never seen them?" I pulled them out of my pocket. The glass spheres had twists of colors inside. "These are cat's eyes. Want to play? I'll teach you."

"Certainly."

Librarians, it turns out, have uncanny mathematical aim. Luckily I only bet my watch, my jacket, all my worldly goods and the rented motorcycle. When I dropped Prue off at her apartment she kindly returned her winnings to me. I had the urge to touch her but settled for a pat on her shoulder. "See ya 'round, pardner."

"Goodnight, Mr. Gannon."

I grinned all the way home.

~ ~ ~

It was Solstice. I must have been insane to bring Prue — we'd only gone out a handful of times — but when she'd claimed she liked being alone with an old book on Solstice evening, I couldn't help myself. I dragged her to Solstice dinner. *Really* dragged. In fact, I pretended I couldn't get out of it, and sort of tricked her into coming. Perhaps in front of other people I'd be able to get a sense of how she felt about me.

"Don't be overwhelmed. They're noisy," I reminded her, brushing snow off her glossy hair. We were standing on my parents' front step. "And there's a lot of them, but don't be nervous."

She stayed my hand. "It's just popping in, right? An hour or so?"

Ahem. I nodded. "But my mother will try to talk us into dinner. Nod at me if it's okay, and frown if you want me to make an excuse." What if Iris said something stupid, or Mom called me Ernie, or my nephew snorted juice out his nose? In other words, what if they all acted normal? I'd ordered my mother to act very casual. No fuss. No embarrassing scenes.

"Will they like me?" She bit her lip.

"A terrifying librarian." I grinned at her, wishing that I could hug her but there was that *you people kiss too easily* thing between us.

The door flung open, and my dear mother was revealed in a stretchy parrot pink jumpsuit with hair to match. "Ernie!" she cried. "You've finally brought a woman home!"

It took a moment for my brain to re-enter my head. "Mother," I sighed. "This is Prue."

My mother yanked Prue in as if she might get away. "Come in, come in," she said. "And tell me all about it. Where did you two meet? One of those new dance clubs? A stranka?"

"A library, Mother."

Mother hid her disappointment. "Well, let me take your coat. My, what lovely hair you have," she continued, ignoring me. She touched her volcano shaped hairdo lightly. "I can't do a thing with mine. Ernie's old fashioned. He doesn't approve of hair color, I can tell. But I like just a little sometimes, don't you? Just a touch up? Though you certainly don't need it."

I winced. What would Prue think of such nonsense?

She surprised me. "I think the pink suits your skin, Ms. Gannon. It creates a pleasant contrast with your lilac eyes."

Mother leaned forward to whisper loudly. "Contact lenses. Such fun, aren't they? I see you—"

Amy interrupted this tête-à-tête by poking her head between them and whispering even more loudly. "Did Grandma have to pay you to come?"

Prue laughed. My mother looked at her anxiously, then joined in.

"I heard that, bug," I said, looking sternly at Amy. "Prue, this is my niece, Amy."

"Nice to meet you," began Amy.

"Does she know you're gay, Uncle Deck?"

We all turned to gape at young Harry, who was poker-faced. If I laughed, it might seem like I was trying too hard to be convincing. Luckily Haley appeared, wiping her hands on a dishcloth. She was dressed in a white fuzzy thing over lime spotted tights.

"Hi, I'm Haley, Deck's sister. He's not gay, or he'd be bringing your brother. Ignore this kid." She shook hands with Prue, who looked a little startled.

Iris appeared. "And I'm Iris, Deck's older sister. Smarter. A brain surgeon."

Prue blinked and shook Iris' hand. "I'm Prue. A harmless librarian."

Everyone laughed, including my father, who had entered in an apron which proclaimed, "Keep Uranus a Planet, Mine's a Bum." Mother wanted us to sit in the living room, but the teenagers had the tri-vids on there, so we trailed after Dad into the kitchen. Iris fetched Prue a sherry while Mother dragged a chair out for her. Amy had her dead bug collection handy and was shoving plasboxes at Prue, and Harry was already playing his trecorder for her. I might as well have been invisible.

I tromped downstairs to find a beer. Dad's 472 power tools were lined up on hooks and shelves, which reminded me of lawnmowers and Spanish-speaking janitors and Prue speaking Spanish and Mandarin.

When I came upstairs, Harry had finished his fifth run through "Twinkle Twinkle," and Amy, talking with Prue non-stop, had replaced the dead bugs with her collection of fingerprints.

"And this is my dad's. He's in Ottawa right now. And this is my teacher's. And this is Uncle Deck's. A cop's fingerprint. Funny, eh?"

Prue's head snapped up to look at me just as my mouth fell open. Luckily, Harry took that moment to stare at Prue and announce, "She has weird eyes!"

Prue tucked her chin down, flushing scarlet.

"Harry, that's just plain rude. They're lovely eyes," corrected my mother, her hands on her violent pink hips. "Now Ernie, get yourself a drink."

"My name's not Ernie," I replied automatically and raised my beer in answer. Harry, already bored with adults, ran out of the room and knocked over Amy, returning with her space rocks collection.

"Har-ry!"

"This is just about the lot," I said to Prue, waving my beer at the group. That's when Iris' oldest boy, David, head-butted his twin, Xan, into the room.

~ ~ ~

"So, son, what's with the beard and long hair?" asked my father, passing the meat platter to Prudence on his left.

I glanced at Prue, seated between my parents, then swallowed. "Well, actually, it's undercover month at the office."

"Trying to break into that mafia? That's dangerous, son."

Prue looked at him, frowning.

"No, um, just a small-time smuggling group."

"That Andromeda drug?" asked Amy, leaning forward. "We've been warned at school to watch our drinks."

"Um," I replied, looking studiously away from Prue. She was probably furious at me for lying. "I'm not supposed to talk about it."

"Police officers lead such *glamorous* lives," gushed Amy. "Like in the vids, chasing aliens across the galaxy..."

Chasing lawnmowers, more like.

"So, what do you do, Prudence?" asked my father. "Here, have some cranberry sauce. Made it myself."

"I'm a librarian," she offered quietly. Then, louder, she added. "*Officer* Gannon has been doing some vital research at the library."

I cringed. Just how mad was she?

"Oh, cool! He came to you, like, for help?" Amy elbowed her cousin Harry.

"That's right."

"Then *you* can tell us what this top secret investigation is, right?"

Prudence plopped mashed purple potatoes onto her plate slowly, then looked up. "I *can* tell you that it involves more than this planet," she confided across the sea of faces to Amy. "But you're absolutely right. It's *top* secret."

"Ooh!"

The kids conferred. My sisters and parents all shot meaningful glances at each other.

My father leaned forward and spoke in the loud whisper my family seemed to think actually signified privacy. "Son. I hope you're not involved in anything too dangerous. The intergalactic treaties haven't all been ratified. You're not chasing pirates now, are you?"

Everyone turned, open-mouthed. I could sense their new awe of Uncle Deck and straightened in my chair. It was tempting to leave matters as they were, but the idea of me in a silver one-piece sneaking aboard a spaceship was absurd. Me, who got motion sickness the one time they let me canter on one of the beautiful black thoroughbreds reserved for the Musical Ride. "Give it up, Prue. She's pulling your legs. All of you. Truth is, I'm looking for a thief who's into garden equipment. It's local and very boring. Now get those potatoes over here. Some of us dull, ordinary cops are starving over here." I picked up the platter of squash, decorated with slivers of lime. "This looks like it's for you," I said to Iris.

"Gee. Thanks."

The conversation recovered as Iris asked Prudence how we really met, and Prue asked Iris about her work as a skin (not brain) surgeon. Dad asked Haley about her leaking basement, while my mother argued with Harry about pickles.

"You can't eat *just* pickles, Harry. Some *regular* food too."

I caught Prue's emerald eyes across the table and gave a tentative grin. She winked back. With relief, I tucked into my supper. Things were going to be okay.

"I'm so sorry your parents are gone," sighed my mother to Prue, heaping extra squash on her plate as though to make up for lost parents. "I've lost mine too. Such a shame."

"She's religious," whispered Amy.

"Ssh. What makes you think so?" Haley glanced at Prue. "She's not wearing one of those rope-thingys. And there's no tattoo."

I had to interrupt there. "Why do you think she's religious?" I whispered to Amy, leaning over. My whisper really *was* a whisper.

"She said her parents were in the heavens." She pointed up.

"Could be the North Pole," Haley offered. "Died studying the earth's axis."

Why hadn't I thought of that? It explained her finding those books for me. The last one was at home under my orange feline. *War and Grease: Arctic Oil Exploration, a Galactic Mistake.*

"She's an alien. Look at her eyes," stated Harry. He put two more pickles in his mouth.

I glanced at Prue to see if she'd heard. She had the most peculiar expression on her face, almost of panic. Yes, panic. She glanced from Harry to me, to the door, to her food, then from Harry to me. A silence spread across the table, broken only by the crunch of pickles.

"There, there, dear," began my mother. "Harry didn't mean…

Prudence pushed her chair backward and stood up, clutching a large poinsettia napkin to her stomach. "I'm sorry. I—" She turned as if to flee.

"Prue!" My chair tipped over loudly as I rose.

My mother was one step ahead of me, dragging Prue gently back into her seat. "There, there, it's no matter. Nobody minds." She looked directly across the table at my ten year-old niece Amy. "Right, Amy?"

I glanced from my librarian's stricken face to my mother's, to Amy, calmly wiping her mouth. My brain was smothered in thick fuzzy fur. *You people kiss too easily.*

"It's cool. But warning: Grandma seriously wants more grandchildren."

There was another awkward pause. My mother placed one arm around Prue's shoulders and patted her hand with the other.

"Will that be a problem, dear? Grandchildren?"

Prue blushed deeply and bit her lip. "Well, no. But most people are uncomfortable with us. I should have told—"

"Nonsense!" bellowed my father. "Here, top up your wine. Now hurry up and eat this stuff. I didn't cook all day for it to get cold. And Ernestina, quit pushing poor Deck into fatherhood before he's even married. Who's got the gravy?

~ ~ ~

"I should have told you," she began the moment we were alone in the back hallway, ostensibly fetching cider.

"I should have told you," I replied, lifting up her chin. "Do all aliens have crooked noses?"

She laughed. "Oh sure. We all look alike."

"And grandchildren are a possibility?" I teased.

She blushed but looked me straight in the eyes. "I think its best we start with kissing," she offered, and started right then.

Pretty soon I was seeing stars, moons, even galaxies far away. No wonder they didn't kiss on the first date! I wasn't sure I'd be able to stand up straight afterward.

She pulled away for a minute.

I peeled my eyes open and tried to focus. "Um," I said, brilliant as usual. There *was* something weird about her eyes. The ceiling light was shining in them, and her pupils had shrunk to a slim, pointed oval. "Like a cat," I murmured, surprised. Pepper would be so pleased. I moved back in for another long kiss.

"Definitely a possibility," she purred.

—— « O » ——

Jerri Jerreat

Jerri Jerreat's fiction has appeared in *The New Quarterly, The Dalhousie Review, The Antigonish Review, Fireweed, Canadian Storyteller Magazine,* and won a *Room* fiction competition. She has a Masters degree in Creative Writing from the University of British Columbia and has taught a variety of writing courses at St. Lawrence College, in Kingston, Ontario. She now teaches younger students, and each year, mentors a class to create a play together, then directs it. She read *A Wrinkle in Time* and other fine books aloud to her own kids, Tanner, Adan and Haven, walking them to school, and is proud to say she can still walk and read at the same time. When her family canoe trips somewhere like Algonquin Park, they all stuff massive books secretly into their packs.

Across the Seas of Sand

Jason Lane

The buggy climbed over the dune, its engine roaring, eight wheels turning, leaving jagged trails like two long snakes in its wake. The desert stretched out on every side. Hills of dunes punctuated with rusted metal hulks of things that once were. Leviathans in a sea of sand, dwarfing the small vehicle as it lumbered through the graveyard of iron and rust.

"Used to be all ocean here!" Old George called jovially. He smiled, showing the three teeth left in his head, his goggles flashing in the sun. He wore a bandana to keep out the dust but had pulled it down to better be heard. "All ocean! Made it in the tenth year after the first colony ship arrived. Course, they say there was always oceans here. Called it the Jonah Sea! I was here when they made it. Born on the trip. Pod babies they called us! When we first landed, I practically pissed myself! Never felt the disturbance of the earth, the shaking of real proper gravity until we started to land. Whole trip through space was smooth. Smooth as glass!"

"Huh," Jack said.

Alice shook her head with wonder.

Beneath their voices, the radio crackled. *"Thirty seven left and counting. Make your way to coordinates 12-36 by north. Waiting there…Repeat. Thirty Seven left and…"*

Old George jerked the aged stick and gunned the engine, and the little buggy roared as it crawled its way across the desert. Salt crystals flashed in the sand that flew in their wake.

~ ~ ~

They drove until night and then parked in the lee of a mountain of rusting metal. The three of them gathered around a fire built against the cold.

"Let me tell you about the first colonists," Old George said eagerly. "We landed all over the planet and across the deserts. Everything had been prepared for us. They'd been waiting! Grand thing it was. Converted the old ships into settlements. Best way. Best. Came pre-equipped but the numbers were larger after the trip. A long trip. Had to be made. And you know how men and women get on those long quiet nights eh?"

He wiggled eyebrows white as snow. Alice blushed and ducked her head but Jack sat rigidly, jaw clenched. When Old George wasn't yapping the night was quiet but for the fire and the low drone of the radio.

"Thirty left and counting. Thirty left. Make your way to coordinates 12-36 by north. Waiting there. Repeat..."

"Should we drain the battery like that?" Alice asked.

Old George struck a match and lit a cigarette. The tip glowed cherry red in the dark. Jack glowered. Those had been his cigarettes.

"Don't you worry. We have enough. Plenty of power to get you there. Fuel too. Have three cans still full from the old rest stop. Won't need it much longer. Nope! May as well use up what supplies we have. Waste it otherwise. Just need to get there."

Old George settled back on the rock, hooking his thumbs in his belt. When he continued his voice took on the familiar groove of the story. Slow. Steady with the familiar words. "Come to think of it, did I ever tell you about the old caves we found? They ran deep indeed. One night I went into one. Just a lad, younger even than you two. Terraforming had just finished. The air was still stale. Kind of like now really. But there was the beginning of freshness in it. Oh yes there was. Just the beginning."

Jack opened his mouth and breathed in the dusty air. He coughed a little.

Old George spoke late into the night about the caves. About how he and his friends had ventured into them and found paintings. Old drawings of things that'd come before the first man's boots disturbed the dust of the world. The fire crackled when he finally fell silent and they bedded down, covering their faces with sheets to keep the sand from suffocating them in the night.

They slept 'til dawn. Then they loaded themselves back into the old buggy. Old George took the wheel again — he was the only one who knew where they were going. As they drove on, the radio continued in its measured voice.

"Twenty six seats and counting. Twenty six left. Make your way to coordinates 12-36 by north. Waiting…"

~ ~ ~

They left the desert with its behemoths of orange-tainted iron behind and crawled across the later dunes tufted with dry yellowed grass. They made particularly good time when they found an old highway. Skeletal trees wrapped in gray bark like mummies stood here and there in the parched earth. They camped beneath one that night and when Jack touched the trunk, its bark broke away like charred paper.

"Canals ran through the whole avenue this way," Old George said amiably. He stuck his thumbs into his belt and hefted it around his girth. "Oh yes! Needed them in the beginning. Atmospheric generators could only keep the water from flying into space. We needed it to run though. Found it buried deep in the ground. Why!" he called, eyes misting with memory. "I recall the pools. My old friend Richie had one. Used to play in there during the hot months. Course, there were only ever hot times. Not much for seasons here. Back on Earth, so's my old gran said, we had four at least! Summer, which was hot, spring when things would bloom, autumn when things would die, and winter when things were buried under snow."

"Snow?"

Old George's eyes snapped back to the present and down to Alice. He smiled. "Well, snow was…a kind of white powdered water. Icy cold like the nights like this."

"Suppose we're in autumn, then," Jack said moodily, his head cocked, listening to the radio murmur through the dark.

"*—teen seats and counting. Eighteen left. Make your way to coordinates…*"

Old George nodded slowly. "Suppose so. Suppose so. Wouldn't know myself. My gran. But don't worry. Don't you worry. There's better waiting for us. Up there's where the future lies." Old George waved his hand to the heavens, the stars clear and visible, bright as diamonds on black velvet. "Up there, they found the way. We just need to get to them. Need to reach them. We'll make it. I know the way! The old stomping grounds hereabouts. Don't you worry. Have a good feeling. Real good. Hear me?" Old George tapped his forehead. He laughed, hitching his belt again. "Now then. What'll we hear about tonight. Hmm…" Old George's voice lowered into the familiar drone. "Oh yes. How about the naming? The old surveyors who prepped the place named most of the mountains. Gave them old earth names. Names they remembered. Things like Mount Washington and Jonah Sea. But there were others that still needed it. Hills and lakes and smaller things. We all got to name those. Suppose you'll get to do the same to the new ones. Well, when I was about thirty…"

~ ~ ~

Jack woke in the morning, tense. The sand that had blown over him during the night made a dull weight on his chest. Something felt wrong. Something was different.

He listened, his head in the sand, and suddenly knew. The radio was silent.

Jack sat up quickly and saw Old George at the buggy. The old man looked back. "Oh! Morning Jack. Seems the radio died last night. Shame. Spark plugs burned out. I guess your girl was right."

Jack stood up, quieting the tremor inside him with effort. "But…you said the buggy was fine. How'd it break?"

"Spark plugs. Didn't you hear me?" Old George tapped his temple. "Gotta listen better lad. Gotta listen. Who knows what you'll miss if you don't pay attention to what goes on." Old George laughed.

Jack kept quiet, wandering about as they broke camp, idly kicking the sand as he watched the old man wake Alice and prep the buggy. Spark plugs? Spark plugs! He scowled. Oh yes. Spark plugs in the radio. What a farce. He shook his head, and spotted something out of the corner of his eye. There! Something gleaming beneath the punishing sun. Jack stomped over and picked it up.

He stared at the torn-out wires until Alice called him. He pocketed them, and hurried to join her.

~ ~ ~

Old George spoke more enthusiastically than usual as they drove onward, as if he was trying to fill the silence left by the radio. Alice listened with all her being to tales of a world forgotten and lost.

"Course," Old George said as they drove. "Atmosphere couldn't be sustained. Oh we thought it could, but the plans they had…Well kids, the plans men make are grand old things but sometimes life doesn't quite work out. Things break down, and when they do, you need adapt. Need to change! We did for a while. We tried. But some things just don't work out. Learn from mistakes! That's the way. Well, too late for me and mine." Old George laughed. "Then of course there was the fear. And well…" Old George said softly, leaning back with a sigh. "Fear can make men do stupid things."

Old George looked out across the desert. "Need courage to brave what lies ahead. But a lot of men lack it. The pioneering spirit. Far easier to be a coward."

Jack watched him closely.

~ ~ ~

The store sat astride the highway like some ruin of other times. The windows were shuttered with ruddy-colored steel and the wooden walls were dry with a texture like bone. A sign stood on the end of a long pole, its letters long dead fluorescent tubes. When they stopped Jack managed to make out the words '*Little Ever*'.

A man stood on the porch with a heavy rifle in hands baked dark by the sun. The desert had sucked the moisture from his face, leaving only pitiless lines which might have been wrinkles. But a smile came to his lips as Old George stepped out of the buggy. "Some more comin' through, eh?"

Jack was halfway out and froze at that. George waved his hat. "Passin' through. Only passin'. Still have some gas?"

The man on the porch, still grinning that smile that stretched his skin taut over the bones of his face, nodded. "In the back, you know. The old jerry cans still have enough for a few trips. But you pay."

Old George laughed and hitched his belt up and looked to Jack and Alice. "Could use a hand with it. Not as strong as I once was, you know."

Jack pretended not to hear. Alice glared at him before hopping out to join Old George and disappear around the back of the store. The dry figure watched the pair, then looked back to Jack as soon as they were about the corner.

"What do you mean more?" Jack asked quietly.

The man cocked his head. "More? Said more didn't I?" His tongue flicked across dry lips. "Some on foot. In cars. Sorts. They come through with all they have on their backs. Where'd he pick you up then?"

"Nestor's Creek. Thereabouts," Jack said stiffly.

"Ah. Surprised anyone 'thereabouts.' Surprise surprise."

"Why do you say that?"

"No reason. No reason. But seen others come this way before. All going that way." He smiled with teeth yellow like old ivory. "Never see them again."

"There's a ship taking them out," Jack said. "Why would you?"

He rasped with something that might be a laugh.

"Is there really a ship that way?" Jack said.

He grinned wider. "Is there? Maybe. Maybe not."

"Do you have a radio?" Jack asked.

His smile grew suddenly hard. "No use in those things. They only play dead sound now. Screaming out lies into the dark. I broke mine ages ago."

"What do you mean?"

"Ruined stations, leaving their sounds floating in the air. Nothing to hear but the crowing of ghosts in the wires, running through what's known. 'Ten seats!' then 'No seats!

Ship has launched!' Ha!" He shook his head. "The world's dying. So's everything on it. We're all going to die on this rock, you know. All of us. Children burned in the dust. We're the last."

Jack glanced back towards the corner where Old George had vanished. Then back to the man on the porch. "You sell things. Have a screwdriver?"

~ ~ ~

They left the mummified shop and its sun baked owner far behind. Jack woke in the dead of night. He listened to the snores of the others — Old George's whistling through his few remaining teeth. Alice's soft and muffled by the sheet she'd drawn over her head to protect against the dust.

Jack rose softly. The sand that had tried to bury him in the night sloughed off with a hiss. He froze, listening, but the cadence of snores never rose or fell.

Jack opened the buggy's side door and leaned in. The seat was contorted to Old George's heavy frame but the man's smell had been baked out of the leather by the blazing sun, leaving only a smell like dry paper. He slid into the seat and by star and moonlight Jack began to open the front of the radio with the screwdriver. Once he took off the panel and opened the radio, he stared at the snipped ends of what had been two connecting wires. Jack returned the front of the radio to its place and sat back in the driver's seat, dreadfully quiet.

~ ~ ~

The next day Jack said nothing while Old George prattled and Alice listened. After they'd stopped and before they bedded down Jack took Alice by the arm and drew her away to collect wood for the fire. In the dark, lit only by the stars, he told her about the broken wires.

"Well?" he asked.

Alice shrugged. "Well what? They're broken. So?"

"They didn't burn out. They were cut. Old George cut them."

He heard the frown in her voice. "What do you mean?"

"I mean, I think he cut them on purpose. To quiet the radio. I don't think he want us to hear what's happening."

"Hear what?"

"About the ship. About the colony. Alice, I'm worried. What if there isn't one?"

"He brought us this far."

"And how much further will he? What do we know about him?"

"He found us Jack. If he hadn't, we'd be dead now. Left in the sands to die. We have to go on. I'll not hear anything else."

"Will you listen! We're—"

"Jack."

She put her hands to her stomach. Jack saw the movement.

"We have to," she said softly. "We can't stay."

~ ~ ~

While they drove, Old George's mouth was always moving, spouting tales and stories of the lands they passed through. Lands he'd come through before. Had heard of. Knew someone who'd been. Everything had a story and he was eager to tell them. Alice listened from the back, soaking in his every word. She didn't look at Jack where he brooded in the front beside Old George. While the old man spoke through cracked lips, Jack stared at the silent radio.

~ ~ ~

That night, Jack found an old iron bar in the back of the buggy. He felt its weight, hefting it, and swung it twice in the dry air. He nodded, satisfied, and stowed it under his seat before they started out the next day.

~ ~ ~

Two more days they traveled, miles vanishing under their treads until finally, they crested a cliff, and they were there.

The ship sat in its berth. Shining chrome and glittering steel. So new. So fresh! As long as the largest behemoths in the sea of rust. As tall as the mountains once seen in the distance. It pointed upward like a spear to pierce the sky.

Around it lay a wash of gray. Buildings aged and broken. Workshops and assembly yards. Cranes drooping like tired arms. But the ship gleamed, glaring in its newness while surrounded by the detritus of the broken city.

Old George gave a great whoop and again he gunned the engine. No one spoke as they drove quickly down the lonely road, passing broken down cars and left to rot and buildings blasted bare of paint by desert winds. Sand flew beneath their tires and asphalt rattled as it chipped away.

They slowed as they came upon an abandoned camp. Old George guided the buggy around listless tents, many knocked down by wind or half-buried in the sand. Old cookfires formed pits, and vehicles crouched in ruin, abandoned and still.

A huge wall with a single gate surrounded the ship, and as they drove up, men with guns came out and fanned about.

Old George slowed. Jack tensed. The men were dressed in the worn remains of uniforms. They held themselves in grim silence.

Old George stopped and stepped out, ambling towards the soldiers. One in a peaked cap of office walked away with Old George and fell into conversation.

Jack looked at the men surrounding the car. He reached for the bar under his seat before realizing its futility in the face of the shining guns. He abandoned it.

Alice's hand found his arm and gripped it. "What's happening," she murmured.

Jack eyed the soldiers. "It'll be okay," he said.

"Jack?"

"It'll be fine."

"Oh God," Alice whispered. "Oh God."

He took her hand and squeezed it.

Old George finished speaking with the officer. A package passed between them and they came back towards the buggy. Old George leaned in. "Alright. Everyone out."

Old George was still smiling, but there was a sag to his face that hadn't been there before. A look of something finished. Jack put his arm around Alice as they left the buggy, their feet kicking up dust on the old road.

Old George stood back. "In you go," he said, making a sweeping gesture to the gates.

"George?"

"Go on kids. Remember everything I told you. Courage kids. Courage!"

Alice stepped closer to Jack. She opened her mouth to speak, but the men with guns closed about them and ushered them away. In the silence of the dead city, they walked towards the doors. They opened with a hiss. Jack looked back to see Old George standing by the buggy, waving his tattered hat farewell.

They passed through the gate and into a large room with the soldiers, and Jack heard a familiar voice drone through the silence.

"Two seats and counting. Two seats left. Make your way to coordinates 12-36 by north. Waiting there. Repeat. Two left and..."

One of the soldiers went behind the desk and tapped the keys of a terminal. The voice crackled, changed.

"No seats remaining. The Arc has launched. There are no seats remaining. Repeat. No seats remaining. The Arc has launched."

—— « O » ——

Jason Lane

Jason Lane has lived in Whitehorse, Yukon all his life except for occasional visits to the southern climes, always to gravitate back towards the pole when winter calls. Weird tales and fantasy are his lifelong loves but science fiction always has a special place in his heart. He is a huge fan of Ray Bradbury and Terry Pratchett, and when not writing, can be found perusing the local used bookshop or libraries. Across the Sea of Sands is his second published work.

Lt. Anderwicz Goes Applepicking

Natalia Yanchak

Andy rides the yellow school bus out to the apple orchard, bouncing along the highway into the countryside. Less than a hundred meters back up the driveway he spots a telecommunication tower. A metal red-and-white structure, a thin triangle pointing up into the sky.

As the rest of his kindergarten class climbs onto the hay ride wagon, Andy slips away and runs between the widely spaced McIntosh trees to the tower. Only five in human years, but developmentally middle-aged, he curses the limited speed his tiny legs are able to achieve. Scuttling under a wood fence, he runs to the base of the tower. Andy smashes open the switching box with a rock to access the communications equipment inside: a black phone receiver, an array of PCBs, and a tangle of thin, multi-colored wires.

Using the entire weight of his body, he tugs out a handful of wires then braids them following a specific pattern: far left, over; second right, under; far right, center; second left, under; and so on until the braid is nearly two meters long. He sets it down it atop the dewy grass to form a closed circle, then steps inside.

As his classmates pose for their group photo down the road, Andy's body electrifies, and he floats a few inches above the ground. Glowing gently, he connects to Base, informing them of the success of his mission. They can come collect him.

He runs quickly back to the parking lot and slips back in line to board the school bus as the educator checks each student's name on her attendance list.

~ ~ ~

"Andy, do you want your snack?" The educator hands him a paper bowl, filled with crackers and yellow cheese. But Andy is not in his seat; he is at the toy kitchen set, pretending to fix his own snack. He shakes his head and returns to his role play.

He picks up the pink toy phone and puts it to his ear. The buttons are molded in hard plastic and there is no cord. He listens intently. The educator catches a glimpse of him beginning to speak, so he turns his back to the group.

"How long?" he demands, in a whisper.

"We're sorry, sir, but the mega-drives are still down, and at nominal speed Base is at least fourteen Julian years away."

"These creatures, their bodies are tiny. My mind is far too advanced for this size," Andy implores.

"We know. The Director is aware and we are working on a solution."

"This embed is tiresome." He looks around the room. "Do you know how many apple slices I've had to eat? Have you ever tried an apple?"

"No, sir." He hears the officer typing. "The system says they are tart yet sweet, appear in any combination of red, yellow or green, ripen in the Last Seasonal Quarter..."

"Yes. Disgusting. They mush them up into a grainy puree that is absolutely repulsive. And if I don't eat it, the creatures get *angry*."

"We understand, sir. We're doing our best, sir—"

"Ah! Circle time. Gotta go." Andy replaces the pink receiver in its red cradle on the side of the kitchen set and runs to the carpet, smiling. He sits cross-legged between Jasvinder and Lauren.

At midday, the educators dim the lights and draw the curtains. It is nap time and the children are resting on their floor-mats, each under their own fleece blanket. Andy pulls his blanket over his head and holds his stuffy, a blue-white snowman named Frostman, tightly. He toggles its orange, carrot-shaped nose like a switch then whispers: "Are you there?" A faint hiss.

"Sir?" the officer's voice answers.

"Yes."

"Engineering has the mega-drives back online. Communications will be down while we are they are engaged. The Director expects you to open a channel in the next 36 to 42 Earth hours, to send your exact co-ordinates upon our arrival."

"Great news." Andy wriggles his legs in excitement under the blanket. "Regards." He toggles the carrot.

"Andy, no silliness," the educator calls, quietly. He stops moving and pulls the blanket back down under his chin. His eyes closed, a large grin on his face.

~ ~ ~

It is nearly midnight, and Andy is tucked up in his small bed at home. A dome-shaped, indigo lamp pockmarked with tiny circular holes projects a star map onto the ceiling. He opens his eyes to the meaningless map, observing how clusters are mislaid by thousands of parsecs. "*As if* Rigel is that close to Betelgeuse," he mutters, listening closely to the clean thread of static emanating from the baby monitor. Two years ago he modified its circuitry, de-coupling from the channel of the receiver unit in his parent's room and enabling two-way comms, a wide-band scanner, and relative clock mode.

"Earth hours since last contact," he commands.

"Thirty-two," the automated voice calls from the monitor.

"Hmmm." He grows impatient, waiting for Base to come out of mega-drive, and looks over at the bookshelf lined with wooden puzzles and picture books. He wishes he had learned to read since arriving here, but he'd found human literature fraught with imagery, abstract drawings and blocky pictograms, as if they didn't even *want* him to learn their language. He gets by with the words he picked up along the way, but there was definitely a period of nonsensical babbling when he first arrived. He reaches for the avant-garde volume resting on his side-table: *The Very Hungry Caterpillar*. The chunky, board book accidentally falls from the ledge to the floor with a thump.

A moment of silence, then his mother's voice: "Andy?" Hearing her footsteps come down the hall, he quickly lies back down, faking slumber. She peeks her head into his room and sees the book on the floor. She returns it to the side-table and kisses his warm forehead. For a moment she stands over him, gazing at him lovingly.

A sudden crackle bursts from the baby monitor: a garbled voice speaks urgently, but the signal cuts in and out. She reaches over and switches the unit to the OFF position, then sits in bed next to him, stroking his back softly.

He tightens his eyelids yet remains otherwise motionless. His heart races, and his whole body begins to perspire. He can barely stand it and stirs slightly. "Poor guy," she whispers, pulling up the blankets. "Must be a bad dream." She remains for several minutes, rubbing him gently as he wills his body into a calmer state. His mother yawns, then stands and leaves.

He waits to hear the bedroom door close then scrambles over to the baby monitor, turning it back to the ongoing broadcast: "...please respond! Lieutenant Anderwicz, is your channel open? What is your location?"

"Yes! I'm here!" Andy yelps. "I am at 45.626441, -74.591066. Do you copy?" Silence, under a wheeze of white noise.

"45.626441, -74.591066, coordinates received," the officer states. Andy breathes a sigh of relief. The voice continues: "Sir, we have to hold until the atmosphere improves. There is an abundance of ice crystals interfering with our sensors."

Andy gets out of bed and pops his head under the tow-truck curtains to look out the window: light wet snow falls as dawn breaks.

"Unfortunately, Sir, we must wait in holding pattern for a full diurnal cycle." The line goes dead. Andy switches off the baby monitor and gets back into bed. He stares at the ceiling as daylight causes the questionable star map to fade into oblivion.

Hours later, his mother comes to wake him. She draws the tow-truck curtains and sun glares in. Andy, who had just dozed off, stirs as she collects his clothes for the day, laying the outfit at the foot of his bed.

"You okay, honey?" she whispers, stroking his fine hair.

"Mm-mmmm," he mutters.

"Time to get up!"

"Mom," Andy sits up, his Earth mother glowing in the morning sun. "I love you. I'm gonna miss you."

"While you're at school?" she scoffs, then stands to leave. "Now please, get dressed."

"Okay, mom." He smiles, and begins struggling to pull his pajama top over his head, cursing under his breath: *Stupid... short arms...*

~ ~ ~

In the school vestibule, Andy's mother collects the jacket and outdoor shoes from his cubby. She notices a collage of photographs from last week's apple picking trip on the far wall: children in their blue pinnies emblazoned with the name and phone number of the school; kids holding apples, riding in a red cart pulled by a green tractor; farm animals behind a wooden fence. There is also a group photo.

Waiting for the dismissal bell to ring, she approaches the collage to locate her son in the group, but he's not there. "Maybe we can't see his face, kids never stop moving," she concludes. As the bell rings, she thinks: "I just hope he had fun." The children cascade into the vestibule area, a flutter of running feet and pleased squeals.

Andy hugs his mother tightly; they hold hands as they walk down the steps and into the parking lot. As she clips him into his booster seat at the back of the minivan, he wonders how she will manage when he leaves, what she will do to pass the time, the mornings and afternoons without him. It occurs to Andy that maybe it is selfish to leave, and how his species would never understand the emotionally benevolent connection he has with this human woman, his "mother."

He stares out the minivan window, his throat tight, knowing the responsibility and promise he made to the

Director. And how the information he collects, including these feelings, are invaluable to the mission.

At home he patiently waits in the kitchen as she prepares his after school snack: a slice of thick cut bread with butter and strawberry jam. He stuffs the food into his mouth and runs upstairs, still chewing.

~ ~ ~

"Modular mind replacement?" the officer hisses over the baby monitor.

"Yes, somehow, this body must stay. Anyhow, it is tiny and useless," Andy commands with a forceful whisper.

"This is highly unusual. I will have to check—"

"There's no time to check. I'm leaving tonight, but the humans here, they will be negatively impacted by my departure. Transfer the mind files from my initial Earth implant. My mother just— I can't disappear."

"Sir, I—" A long pause on the other end, before a new, stern voice comes on.

"Director Park, here."

"Yes, ma'am." Andy stiffens up, despite his hiding under a lean-to tent he made hastily with a bed sheet and pillows.

"You're not the first to succumb to human emotional reciprocity, Anderwicz. We've seen this before with Earth embeds. We do not condone leaving mind files behind but understand the complexity of the situation. Humans are social beasts. Where we collect emoticons, they experience feelings. Their every interaction is a permutation of a previous action, and these minuscule emotional adjustments inform every action that follows. We hope to one day understand them, but the full data set is overwhelming."

"Yes, ma'am." Another pause.

"You've run an excellent embed, Anderwicz. We value your dedication."

"Thank you, Director."

"I've instructed the officer to provide a seamless transition for your human host family. They won't know you've gone. We will leave files that maintain a believable personality quotient. See you back at Base, Lieutenant."

"Looking forward to it, ma'am." Andy drops the baby monitor after turning it off. His face flushes, and tears pour from his eyes. He sobs, quietly, under his makeshift tent. His body glows with a violet-white bioluminescence as he begins his passage to the ship. Andy's consciousness, floating above his human body, looks down as the child curls into fetal position and falls asleep. He floats beyond the percale roof of the tent and hears his mother's voice: "Everything okay up there?" She enters the room and looks straight into his dissipating spirit. He is overcome with heartbreak, a panic that this journey is irreversible.

"Andy," she whispers, staring into a rainbow cast by the sun onto the ceiling from a crystal diffuser hanging in the window. She leans into the tent, checking in on her napping boy.

—— « o » ——

Natalia Yanchak

Born and raised in Toronto, ON Canada, Natalia moved to Montréal, QC to attend Concordia University's Creative Writing program. After graduating (B.A., Hon.) she focused on her rock band The Dears. Finding moments between international tours and recording sessions, she completed her first sci-fi novella. She is presently working on her second book. Natalia lives in Montréal with her husband and two children. (nataliayanchak.com)

With Two Left Feet

Lisa Timpf

careful as cats walking on glass
they stand at the edge of the cliff
that drops off echo-distant

smoke pluming up
from the distant city
catches and scratches
raw in her throat
and the sirens' screams
still echo in her mind
like the knell of something dying

there on the earth's stone heart
he drops a knee
and opens a box
with a ring that gleams
like dreams she'd thought
forgotten

and she smiles for she knows
despite the smoke and broken glass
there will yet be a time
for dancing

———— « O » ————

Lisa Timpf

Lisa Timpf is a retired Human Resources and communications professional who lives in Simcoe, Ontario. Her writing has appeared in a number of venues, including *New Myths*, *Third Flatiron*, *Star*Line*, *Liquid Imagination*, and *The Martian Wave*. When not writing, Lisa enjoys bird-watching, golf, organic gardening, and spending outdoor time with her border collie, Emma.

A Threadbare Carpet

Kate Heartfield

Baz drops the drunk students off at their lodging, lights her pipe, and turns her carpet toward the Magadd Central Hospital. It's been a long shift, back and forth over the city, one of those days when the gray gets into your bones. But soon she'll be at her brother's side.

Aunty Baz. It doesn't sound like her, exactly, but it doesn't sound bad.

A pigeon flutters onto the carpet and looks her in the eye. Damn. She hates these goddamned pigeons.

The birds are never around when Baz is desperate for a fare, and they're in her face when she wants a bit of quiet alone with her pipe, high above the city. If only Tarquinna would assign one pigeon per carpet, so the filthy birds would always be there, ready to squawk their mistress's orders as they came in. But telepathic pigeons don't come cheap, so Tarquinna only has a half-dozen to cover all twenty of her carpet-drivers.

"I'm done, pigeon," says Baz.

"Dove," says the pigeon.

"Watch those feet, will you? This is silk, you know. Heirloom. My shift ends in five minutes."

Baz pulls her battered watch out of her pocket. Three hours before dawn. Eleven hours since Joylin went into labor. She turns the watch-face toward the pigeon.

"Right," says the pigeon. "Five minutes. Tarquinna has one more fare for you. Corner of First and Ninth."

Baz shuts her eyes so the pigeon won't see her roll them.

Her sister-in-law doesn't want her at the hospital anyway, probably. Doesn't trust her, still. Baz has an apartment now, with a working door and a working toilet and nobody unsavory sleeping in it — unless you count Baz herself, which Joylin probably does.

Baz also has, for the first time in her 42 years, a legal job that pays. She's off the potions now, clean for six months. She's in Radi's life again, for good and always, and she'll be in the baby's life too. But to Joylin, bloody Baz and her dirty carpet will always be a reminder of what family she married into, even if Radi has long since changed his family name.

The bird takes a few steps toward Baz, so that it's well inside the shelter of the canopy. Ah, the rain has started. Spoiled creature.

"It's raining," Baz says.

"You have a canopy," retorts the pigeon.

She does indeed, rented from Tarquinna because this carpet didn't come with one.

The first owner, the Venerable Kishyf, had no need of a canopy. He controlled not only the larger and brighter carpet from which hers was cut two generations ago but also the weather, the tides, and most of Magadd's politics too, if the stories are to be believed.

Baz does believe them. She believes in all stories with unhappy endings.

The rented canopy is a bleak beige square of canvas that barely reaches the edges of her carpet. From where Baz sits in the middle, she can't see the four harnessed nightingales, each leashed to one of its corners. Tarquinna was only a first-level wizard before the Stone Gangs put all wizards out of — or into — business. Now she runs a third-rate carpet-driver company, but her control over birds is peerless.

So Baz has a canopy, such as it is. The rain is getting heavier now, and Baz can hear it drumming on the canvas overhead.

"This carpet belonged to the Venerable Kishyf," Baz grumbles to the pigeon, although her real audience is Tarquinna, listening in somewhere to the pigeon's thoughts.

"This shade of green doesn't exist anywhere else. Not in nature, not in dyes, not in the dreams of mystics or bunny rabbits. It's magical green, pigeon. I'll never get the stains out if it gets wet."

"This rag? It's more stains than not. Yes, it's raining! That's no reason to end your shift early. Why would we shut down precisely when people want our service? Take this fare, Baz, or no more shifts for a week."

With telepathic pigeons, you can never tell who's talking, them or their masters. Baz suspects they editorialize.

"The truth is," Baz admits, "this carpet gets slow when it's wet. Heirloom, you know. Temperamental."

"Then you'd better get moving," says the pigeon, and flies off.

She can't lose shifts, not if she wants to buy a decent gift for the baby. Any gift at all, really; she's barely clearing this month's rent as it is.

As Aunty Baz, she's not off to a promising start.

Baz clamps her pipe harder in her teeth and urges the carpet through the canyon made by the buildings of downtown Magadd.

The pigeon might be prone to hyperbole, but it isn't exactly wrong about the state of the carpet. At a glance, it's mercifully hard to distinguish the marks of Baz's tenure from the intricate green, brown, and gold motifs of the carpet's original design. Right under Baz's left toe? That's old blood. Baz's own, probably, from the night she and five other members of the Bezoar Gang went to rough up a double-crosser and found him prepared. They all bled that night, and many others. Baz is as scarred as her carpet, but she's easier to cover up.

In some spots, the carpet is worn right down to a lattice of thread drained of all color.

If she had been able to sell it, she would have, many times over, in her younger and more desperate days. But the bequest of a carpet is a yoke that neither driver nor carpet can break. No one else can drive this carpet.

The carpet resents being yoked to Baz. It has been sluggish and willful lately, as if it preferred their former life of getaways and abductions. It finds any excuse to rebel.

Another carpet-driver whizzes past and holds up a hand in greeting. Camaraderie between the drivers is a small bit of light in a gray city. They look out for each other, warn each other about bad fares. It's been years since Authority officers in Magadd might have listened to a report of assault on a lowly carpet-driver. These days, the Authority are all hired thugs for one Stone Gang or another.

The fare at First and Ninth doesn't look like the type to hit a driver over the head with a lead pipe, but she does look like trouble. It's a white woman, looking up, pacing. That fancy black wool coat might mean a good tip or, more likely, no tip at all.

Baz banks the carpet. Rain slants in under one side of the canopy, soaks her arm and thigh, extinguishes her pipe. She offers the fare a hand.

"Your bag first."

The woman's carrying a shoulder bag so heavy it's cutting deep into her coat. She shakes her head and puts her hand in Baz's instead, clambering up onto the carpet.

Baz indicates the passenger cushion.

"Just fly," the woman barks, still kneeling on the edge. "Fast."

Rich people.

Rain has soaked the edges of the carpet, and it's starting to drag. Baz maneuvers between the city's towers, barely clearing the lampposts. Kids throw pebbles as she whooshes over their heads, but the pebbles mostly don't connect, and the ones that do hit the underside of the carpet.

"Can't you go any higher?" the woman grumbles.

There are certain lessons a carpet-driver learns early. Tarquinna does not insist that her drivers know the streets and alleys of Magadd particularly well. She does not insist that their carpets be clean or new.

She does insist that the fares not complain.

So Lesson Number One for every carpet-driver is distraction.

Baz launches into her history spiel.

"This carpet belonged to the Venerable Kishyf. You've heard of him, I'm sure? Or are you a visitor to Magadd? A tourist?"

Baz keeps her face as straight as only a tout can. Magadd has not had a tourist in twenty-five years, not since six mages went far from the city — to slay a dragon, they said — and came back bearing six enormous magical stones. Bezoar and Beryl, Carbuncle and Chalcedony, Tourmaline and Topaz.

Each mage hoarded their great stone and used it to imbue all smaller stones of like kind with rage and bloodlust. They fought each other for power and influence, and they taught their acolytes to spurn the Authority's laws, for it was war.

Though all six mages were soon dead, the Stone Gangs live on, like great dragons themselves, the city crumbling and burning beneath their mighty brawls.

No one would come to this crime-torn city unless they had to. But Baz always asks, because it makes the fares feel as though they're in the sort of conveyance a visitor might use, if such visitors were suddenly to appear.

"Of course, this is only one-sixth of the Venerable Kishyf's original carpet," Baz says, continuing her spiel. "His children cut it up after he died. But it isn't one-sixth of the magic, see? It doesn't work that way."

The woman isn't listening. She's on her knees, looking behind them.

Blast.

Three Authority carpets are coming in fast behind.

"I'll have to land," Baz says, peering at the rooftops ahead.

"You'll do no such thing."

The woman crawls to Baz and puts a knife to her neck. The carpet ripples like water. Baz breathes, calms her own heart, calms the carpet as best she can.

Rich fares. Always trouble.

The woman's nostrils flare, round as pearls.

"You'll get me where I need to go," she hisses. "Tarquinna is a very good friend of mine. She won't be pleased if I'm caught."

The hand that holds the knife, just at the edge of Baz's vision, bears a ring: a ruby at the center sharpened to a point, with a ring of dull silver around it. A weapon and a sign. Damn her luck.

Magadd is breaking itself apart, and blood is bubbling up through the cracks. Baz should have left this city years ago.

"You're in the Carbuncle Gang," Baz whispers. The Carbuncles have been feuding with the Bezoars for weeks; no one counts the dead these days, but it's a bad one.

The woman has come from some kind of job. A dangerous job. She must have had a getaway. Something went wrong — the getaway was killed or didn't show — and she called Tarquinna.

"Never mind who I am," the woman barks. "Close your eyes and you'll live. Just get the damned carpet up and away."

"There's nothing I can do. The blasted thing is soaked around the edges, and it's like a cat — it doesn't like to get wet."

"Shut up and get this thing higher," the woman says. She shifts the shoulder-bag onto her lap, as if it's a child she's protecting from the elements. Her perfume smells like lilacs. "If you think I will hesitate to kill you, I can happily cut off a finger to settle your mind about that."

Baz tries to bury her hands in the carpet, but it's worn so thin it might as well be velvet. She's sorry for it. She's sorry for the whole world.

The woman yells some wordless curse and shifts the knife to her other hand. Then she holds her right hand up, palm toward her own face, carbuncle-ring facing behind them.

Oh hells no.

The red stone glows, flickers, shimmers with flames that lick the woman's hand. The fireball gathers and rushes past Baz's cheek, a blast that incinerates a chunk of her own hair at the edge of her vision but doesn't warm the knife-edge at her jugular.

With that knife at her neck, Baz can't turn her head to see if the fireball hit its mark, so she banks the carpet instead.

She half-expects to see the lead Authority carpet consumed in cinder beneath burning, screaming people, but it remains untouched, surrounded by a red glow rapidly fading into nothing. The fireball was well aimed, but the carpet and people on it are protected. They must be dry in there too, damn them.

"Shit!" yells the Carbuncle woman. "They've got Bezoar scum aboard. I should have known. We have to outrun them."

If Baz's old gang find her spiriting a Carbuncle away, they'll treat her as a traitor. Goddammit. Tarquinna must have known what she was doing when she gave this fare to Baz, who can't risk getting caught with such a passenger. Baz had no idea Tarquinna was mixed up in the gang wars. But then, who isn't now?

"They're gaining on us," growls the woman.

The carpet's so low that a spire scrapes its bottom, like hidden rocks under a boat. It snags, twists, and Baz wrenches it free with all her will. She can hear the Authority whooping behind them now, uncaring that everyone knows they're paid thugs hunting prey.

"It doesn't just go faster because I want it to go faster." She gulps. "It's like an animal, or a child. If it's unhappy, it digs in its heels. So to speak."

"So make it happy. Now."

Make it happy. As if Baz were a wizard of the golden age and not a recovering addict on a cut-up carpet. Smaller and smaller, weaker and ever weaker, until all the magic is gone from everything, even magic itself.

"Let me get my knife," Baz says, the damp air almost choking her words.

"No."

"I have to cut off the wet edges," Baz says through her teeth. "It's the only way. The knife's at my waist."

The Carbuncle woman thrusts her hand under Baz's jacket and pulls Baz's knife from its scabbard, but instead of handing it to Baz, she puts it in her own belt. Then she pulls her own knife away from Baz's neck, pauses a moment, and crawls toward the edge of the carpet.

"I'll do it," she says.

Baz can't watch.

By the sound of it, the knife tears more than it cuts, and the carpet jolts like an injured cat, hunching its back so high that Baz nearly falls off. The nightingales squeal and go flying off in all directions while the canopy flutters to earth. Damn. Tarquinna will charge her for that.

If Baz lives.

If she doesn't, Tarquinna will probably send a bill to Radi. Welcome to the world, child! Here's your inheritance from your dead Aunty: a bill, a scrap of carpet, and a city's worth of stale grudges.

The carpet seizes, goes dead, and drops so quickly that Baz's stomach lurches, and the woman screams and grabs the edge.

Baz grabs fistfuls of slackened carpet, shuts her eyes, and wills life back into it. Sometimes, she imagines the patterns are a map, the lines roads that she could follow if she knew how. Chastened, resentful as a teenager, the carpet whips high into the air, up over the towers of the city, and catches a wind.

For one brief rushing moment, Baz feels something like the memory of joy. Then the carpet rolls itself up under her like an old map on a table. Baz scrabbles with her fingers, grabs the wet, ragged edges, slips off, and pitches forward into the wet sky.

She falls slowly but not slowly enough. She rolls over onto her back, holds the carpet fibers in the air, and watches the wind flutter through them.

The carpet, what's left of it, is falling too. It glances off a gable and shakes itself sideways like a kicked dog. The woman in the black coat is kneeling, urging, whispering. Red flashes from her hands. It's no good. No one but Baz can drive the carpet. And the carpet has decided it would rather bear no driver at all than one who would consent to its mutilation.

Baz, the carpet, and the woman rush toward the streets.

At last, Radi and Joylin and the baby will be rid of her, rid of any connection to their family's angry history. The wound will close. With Baz dead, Radi and his family will just be good solid magic-fearing people living normal lives — as normal as anyone can live in a city like Magadd.

Baz grabs at a fire escape railing, and the carpet threads float out of her grasp. Her fingers grip the wet metal, but they can't hold her weight for long without any of the carpet left to her, without any magic at all.

What she sees, the last thing she expects to see, is the woman still kneeling on the flaccid carpet, opening the flap of her shoulderbag and pulling out two fistfuls of color. Light bleeds through her hands: golden and green, silver and blue, brown and red.

No.

The great stones are battle magic. They burn and break. They cannot make a woman fly, or feed a hungry child, or build a ship. There is little they can do to save Baz or the Carbuncle woman.

This woman is going down, but she's going to use the powers of all six of the stones to take her enemies out with her.

Baz's fingers creak open, lose their grip on the fire escape railing. She drops backwards, shuts her eyes tight, feels the rain beat upon her eyelids as it beat upon her canopy not ten minutes ago.

Beneath her, she feels not hard darkness and pain but a soft, cool caress. Something is slowing her fall, bearing her up, undulating and curling beneath her.

Baz does not believe in an afterlife. She opens her eyes.

Beneath her is a glittering carpet like nothing she has ever imagined. Silver and shining black, every thread as thin as thought, whorled with blue secrets and green sighs and red whispers. It feels like silk and looks like diamonds.

It bears her upward, upward, until she's over her own old carpet, and then the glittering carpet explodes upward so she has to close her eyes again against a chalcedony rain.

She's on her own soaked carpet with the woman, all of them barreling downwards like an angry barn swallow.

"Grab on!" shouts the woman. She's covered in multicolored glitter. So is Baz, Baz realizes, looking down at her arms, every hair of which is decorated.

Baz grabs on and pulls the carpet up so it skids against the pavement. She wills it higher. This time, it does not roll or buck her off.

"Faster!" the woman yells. Baz looks behind: one Authority carpet remains, within magicking distance. She urges the carpet forward, higher. It has never gone this fast before.

They lose the Authority carpet as they whip between two towers, but Baz doesn't let the carpet slow. The glitter washes off in the rain and wind until the carpet is merely faded green and gold again.

She doesn't slow until they reach the necropolis at the city's edge. Then, at last, she circles it downward. She's shaking.

The damn thing is soaked through now, but it does as it is told. The exhausted carpet flutters down. Baz picks up her pipe. The woman steps off and nearly falls over, getting her land legs. She takes a deep breath.

"Will you at least tell me your goddamn name?" Baz says, leaning on her knees because she doesn't trust her balance.

"Sess," the woman says. "You can call me Sess."

"You saved my life," Baz accuses.

Sess shakes her head. "I saved my own life. The carpet wouldn't obey me. And even if I didn't die from the fall, if the Bezoars got hold of the stones in my bag, they would have destroyed me and all my fellow Carbuncles. Then they would have put the Authority's stamp on absolute power. Do you have any idea what that would look like?"

"Something like the Carbuncles having absolute power, I suppose," Baz says.

Sess frowns, then her expression clears. "Perhaps. Well, we'll never find out now."

She opens the shoulder bag, holds it out for Baz to see inside. It's coated in a glittering dust, studded here and there with small gems.

"All that remains of the Six Stones."

Baz whistles. "It — the carpet made of gems. It was made of the stones, wasn't it? And then it just disintegrated."

"I knew something like that would happen," Sess says softly. "Alone, each stone can only mar, not make. Together, they can make, unmake, and remake. The power is greater but nearly impossible to wield."

Baz puts her finger, wet from rain, inside the bag and pulls it out dusted in red and silver. She has a sudden urge to lick it, as if it were sugar.

The woman snaps the bag shut.

"I'm sorry about the carpet," she says. "It must have been very beautiful once."

Baz sheaths her knife, wipes the glitter inside her pocket, and pulls her tobacco pouch out. It's damp, but inside there's enough dry stuff to smoke.

"I don't know what it looked like," Baz says. "The Venerable Kishyf had six children, and they all hated each other. He tried to trick them into getting along by yoking them all to one carpet. The inheritance didn't have the intended effect, though. They quarreled all the more, until at last they cut the carpet into six pieces."

Sess nods. "They rode together to the dragon's lair," she recites softly. "And came back, each on his or her own scrap of carpet, each bearing a stone. All of the carpets are lost."

"Not all," says Baz.

"I thought all your spouting about Kishyf was just patter."

"It was," says Baz with a shrug. "There are at least thirty carpet-drivers in Magadd who will swear their carpet is one of the mages' six. But I'm the only one telling a family story. Kishyf was my great-grandfather. My grandmother was Ananna, the Topaz mage. I joined the Bezoars to be difficult."

And difficult it was. She got all the shit jobs and had to prove herself again and again, in ways no potion could ever help her forget.

Sess stares at her, swallows, and pulls Baz's knife out of her belt. She wraps a few grimy bills around it — just the fare, nothing extra. She hands the knife over to Baz, handle-first and wrapped in money, as if paying for the story.

As Baz pockets the money, Sess sits down on a tomb; it's wet, but so is she, now. Soaked through just as Baz is.

"Will someone come to collect you?" Baz asks.

"Someone will come, yes, but not to collect me. I destroyed the great stones. I... I destroyed the great stones!" She shakes her head.

"Well, they're not destroyed, exactly. But they are definitely very broken."

Sess doesn't laugh, merely arches her brows. She looks very small against the great tomb, and the stone in the ring on her finger is dull as brick.

"Listen," Baz says. "I have somewhere I would very much like to be, as soon as possible. But I can take you a little farther first. There's a caravanserai an hour from here. You can try to get lost."

Sess looks up, and after a long moment, nods once.

They clamber back on the carpet and travel in silence, going quickly. Dawn silvers the distant mountains. Out here beyond the city, there are older allegiances than the gangs, and other magics.

"You won't be safe in Magadd either, you know," says Sess as Baz banks the carpet to let her down. "The Carbuncles will come looking for you, even if only to ask about me. The Bezoars will come after you for protecting me."

Baz nods. "They'll try. But Tarquinna hasn't kept her Carbuncle allegiance secret this long without knowing a few tricks to keep her name out of things, and if they have a hard time finding her, they'll have a hard time finding me. And even if they do, they'll have less power now, with the great stones broken, right?"

Sess looks off into the distance. "Yes. The stones' magic is dispersed. Mingled. Harder to grasp."

"There," says Baz, as if that solves it. "I'll be fine."

Still, as soon as she flies back over the crumbled city gates, she lands. The Authority, the Bezoars, the Carbuncles — they'll all be looking for Sess and her accomplice in the sky. So Baz sends the carpet home on its own, watches it gambol up and away from her. It's always happiest without her.

Baz smokes a fast, shaky pipe as she walks toward Magadd Central Hospital.

On the way, she picks up three scraps of green-and-gold carpet and wipes the gutter-grime off them. There must be more scraps from the edges of her carpet, scattered and trampled, but she only finds three. The world gets smaller and threadbare, but there isn't less magic in it. That's not how it works. So many scattered pieces could be found, and gathered, and made into something new. Someone could do that.

Baz braids the scraps together. A gift for the baby.

———— « O » ————

Kate Heartfield

Kate Heartfield, a former newspaper journalist, lives at the rural edge of Ottawa. Her first novel, *Armed In Her Fashion*, was published in 2018 by ChiZine Publications, and her interactive novel, *The Road to Canterbury*, is coming out the same year from Choice of Games. Her short fiction has appeared in *Strange Horizons, On Spec, Lackington's, Clockwork Canada* and elsewhere. In 2016, Abaddon Books published her novella "The Course of True Love" in the shared-world anthology *Monstrous Little Voices: New Tales from Shakespeare's Fantasy World*. Kate grew up in Northern Ontario and Manitoba and spent a year in Belize. She now teaches journalism at Carleton University and works as a freelance writer and editor. Her website is heartfieldfiction. com and she is on Twitter as @kateheartfield.

Green Leaves Don't Fall

Stephen Geigen-Miller

Jason leans back in the driver's seat and takes another hit of his joint, the air streaming from the AC cold on his face. It's a pointless, wasteful indulgence on a cool barely-summer day. Hell, he's still got the engine idling, and that's unconscionable, pure planet-killing wrong. He chuckles, and guns the engine just because. It's not like the oil is going to run out anytime soon.

Everyone has everything they want now. Nobody's homeless; iPads and smartphones are free for the asking. And even though nobody's going to have a job making cars or a whole bunch of things that now have supplies vastly in excess of demand, nobody is out of work. Plenty of jobs for everyone, with six billion bodies to bury.

Or burn. He remembers the smoke from the mass pyres, the thick, smudged black of fuel oil and something else. And the smell — Jesus, the burning-fat stench — and everyone who could still walk and talk making sick jokes to keep themselves going in between bouts of helpless crying or puking.

~ ~ ~

There's a knock on the window. Old habit makes him try to hide the joint, but it's just Deena, her smile showing plenty of crooked teeth. He gestures towards the passenger seat, and she opens the door and slides in beside him.

"The fuck, Jay? You're gonna catch shit if they find you smoking up on the job."

He shrugs. "What are they going to do, fire me?"

It's simple economics. There's plenty of demand for people to do dull, crap jobs like getting dead people's cars off the road. Jason and Deena are un-fireable, as their supervisor knows perfectly well. Everyone takes all the cigarette, pot, booze or sex breaks they want in this job. It's the only way to cope.

"Besides, what do you care?" he asks.

"I just wondered," she says. "I looked for you, and you were gone."

He nods. People don't leave you alone for long these days. Spend five minutes in the bathroom and you'll get twelve people knocking on the door, 'just making sure you're okay.'

"I needed a break." He waves the joint towards the backseat. Deena looks back, sees the booster seat, the faded but obvious bloodstains.

"Fuck," she says eloquently, and reaches out her hand. "Pass that shit over."

~ ~ ~

Dulled pain is still pain, and no matter how much he distracts himself with drugs, booze, or Deena's body, he remembers Kirin. He remembers her long hair — no one has long hair anymore. He remembers her body, soft despite spending half her day on a bike, so different from Deena who's all muscle and sinew covered with piercings and tattoos. He remembers her face, gentle and thoughtful, and her passionate intelligence.

And every night, no matter how much he drinks or smokes, he remembers her last words.

~ ~ ~

Deena takes another hit, kicks off her shoes, and waves towards the dashboard. "You shouldn't be doing that."

He takes the joint. "Doing what?"

She points a bare, black-painted toe at the key in the ignition. "Running the engine and shit. Isn't that against the smog law or something? And it's, like, bad for the planet."

"Fuck the planet," he says, smiling.

She sits up. "Weren't you a professional tree-hugger? With that GreenFuture place."

"I was researcher and an activist, yeah. But that was before. Nobody cares about the environment now."

"Even you?" When he doesn't answer, she holds out her hand. "If you're not going to smoke it, pass it." He gives her the joint. She takes another long hit, finally exhales. "I was thinking I should go back to school."

"Really?" he asks. Deena — who's always been vague about her job before the Dying — has never mentioned any aspirations beyond spending her time off in various combinations of alcohol-, drug-, and sex-induced altered states. She never speaks of the future at all: a perfect citizen of the Dying, living only in and for now.

"Yeah, man, you know that eventually they'll have all these cars moved, and then what are we going to do? So I thought, shit, maybe I should, like, go be a nurse or something, and help retarded kids."

He can't help laughing, despite the hurt look she gives him. "You want to be a nurse? And work with...." No, he decides. Even with Kirin gone and the environment welcome to go screw itself, he can't be quite that insensitive. "...with intellectually disabled children?"

"I'd be a great nurse, asshole," she says. "Or a, what-do-you-call-it, RMT. A massager."

"You know that a RMT is the therapeutic kind of massage, right? Not the hand-job kind?"

"Fuck you." She laughs and punches him in the arm.

"Why not do both?" he asks. "Deena Benson, providing manual release for your intellectually disabled loved ones,"

"Shit," she says. "That would look fucking wicked on a business card."

"You think there's a lot of demand for that sort of work?"

She leans over and kisses him. Her hand goes to his crotch and she starts kneading. "You tell me." She puts out what's left of the joint in the cup-holder and undoes his belt.

"What, here? Now?"

"What are they gonna do? Fire us?"

Good point, he thinks, and leans back to enjoy the ride. There's nothing but now. Forget worrying about the future, or the fate of the planet. Just live in and for now.

It's then, leaning back, pleasure building and head rolling, face turned towards the window, that he opens his eyes.

And sees a ghost walk by.

~ ~ ~

His erection wilts, but he barely notices as he opens the door and scrambles out of the car.

"What's wrong?" Deena shouts.

He manages an awkward tuck and zip as he runs after the green-cloaked figure. It's not a ghost; ghosts don't wear green, and their boots don't clomp against the sidewalk. But is it her? He follows north along Bathurst and catches up half a block north of the subway station, near the vegetarian Jamaican restaurant Kirin once loved.

"Lindy," he calls. "Lindy Comeau!"

She doesn't react, and he wonders if he's made a mistake. It happens, people thinking they've seen old friends on the street. Colleagues. Children. They're always wrong.

But then she stops and turns back towards him, and he sees that he isn't wrong. It's her, really her.

"Jason?" she asks, and her face is so tranquil, her smile so serene that it shocks. No one is serene, and if anyone was going to be tranquil after the Dying, he would have bet hard that it wouldn't be Lindy.

"Oh, Jason," she says. Then opens her arms and enfolds him in a hug.

He couldn't stop the tears if he tried, and she holds him in a mothering way that's unlike the Lindy he remembers, but isn't unwelcome.

He touches her hair, her long hair, like he hasn't seen since before. He wonders how she did her time at the pyres with hair like that, then puts the thought away. It's not important.

"You're alive," he says, "Thank God."

"Thank the Goddess," she says, "so are you." Her every word and gesture seems so much stronger, so much more certain, than anyone else he can think of.

He answers the question before she asks it. "Kirin died in Wave One," he says. "One of the lucky ones."

Wave One had been bad, so bad, suddenly and painfully killing Kirin — and ten percent of the global population — via massive internal hemorrhaging.

The next waves had been worse. The whole bloody process, the swift death of nine of out every ten human beings, had taken less than four weeks. And a few hundred million devastated survivors had been left to carry on.

Kirin would have hated this traumatized new world.

Lindy shakes her head. "No. You're one of the lucky ones."

He steps back, shrugging her off.

She looks up and down the parking lot that Bathurst Street has become. "What are you doing here?" she asks.

"Moving cars," he says, half-defiant, but half-embarrassed too.

"Oh, Jason," she says, and her pure, unfeigned compassion is like an icicle to his gut. "You've lost your way. I'm sorry."

"Were you always this self-righteous? Or did everyone dying turn you into a bitch?" He's gone too far, farther than anyone decent would go after the Dying, and he looks away from her in shame. When he looks back, he still sees that same cool, compassionate gaze. The old Lindy would have been a puddle of tears at a sharp word.

He fumbles to explain. "Don't you get it? It's dispose of the corpses first, forget second, everything else third, and climate change or endangered species a distant fucking fourth. The environmental movement is dead. So yes, I'm doing something useful and moving these cars off the road. At least I'm not wandering the streets like Starhawk the feel-good witch of the year."

She shakes her head and — is she smiling?

"The old environmental movement is extinct," she says. "But there's a new movement, and our purpose is more important than ever. Six billion fewer consumers to drain Gaia of irreplaceable resources. That means we have a chance. To get it right this time. And we need you."

Hope is the one thing he doesn't ever want to be drunk on again.

"Nobody needs me," he says.

"I remember your passion. Your intelligence. How we all listened when you spoke. I had a crush on you, I guess," she adds without a hint of self-consciousness. "But you were Kirin's, and anyway I was too shy then. But what you said made a difference." She looks into his eyes, as if she thinks she'll see the old Jason looking out. "It can make a difference again."

She hugs him close. "There's a place," she whispers, "if you want to know more. You remember my parents' cottage?"

"Up by…" She squeezes him hard, and he whispers the rest of his reply, "Owen Sound?"

"We can talk there. In the city I'm being watched." She releases him. "I'm so glad I found you, Jason. Blessed be."

She turns and resumes her path north up the street. He watches until she disappears from sight, and a hand lands on his shoulder. It's Deena, tears collecting around her piercings.

"Jay?" she asks, her voice trembling.

"I'm sorry," he says, and puts his arms around her. "I saw someone I knew. Someone from before." She's tense, her lean body resisting his embrace, and he tries not to compare her to Kirin. Or Lindy.

"You didn't even say nothing," she says to his shoulder.

"Sorry. Look, I might need to go out of town."

She pushes off him and dries her eyes with a swipe of the back of her arm. "I figured," she says.

"No, you don't understand. That girl, she used to be such a flake. Now… I think she's found something, a way forward."

"Whatever. Fine," she says, and turns away. "It's just, I would have let my hair grow and put on a Game of Thrones costume if I knew that's what you were into."

"Hey, it's not like that." He puts a hand on her arm. "It's… do you remember the last time since the Dying that you really cared about something, Deen?"

She shrugs his hand off. "Yeah, Jay. I do."

And then she's walking away, back down towards the cars, and the job, and everything he's been since the Dying and suddenly hates with an intensity that twists up his stomach so hard he can barely stand.

This time, nobody comes to check on him. Not even Deena.

~ ~ ~

The highway running north from Toronto is dark.

It's slow going. Always the risk of an abandoned car in the middle of the lane, its driver long-dead. And he's going by memory. He was at this place — a cottage, near the lake — once, but that was with Kirin, before the Dying. It had been half party, half staff retreat for GreenFuture, hosted by Lindy as she was then, shy and painfully earnest in her commitment to the usual roster of lefty causes.

He remembers sitting around a campfire, staring into the flames. Kirin's head on his shoulder. There'd been some pot, some wine, and lots of talk. About hope, he remembers. They had talked about hope. It had pissed him off.

"There is no hope," he had said. "We tried, but it's too little, too late."

"You can't believe that," one of the others had said, a white kid with dreadlocks and a beard, Jason forgets his name, "or you wouldn't be here. You're still part of the struggle."

"That's because I want to go down swinging," he'd said, and Kirin had snorted at his attempt at machismo.

"There has to be hope, Jason," Lindy had said, sounding on the verge of tears. And because he was a little drunk, a little high, and never could resist needling Lindy and her humorless sincerity, he had laughed.

~ ~ ~

It's another fire, bigger and brighter than the one in his memory, that helps him find the place. At the end of a road off the highway, the night is smeared with orange and yellow, and he turns the car towards it. Someone might need help. After the Dying, and the pyres, nobody lights a fire just for fun.

Nobody, apparently, except Lindy and her new movement.

The blaze lighting up the night sky looks like a tower aflame, but it's clearly controlled. The road runs out, and he stops where a wooden gate bars a laneway. He gets out, hops the gate, and walks towards the fire. Finally, he's close enough to see the shape of the tower, a tall structure of wood, or maybe osier, vaguely human in shape.

"That's the amazing new movement?" he asks the fiery figure. "Re-creating Burning Man?"

If being here was going to bring up the past, he had hoped it would be of happier times. Instead he's remembering the piles of dead, and that awful clinging smell. He turns back towards his car. Why bother? Why subject himself to bad memories and crystal-waving neo-hippies when he has a life back in the city?

And yet, he turns to face the fire.

"This is private property," says a voice in the darkness.

There's a man on the path ahead of him and as he gets closer, Jason can see a flowing green robe. Long hair. Suspicious eyes. He has a hand concealed in the folds of his robe, as though hiding something. A weapon? Seriously?

Jason raises his hands, tries to smile. "Is this the Comeau place? Lindy asked me to come. I'm Jason Fry."

The man steps forward and peers close to see by the flickering light of the distant fire.

"You've come," he says, his smile wide and eyes shining. "Just as she said, you've come to join us."

Jason takes a step back, wonders if that might seem insulting, steps forward again. "Is Lindy here?"

"Let me take you to her."

~ ~ ~

Lindy stands a not entirely safe distance from the fire. All around her sit her... followers, he supposes. That word will do for now. It still looks more like summer camp for granolas than a new green movement.

The man leading him to Lindy fawns like a dog as he approaches her. She turns, sees them, and smiles that remarkable, serene smile.

She's carrying a large wicker basket but hands it off to one of her green-robed acolytes before taking a step forward to meet him. She opens her arms, and Jason nearly trips over his feet rushing to her embrace. Part of him knows he should be embarrassed, but the rest of him doesn't give a damn and just wants the strength she seems to have to spare.

"I'm glad you've come," she whispers, and gives him a peck on the cheek.

"Me too," he says, and his eyes dart to the man who guided him here, who's still hanging around with the others. "Was everyone expecting me?"

She laughs. "My people know how instrumental you were to the formation of my thoughts. They're excited to meet you."

Lindy has changed, but she's still not all that subtle. There are things she's not telling him. She wants to milk a dramatic moment for her crowd, fine, but he needs more data if he's going to understand.

It's just so hard to think with that fire blazing, bringing back the horror.

"Can we talk about what you're doing here?" he asks.

"Of course," she says. "I want to tell you all about our work. That's why I prayed to the Goddess that you would come." That sounds more like the Lindy he remembers.

"I'm...." He glances around. Every eye is on him. "I can see you've found something that works for you. But maybe you remember that I was never really religious? I'm still not. No offense."

"Jason thought that pagans and Wiccans were the hurting the environmental movement," she says, her voice pitched for her followers to hear, but her eyes fixed on him. "Distracting ourselves and others with silly make-believe."

The only sound, after she stops speaking, is the roar of the fire. And all around him are Lindy's green-robed followers.

"I always respected your commitment to the cause," he says.

"Do you remember the last time you were here?" she asks. "With Kirin, and everyone? I wanted us all to form a circle, do you remember? And pray to the Goddess and ask her to bless our efforts."

"I remember."

"You laughed. Out loud. I invited you here. And you laughed." Her tone is as mild as ever, and her followers still surround him.

"I didn't have a lot of patience for that sort of thing, then," he says. "But I'm sorry."

"Sorry? No, don't you see? You were right. About everything. The world was burning, and I was just pretending. You studied the evidence. You knew."

He nods. His work at GreenFuture had been examining the state and impacts of climate change. He'd had no doubt about what was coming.

"You helped me realize I had to do something. To show you there was still hope. So I worked, and I studied, and I practiced, and I sacrificed. And you see? I did it. I saved the world."

"You think you're responsible for the Dying," he says in his gentlest voice, the one he learned to use with the people who broke down as the bodies were being burned.

"It came without warning," she says. "Reduced the human population to a sustainable level. Science and reason can't explain it. Thanks be to the Goddess!"

"Thanks be to the Goddess," comes the refrain from all around, and they all still sound so happy.

"Lindy, I'm sorry. I know you want to find some kind of meaning in the Dying, but you didn't kill six billion people by praying or wishing."

"Of course not," she says. "That was the old Lindy. Hoping the human race would get its act together. Wishing you'd see how much better I was for you than Kirin. But you made me see. Nothing was ever going to happen unless I made it happen."

"So you...?"

"I started to think about magic. Read about it. How it worked, and what used to be done that we weren't doing anymore. You see? I researched. I formed a hypothesis. I tested. And I was successful beyond my wildest dreams. Even you couldn't have asked for more."

"Even me?"

"Especially you. It was your idea, after all. We owe it all to you."

~ ~ ~

"There doesn't have to be hope," he had said that night by the campfire. "There doesn't have to be anything."

"People understand now, though," Lindy had said. "They want change."

"Everyone wants change, but nobody wants to have to change. Nothing will ever fix that, not as long as all of us, billions of people, just keep wanting more stuff that takes more energy and more oil. No, the human species is doomed. We're done."

~ ~ ~

His throat is constricted but he couldn't find the words even if he could speak. "You... you think..." he manages to croak.

"Give him some water," Lindy says.

A smiling South Asian girl hands him a cup. He drinks.

"I did what you wanted, and the Goddess sent the Dying to set us free, so we could rebuild a better world. I knew She'd spare you. When the weaklings and the cowards and the unbelievers fell, I knew you'd still be here, trying to understand, waiting for me to give you the key."

She doffs her robe and throws it aside in a swift, sudden motion and stands before him. Completely naked, and completely in control. Her body is lush and full in a way that he hasn't seen since before, since Kirin.

But mostly, he sees someone who just said that the six billion victims of the Dying all deserved what they got.

"You think Kirin was weak?" he asks her.

"Maybe," she shrugs. "It doesn't matter."

"Doesn't matter?" he says, and can't hide his rising anger, cultists on every side or no.

"Don't be naïve, Jason. Gaia doesn't care about us as individuals." He can hear the same condescension she must have heard from him, about her most cherished beliefs. "She's a planet. She does things on a larger scale. The point is, there are no weaklings any more, and all of you in the city, you're so hungry for something to believe in that it's killing you. That's why you came here, to join me. Join me now."

"I'd rather keep my clothes on. Or do you intend to force me?"

It turns out she does. Lindy gestures, and it takes an embarrassingly short time for them to overpower him, strip him and shove him towards her. At least the huge fire is warm, the only small mercy he's likely to get tonight.

"Once we consummate," she says, her tone entirely conversational, "we'll be married in the eyes of the Goddess. But first, the night needs to be hallowed, the Goddess invoked."

"Do you even understand how insane you sound?"

"Yes," she says, with a glint in her eyes that might be lust. "Fight me. Then fuck me. A union of opposites to bring forth a new world. Together, we'll take the word of the Goddess to a planet that's hungry for meaning and something new."

She holds out her right hand, and one of the flock hands her the wicker basket she'd set aside before.

There's a baby in it. A baby.

He can't imagine what she.... No, he can, but that...

"How," he whispers, because it's that or screaming. "What did you do? Your magic, to bring the Dying?"

"I told you," she says. "I studied. And I sacrificed. Do you even know how many sacrifices that was? Gaia's a hungry mother."

"You killed..." he begins, and then stops as something else occurs to him. "The baby. Where are its parents?"

She glances at the huge, burning wicker man, and back to him.

And oh God, her smile.

And then he's throwing up everything in his gut, because what he thought was a sense memory is too fucking real, and he's puking like he hasn't since the last time he smelled human flesh and fat burning on the pyres of the dead.

He forces himself to stay on his feet. Looks at her through eyes frosted with tears as the flames glint against the knife she now holds in her other hand.

"I know I said to challenge me," she says. "But there are limits. Are you ready now?"

He looks at her. At the baby, sleeping in its basket.

And the memory he works himself to the bone to forget, drinks and drugs himself stupid to forget, is as clear as day.

~ ~ ~

It was a good day, the last normal day before the Dying. Kirin had seemed so happy, the way she did before his birthday, or when she had a secret to tell. They had gone to a farmer's market to buy fresh vegetables, and she'd been stir-frying dinner.

Then she had dropped the spatula, and gasped. He remembers looking towards her, asking what was wrong.

She had turned to him, pain and fear in her eyes, and said, "I think there's something wrong with the baby."

"What baby?"

Those had been his last words to her in this life.

~ ~ ~

He walks towards Lindy, and she smiles.

He reaches out to her.

Grabs the basket and pulls it from her hand.

She barely has time to change her expression, smug triumph turning to shock, as he leans in and shoves her hard.

Towards the fire.

And her hair, her long, flowing hair, the kind nobody has anymore, catches.

No way she'd done her time at the pyres. There's a reason everyone who helped burn the bodies wears their hair short.

Her knife falls to the ground. He scoops it up. She's burning and screaming, and the baby's screaming, and her acolytes are screaming and rushing around. He doesn't need to use the knife; he barely has to brandish it to get past them.

He runs for his car, basket in one hand, knife in the other. Stopping for his pants would be pushing his luck. He has a spare set of keys in the glove compartment. And a lot of ground he needs to cover before the cult gets its act together.

He slams the door, fumbles for the keys. "Shh, it's okay," he says to the baby as he guns the engine and drives into the night, back towards the city. "I've got you. You're safe."

He knows it's a lie. There's no safety in the world; every survivor knows that. But saying it seems to help them both.

~ ~ ~

It's a warm day in Toronto under cloudless blue skies. There are fewer cars on Bathurst than there were yesterday. One day they'll have moved all of them, just like they moved all the bodies, and everyone who's been distracting themselves with busy-work and altered states will need to find something else to do. Something, maybe, that matters a little bit more.

He glances at his car, parked nearby with considerably more care than he's taken in a long time. The baby — Kirin — is sleeping inside, in a salvaged car seat.

He finds Deena in a Civic by the side of the road and taps on the window. She glances at him and mutters something to herself. Rolls the window down.

"What, it didn't work out with your hippie girl, and now you figure you can just pick up where you left off? I don't play it like that, Jay."

"I love you," he says.

She opens her mouth. Closes it again. "You asshole," she says. "I love you too."

"Do you want to get out of here?"

"Now?" she asks.

"Right now. Permanently, if that's okay with you. There are some people after me. And we have a lot of work to do."

She smiles, a little suspicious. "What, you want to, like, start a commune and raise goats?"

"Not that," he says. "But I think I might need to save the world, and I could use your help."

She bites her lip and gets out of the car. "Jay, I'm not like you. I didn't even finish high school. I'm not the kind of girl who saves the world."

"Yes, you are. You care. And you're ready to do something that matters. Well, the Dying broke a lot of people. They're lost and scared and alone. They could get taken in by... dark forces. Unreason and superstition. They could start making the same mistakes again, or worse ones. Or they could get taken up by us."

"Man, when you make up your mind...." She shakes her head. "Fuck it, I'm in. Now what?"

"We communicate. Educate. Stand up for reason. And make a better world."

She sighs. "At least this way I don't have to give nobody a hand-job."

"Almost nobody," he says.

She laughs, but then her smile falls away. "You really think we can do it? Like, fix the world?"

"We can," he says, with conviction he doesn't feel. "We have to. And if not... at least we go down swinging."

—— « O » ——

Stephen Geigen-Miller

Stephen Geigen-Miller writes prose, comics and free-associative paragraphs that seemed to make some sort of sense at the time. Stephen is a contributor to the Skiffy and Fanty blog, where he writes a monthly comics review column. He co-created and co-wrote the comics *Xeno's Arrow* (with writer/artist Greg Beettam) and *Cold Iron Badge* (with artist Patrick Heinicke). Stephen lives in Toronto, works at the University of Toronto, and has two children. He writes in the bits and pieces of time in between everything else.

Proteus in the City

Fiona Moore

Stan saw it first while walking on the beach on the Island, silvery and glittering, amorphous. Resting against a log of driftwood, looking a lot like that weird soapy foam that sometimes washed up from the lake (nothing to do with industrial pollution, the city council kept saying). He might have thought it was that foam, but it was sort of shining, and large, a patch the size of a man. Hero had trotted on ahead and was tentatively sniffing at the thing with his long gray muzzle, ears back; Stan shouted at the dog to come away, worried the stuff might be dangerous, and cautiously stepped forward to check it out on his own.

At first Stan thought it might be some kind of chemical spill, maybe an oil slick the way it was shimmering and changing, but it was too big, too cohesive, for that. He found a long stick and prodded it; it quivered. Not PVC or plastic, then. His mind went back to his childhood and adolescence, the monster matinees he'd sat through. *The Silver Slime*, he thought. *It Came From The Lake*.

He got closer, crouched low, and sniffed, aware that Hero was watching him with puzzlement. No odor bar a faint fishy, pondweedy smell; normal lake smells, not industrial or toxic. Perhaps some new kind of lake weed? He'd never heard of a silver plant before.

The thing shimmered, almost glowed, and he felt an odd compulsion to touch it, to sink his hand into it just to see how it felt. Then he realized what he was doing and recoiled.

Stay away, he thought. Too dangerous. It could poison you, kill you even.

Troubled, he stood up, backed off, and continued on his way, walking along the sand under the shade of trees starting to turn yellow and orange, dog at his heels, until the reddening sun in the West marked the inevitable time when he had to catch the ferry, board the streetcar, and return to the apartment.

~ ~ ~

Stan had been born in Kingston — the one in Jamaica, not the one on the St Lawrence River, as he had said far too many times over the past twenty years, the laugh accompanying it now a little bored and strained. His mother had thrown his father out when Stan was an infant and she'd found out about his father and the owner of the launderette. She had raised Stan largely at arm's length, not hostile, but not really taking much of an interest in him either, apart from making sure he was fed, clothed, passing his exams, and not falling in with the local gang — until the incident with Ron behind the bike-sheds in their last year of school.

His mother had been furious, eyes afire. "I'm not raising a batty boy," she'd said, and before Stan had been able to think of a rebuttal she had arranged to send him to live with her sister who, seeking money, power, and a lack of scrutiny, had moved to a city in the frozen North. Thinking back, Stan was never quite able to follow his mother's logic; perhaps she thought the cold air would dampen his misplaced ardor. As for himself, he'd been frightened at the idea of such a change, pleaded with her to change her mind. But before long he was headed North into an amorphous gray mass of snow and slush from which the occasional building protruded.

His aunt, like his mother before the incident, had been kind but slightly detached. She was in her thirties, single, working as a secretary in a downtown law firm, and hadn't anticipated having a nephew in her West End spare room. Still, he was a family responsibility, so when he arrived on her doorstep that autumn she helped him find a job at a health-food store near the university, working the cash register, cleaning, unloading, taking inventory as the owner needed:

respectable if not prestigious, and with the promise of better jobs to come once he knew the city better. She helped him enroll in weekend classes in book-keeping, to help with that better job to come. Otherwise, and once it became apparent that he was not likely to interfere with her own social life (which seemed mainly to involve men at other firms in the same building), she more or less left him to his own devices.

Stan liked working in the health food store. It meant some physical labor, but it was undemanding and paid well enough that he could contribute to the rent while still putting a little away for the future, and the customers were fun. So was the neighborhood. He'd go out on his lunch break and enjoy watching the mix of people: students from the university or the technical school nearby, businessmen in their suits, rich women in furs flowing in from uptown to mix with poor women in jeans flowing in from the still-hanging-on hippie colony near the university. Sometimes he'd go for a walk, first along the university campus and then, as he got bolder, further downtown, with its grimy second-hand bookshops and used-clothes stores, dark and shuttered strip-clubs and bars, all the way to the bright façades of record stores and amusement arcades.

On weekends, missing the sea, he'd go to the lakeshore and walk, watching the waves crash, even on days when the depth of the snow reached three feet and his aunt, muffled in blankets and duvets, informed him he was crazy.

~ ~ ~

Winter gave way to spring; the trees blossomed in the park, shorts began to make an appearance, and the ratio of students to tourists patronizing the health-food shop adjusted slightly but noticeably. The ferry to the Island started, giving Stan a whole new set of beaches to walk. Weekdays, Stan began taking longer and longer lunch-break walks, but he always made it back within the hour — until that one day.

Stan had decided to walk downtown, towards the strip clubs. As he approached, he saw pylons, policemen, a small crowd lining the sidewalk. A protest, perhaps. Stan had seen a few of these filing down the university campus. But no, the distant music wasn't the thumping drumbeat and chanting slogans he associated with protests. Nor was it a marching band. He asked one of the people in the crowd what was going on.

The man looked at him like he was an idiot or a tourist. "It's Gay Pride," he announced, then turned back to watching the street.

Gay Pride? Stan had never heard of such a thing. He stood and watched, enchanted, as the parade approached and passed: women on motorcycles, driving ahead; men in beautiful dresses, hair and makeup, *en travesti*, on floats; other men in black glittering leather and plastic; men disco-dancing in shimmering silver jumpsuits; speakers, posters, banners, red ribbons, and bands. The crowd danced, reaching their arms up to catch things thrown from the floats.

"Hey!" Stan turned, looked. Somehow, he had gotten pushed to the front of the crowd, almost touching a float. *Caribbean Lesbians and Gays*, read the handmade banner on its side. On top, a pale man with a skinny mustache, hair like a black cloud, and a smile like a box of sugarcubes was reaching his hand down to Stan. "Come on up!" he was saying.

That was how Stan met Tony.

~ ~ ~

Tony's full name was Winston Antony. But he hated the name Winston and any of the nicknames that might come from it. Tony was twenty-five, handsome, and knew everything. He'd been out — that was what they called it, *out* — since his teens. He could wear jeans and an undershirt like Marlon Brando, or slacks and a polo-neck like a TV detective, and look like two different people. When Tony danced, he writhed like he didn't have bones; he'd flash his sugar-cube smile at everyone. Within seven days of their meeting, Stan moved in to his apartment.

"Stan, you making a mistake," his aunt told him, her usually-precise (and scrupulously maintained) Canadian dialect slipping under the strain. "Don't move in with this man."

"Why?" Stan fixed her with a look over the suitcase he was packing. "Cause he a batty man?"

Stan's aunt shook her curls, tears in her eyes. "Forget that, half my friends are batty men." Stan was thinking this over as she went on, "No, I've seen this type of man; he trouble, whoever he goes to bed with. Stay here for a while. Think it over."

Stan slammed his suitcase shut. "You no better than Mama," he said. He half believed it, too, whatever she said about her friends.

Because he was so in love with Tony. Looking at that handsome man, Stan could never quite believe he was with him, that he'd taken the plunge into Tony's world, been absorbed into everything that was Tony.

Tony worked for a film production company as a location scout. The big Hollywood movie-makers always wanted to film where it was cheapest, and things were pretty cheap here, he said. He promised to introduce Stan to Eddie Murphy someday, and Stan didn't mind that it would never happen. Tony had a beautiful second-floor apartment in an old Victorian house, walking distance from the Gay Village that Stan had no idea existed, décor bare and minimalist. Stan thought Tony must have no time for decorating, and one weekend when Tony was away he decided to paint the walls. Chrome yellow, scarlet, peacock blue.

That was the first mistake Stan ever made with Tony.

After Stan had tearfully promised to paint it all white again, Tony hugged him, curled up around him in bed, apologizing and stroking him. Saying it was just that he was under so much strain, and the apartment, well, it was like his place, you know? "I know things are different in Jamaica," he said. "You'll learn what things are like here."

Tony got Stan a job with the film production company, in the accounting department.

"It's a step up from being a shop-boy," he said. "Come on, you don't want to work in a store all your life."

Stan had, in fact, thought he might want to do just that. He enjoyed working in the health-food shop, even more so now that the regulars had begun to recognize him, chat about their families and their ailments, and ask for suggestions for recipes with kale or black beans. The manager had given him some

book-keeping duties, and had even been hinting he might
make Stan a deputy manager after tax time. But Stan thought
Tony must be right, and he didn't want to fight about it.

He didn't really enjoy his job at the production company
at first. It meant spending all day in a closed office, not out
in the sunshine and snow and weather. Stan could do the
math, but it wasn't as much fun as talking to people. But
after a few months, he made friends with some of his co-
workers. He took to having lunch with Tom, who was Polish,
and Ollie, who turned out to be German (his real name was
Jorg, which he said nobody could pronounce right).

Tom and Ollie liked to eat lunch together, and drink
together after work. They complained about their wives;
they complained about the locals and their strange ways.
Ollie complained about his father, who had lost his legs in
World War II.

"Serves him right," Tom said mildly, sprinkling salt on a
hard-boiled egg. "For bombing half of Lvov."

"Not that it didn't deserve it," Ollie retorted, also mildly.

"Wait," Stan said. "Your father… was in the—"

"Luftwaffe," Ollie said. "Not sure he actually bombed
Lvov specifically, but he did bomb a lot of places."

"And yet you two eat lunch together…"

Tom looked at Stan with placid blue eyes. "No sense
holding on to these things," he said. "This is a place to let
go, to change."

~ ~ ~

Tony was certainly changing. He'd become moodier,
hostile. Inclined to start fights after they got back in at night,
accusing Stan of looking at other men. Or more.

"That's not who I am," Stan said. He knew Tony was, but
he put up with that.

Tony started staying away longer on location trips. Stan
liked that. It was quiet around the apartment; he could bring
his friends back, play his own music — the calypso from
back home that Tony said was corny and clichéd — and, not
for the first time, he thought about leaving Tony. It had been
a few years now; Tony was his first serious relationship, but
perhaps he'd outgrown it. Perhaps it was time to move on.

Then Tony got The Diagnosis. That was the way it was, in capitals.

Stan put his arms around him, but he pushed him away. "Don't touch me."

Stan persisted. "It's all right," he said. "They've got things under control now. I'll help you with all the therapies and everything."

"That's it for me," Tony said. "It's over."

"No it isn't," Stan said. Then, more boldly, "I'll take care of you. I will."

Tony looked at him with his beautiful brown eyes, his lips parted over those ice-cube teeth. "Would you?" he asked.

"I will," Stan repeated.

~ ~ ~

Tony quit his job with the production company. Said he had to concentrate on keeping well, and traveling around small towns wasn't helping. Stan thought the fresh air would probably do him good, but didn't say anything.

But Stan quitting his job was out of the question. "We need the money," Tony said, when Stan came in with an ad for a bakery manager at the covered market near the lakeshore. "That job pays peanuts."

"It would be out in the market, selling to people, having fun," Stan said.

Tony shook his head. "Fun," he said contemptuously, screwing up the ad and throwing it at the waste-paper basket. It missed. "You want to change jobs, why not get one with a bank? One that pays proper money."

Stan kept quiet about it after that. The job with the production company wasn't great, but at least it wasn't a bank.

~ ~ ~

Stan tried out for a theater production. He did it secretly, telling Tony he had to stay at work for an extra audit. When he got the part, he had to tell him the truth. He thought Tony would be happy.

But Tony glared at the letter. "What's it about?" he asked, flicking cigarette ash at it.

"It's a dramatization of an ancient Greek poem," Stan said. "At the Symposium Theater. You know, they're the ones that did those musical comedies you liked, two, three years ago?"

"Oh, that," Tony said.

"They do more serious stuff, too."

"Do they."

"It's a good play. It's called *Proteus*," Stan persisted.

"Sounds like some kind of steroid drink for a muscle queen," Tony sneered.

"No, it's a Greek myth. Proteus is the Old Man of the Sea. He lives in the ocean, and he can change his shape. Turn into anything he wants."

"Lucky him."

"So, what do you think?"

"What would you be playing?"

Stan felt a little embarrassed. "I'd be in the chorus."

"The chorus?" Tony laughed now. "Like the dancing girls?"

"Not that sort of chorus," Stan said, but it was too late.

"Well, if you really want to be a chorus girl, then do it." Tony settled back down.

"But you don't think I should?"

"Theater people," Tony blew air out his nose, ran a hand through his thinning hair. For some reason, Stan found himself thinking of his mother, the way she would say things like that, in that same tone: Theater people, tramps, prostitutes, batty men. "I suppose if you have to, then do it. I just don't see the point of making a spectacle of yourself."

So Stan didn't turn up to the first rehearsal of *Proteus*, or any of the others. He made a point of dodging anyone he knew was involved with the Symposium — not easy, in a gay village that small, but he did it — until the whole thing had blown over. By which point they'd all got the message and were avoiding him too.

~ ~ ~

"Where were you on Friday?" Tom asked at lunch.

"Oh, sorry, it was Kay's leaving party, wasn't it?" Stan said. "I guess I just got too busy."

Tom shook his head. "That roommate of yours..."

"He's not well, okay?" Stan said."He needs help."

"Sure he does," Tom said, pointing with a plastic fork. "But you need help too, you know that?"

"I'm fine," Stan said.

But Tom turned up unexpectedly at his apartment the next week, with a dog. A black-and-white mongrel, with a bit of Labrador and a lot of Shepherd. Not quite a puppy, but not yet full grown either.

"Friend of mine works for a shelter," Tom said as the dog worried at a tennis ball tied into a sock. "They're full up, need someone to keep this one for a couple of weeks."

Tony objected. "We haven't got room."

But Stan was willing to go to the wall on this one. "It's just for a couple of weeks," he said, and because Tom was right there, Tony had to back down.

But a couple of weeks became a couple of months, then eventually Tony stopped asking when he was going to leave. Stan named the dog Hero. Taking him for walks along the gray sidewalks under the trees, or through the parks was a reason to get out of the apartment. And on weekends, they walked along the beaches, on the shore or on the Islands.

~ ~ ~

And so the years passed. Tom left for a better job in Europe; Ollie got one in Hollywood. He invited Stan to join him, but Tony wouldn't hear of moving and wouldn't let Stan go.

"It's a strange place, too strange," Tony said. He'd even given up going down the street to buy milk or cigarettes, just stayed at home watching TV.

"It'd be warmer," Stan tried. "And there's be lots of gay men there."

Tony fixed him with his flat eyes. "Thinking of leaving me?"

"No!" Stan protested. "I just meant there'd be things to do. You could join ACT UP or something like it." Though he hadn't joined ACT UP here either, so there was no reason he should join it anywhere else.

So Stan stayed in the accounting department, watching as the people got younger, moved on to other jobs, were replaced by other younger people. Watching computers get faster and flatter, but no better. Stayed in the city when his mother died (Tony argued that he couldn't be left on his own, even for a weekend), when his aunt sent him a postcard from Banff, where she was running a gift shop, urging him to come out for a visit, maybe stay longer (hinting broadly that she'd like some help running the shop). His days spent working, walking the increasingly-arthritic dog, keeping Tony cheered up and happy (he wasn't really sick, not on the new drugs, but he still wouldn't leave the house). Well, it was a life.

~ ~ ~

Stan came back from the ferry docks, thinking about the silver shining thing, the weird compulsion to touch it, the just as strong compulsion to run away. "Hey Tony," he said, as he came in and Hero limped energetically to his food dish. "You won't believe what I saw on the lakeshore…"

But Tony was furious. "What's this, Stan?"

"What?"

Tony brandished a letter under his nose. "This."

"Oh, that," Stan said. "It's Jason, you know, from the Symposium Theater. Wants me to come visit him in New York. He's a producer with an off-Broadway troupe now, thinks I could help with his company accounts."

Tony's eyes slit. "You're trying to leave me."

"No Tony," Stan protested. "You know I wouldn't. It's just for a couple of weeks." He knew he sounded insincere. He'd been hoping the couple of weeks would lead to something longer, something more permanent. But on the face of it, that was all it was, so he said, truthfully, "It's just a visit, I swear."

Tony's hands made fists. "You're two-timing me with this theater person—"

"No—" Stan protested, unheard.

"You don't care about me, just about your own selfish—"

But Tony was interrupted by the sound of Hero throwing up.

~ ~ ~

"That dog will have to go," Tony said, watching as Stan cleaned up the mess.

"He's fine. Just has a bit of a tummy bug."

"Stan, he's geriatric. Limps everywhere, farts in his sleep. Take him to the vet, do the humane thing."

Stan looked up, eyes suddenly sharpened. "You want I should do the same to you someday?"

Tony sighed, and Stan noticed how tight the skin was pulled over his face, almost like the wrinkles were cracks in varnish. "Maybe, yeah," he said.

Stan put his arms around him, hugged him from behind. "Aw, Tony," he said.

Tony leaned into him. "Still," he said, "think about it. He's not likely to survive another winter. Maybe take him back to the shelter. You know it was only supposed to be temporary."

~ ~ ~

Stan was back on the Island the next weekend, walking along the beach beyond where the signs of the amusement park, closed for the season, creaked ominously in the breeze, feeling the cold in the air, watching Hero going on ahead, tail wagging, tongue panting.

For the first time, he felt genuinely trapped. Tony always got his way, and now that he'd started on Hero, there was only one way it was going to end.

He thought about running away. But where to? New York was out now. His mother was dead, his family scattered. His aunt had sold the shop the previous year, retired, God only knew where.

Maybe he could go on the road? Stan snorted at the idea. He wouldn't last five minutes. Besides, it seemed like every time he got a chance to leave, something pulled him back in.

He wished he could just disappear, lose himself within the city.

Up ahead, Hero was barking at something. A seagull, Stan thought, as he navigated another chilly dune.

The barking intensified, then suddenly cut off with a yipe.

Stan broke into a run. "Hero!" he shouted.

The dog was where they'd found the silver shining thing. He'd stepped on it, and was struggling as the material slithered up his legs, onto his muzzle. Looked like something the CGI department did at work, only without the artificial glossiness.

Stan's fear for Hero overcame his fear of the silver thing. He launched himself awkwardly at Hero, tried to pull the dog out of the shining ooze. But all he succeeded in doing was in getting him further in. The silver stuff was covering Stan's arms now; it felt cold, like the air before a snowstorm. He tried to pull it off, but it clung — no, it didn't cling, it was becoming *part* of him, blending into his clothes, into his skin. He couldn't see what had happened to Hero, but he could feel the shiny stuff covering him, enveloping his body, then his face, then his head, until he could see nothing—

—No. He could see everything.

He was part of Hero now, and Hero part of him, and both part of the substance, except it *wasn't* a substance, it was a being, with all the people and animals it had brought into itself, and something more.

Proteus, he thought, and knew he wasn't wrong. *The old man of the sea, who changes shape and brings all within himself. Like the city. Like the lake.*

Proteus wasn't just one man, or creature, or myth. Proteus was everywhere there was water, everywhere things were changing. People came to the North to change, driven by war or depression or mothers or boyfriends, and became someone else — or else they *were* changed, not intending to stay and become part of the scene but, eventually, giving in to the ooze, flowing into the city. The part of Proteus that had been Stan understood that now. Understood that he had come to the city, had changed, and now he needed to change again.

Needed to let go. To become part of the silver thing.

And Tony. Tony didn't want Stan to change, didn't want anything to change for himself, either. But if Tony ever changed his mind, embraced the fluidity of life, then there was always a place in Proteus for him, too. *But you've got to come to me, Tony.*

Larger now, Proteus flowed down the beach towards the lake. Memories of Tony, of aunts and apartments and theaters and jobs and friends were all sorting themselves into the experiences of the whole, gaining and losing context. Stan found that, within Proteus, he could become part of others, share their worlds as they shared his: here he saw life as a white Jewish woman; there as an ancient man, centuries old in objective time, a man who remembered the lake when there was no city on it; and again as the fish saw it, the birds, the coyotes, and the foxes.

Proteus joined the water, and every part of Proteus was one.

And every part of Proteus was content.

———— « 0 » ————

Fiona Moore

Fiona Moore is a Toronto-born writer and academic whose first novel, *Driving Ambition*, was published by Bundoran Press in autumn 2018 and whose second has been acquired by ChiZine Publications. She has written and cowritten a number of articles and guidebooks on cult television, including guides to *Blake's Seven*, *The Prisoner* and *Battlestar Galactica*. She has also written three stage plays and four audio plays, maintains the website for Magic Bullet Productions, www.kaldorcity.com, and her fiction has appeared in, among others, *Interzone, Asimov, On Spec, Unlikely Story* and the award-winning anthology *Blood and Water*. When not writing, she is a Professor of Business Anthropology at Royal Holloway, University of London.

The Garden

Darrel Duckworth

The squeak of fans turning was faint but unmistakable in the desert air. Gar and I stopped a few feet from the chain link fence and looked through at the building beyond. Several feet to our right, the sand jumped. A snake shot out from where it had been hiding and raced away. Gar's gun snapped out. The crack of his shot split the dry air and the top third of the snake splattered away from the rest of its body. The pieces twitched in the sun for a few seconds, then lay still. The softly blowing sand began to gather on the sticky parts.

Soon it would be covered and forgotten.

Gar turned and smiled at me, smug about the shot.

A few days ago, I would have said something about wasting a bullet. Now, I just turned back to the fence.

One bullet or, for that matter, one man, was too small to make a difference anymore. Not on an Earth that human desire and science had 'bio-improved' into desolation.

Which was why we were leaving.

Inside the wire, sunlight glared off the 30 feet of bare, sandy compound between the fence and the one story, flattop, concrete building. Cameras and tracker-lasers hid in the cooler shadows of the roof's overhang, scanning the compound and perimeter.

Thirty feet can be a long way.

"Good setup," I said.

Gar sneered. "Easy to crack. They're depending on those solar panels and wind catchers on the roof for power. I could take them out from here. Then they'd have nothing."

I looked at him out the corner of my eye. Yes, he was serious. Six feet of solid muscle, Gar was one of the best warriors the Clan had produced. But not the brightest. He was fast, powerful and deadly. And he loved to fight. He lived to fight. Nothing and no one was too much for him to take on. Just ask him.

I looked again at the tracker-lasers and doubted he would get off two shots.

As in most things, Gar and I were at opposite ends of the spectrum.

I had no doubts about my abilities as a warrior. I had earned that Clan standing repeatedly. I just didn't buy into the Clan mythos and live for the fight they way he did.

Small, lean, and wiry, I was a thinker. I preferred to win the fight before it started — or better yet, avoid it altogether. The battles Gar loved so much wasted people and scarce supplies the Clan couldn't afford to lose.

Gar learned what made him a better warrior. I "filled my head with useless stuff."

Gar liked to act. I liked to plan.

Gar kept his hair shaggy and wild because he thought it made him look more fierce. I cut mine to keep it out of my eyes.

We were the oddest team the Clan had seen. In fact, the only thing we had in common was that we were the last of the Clan. And we were leaving Earth.

I shook myself out of my thoughts and looked again at the wind collectors. There was something odd about them. Not the fact that they were there. Out here, near the center of the desert that used to be Nebraska, they were the only practical way to make power. But they looked wrong somehow.

I let it go. It didn't really matter. We needed supplies, and this was one of the last outposts before the *Mirta*.

A wooden stake was hammered into the sand a foot or so from the fence. Wrapped around it was the end of a thin, fraying rope. I reached down and pulled. The rope ran under the fence into a wooden box. As I yanked, the sand covering the cord sprang up with it, showering the air, and a loud bell in the box rang.

The sound waves clanged past us, loud and sharp in the desert air. Then they faded away into the distance, chasing the sound of Gar's gunshot. Not much to echo off out here.

I looked at the building — a tiny head was already peeking out of the door.

Of course, I thought. *No need to ring the doorbell when your partner is firing a gun.*

The tiny, Asian face stared at us. Then it responded to a sharp voice from inside the building and ducked back inside. The lock on the gate clicked. I pushed it open.

"Gooks," Gar spat.

I didn't argue with him. It was pointless. To Gar, anyone Asian was a "gook." To me, hating an entire race seemed a stupid way to go through life. But I could understand his bitterness. It was the Chun Minh gangs that had nailed us the second time around, almost destroying the Clan and killing more than half of those remaining, including Gar's family. It would be impossible to ever convince him that not all Asians were part of that. I only hoped he would behave himself until we could pick up supplies and start on the last leg of our journey to the *Mirta* and a new life.

The lasers whirred in soprano as they tracked us across the compound. When we reached the door, the little boy who had peeked out at us opened it. Gar shot him a death look, and he darted away. We stepped inside and stopped.

Several feet away, two Asian girls barely in their teens had shotguns aimed at us, one directly ahead of us and the other a little to the left, positioned behind some shelves. Through an open door behind the first girl, I saw an older girl working in the next room, opening boxes and unpacking. She stopped for a second to check out the situation then returned to work. Against the wall to our right, a thin, middle-aged man stood behind a counter, smiling at us, though his right hand remained beneath the counter.

Clean lines of fire, I thought. *No chance of shooting each other. They work well as a team.*

A pleasant family store.

"Please forgive the weapons, gentlemen," the man said, waving his free hand toward the girls with the shotguns.

"They are a necessary precaution in this business. I am Kian, the owner. How may I help you?"

Before Gar could say something insulting, I answered.

"We're on our way to the *Mirta*. We'll need a few things."

"Ah yes," Kian said, nodding. Carefully neutral, he asked, "Would you like to prepare for the unlikely eventuality that you may have to return?"

"We ain't coming back," Gar spat, taking the question as an insult.

Kian simply smiled. "Of course, good sir. I merely ask because some people are more timid than yourself."

Gar sneered.

"How far is it?" I asked.

"Only two days journey, sir."

I looked around with a raised eyebrow at the copious supplies he had stocked on the metal shelves.

He smiled. "Many fail the testing but choose to live and return to the lives they have abandoned. If they can afford it, I sell them the supplies they need to make the journey back."

"That's where you make your real profits, isn't it?" Gar asked. "Off the weaklings and failures."

Kian never stopped smiling. "Those who do not succeed."

Gar tensed. I touched his arm, and he looked down at me.

"A warrior doesn't make the way harder for the next man," I said.

He grunted and nodded. He relaxed his trigger finger, and I relaxed. If nothing goaded him, we would walk out of here leaving these people alive.

I gave the owner a list of what we wanted and the amounts. Gar looked at me with surprise and contempt.

"We'll eat more than normal rations during these last two days," I said, "so that we will be at our best for whatever tests they have for us. Win or die, we will not disgrace the Clan."

He thought about that and nodded. It was the sort of rhetoric he fed himself daily.

For me, it was just an argument that worked. Truth was, I simply wanted to have the best chance. Win or die, the *Mirta* wouldn't know who our clan was, or give a damn. Win or die, we would be just two more soldiers.

"You are a wise man, sir," Kian complimented me.

I nodded. He was still going to get as little out of me as I could manage. Not that it mattered. Where we were going, they didn't care about Earth goods; otherwise, the Mirta would be trading for something other than human fighters.

Kian indicated that some of the items were in the other room. I told Gar to gather our supplies here while I went to get the rest. One teenaged guard followed me. Her shotgun never wavered from my head.

The next room was cluttered with boxes and goods. Apparently, they had just received a shipment. I wished we had known their schedule. We could have arranged transport and saved ourselves a long, hard walk.

The older girl working back there stopped and looked at me. She was stocky, and her hands had seen years of hard work, the skin calloused and weathered. Her face was similarly weathered, though still pleasant. But it was her eyes that got my attention. They were dark and probing, not nervous and full of false smiles like her father's. These eyes asked questions.

These days, I didn't like questions—but I liked her eyes.

I told her what I was after, and she began pointing to boxes and shelves. Both she and my guard watched me as I retrieved the supplies.

"You are going to the Mirta," the older girl said.

I nodded.

"Why?" she asked.

"Do you ask every customer that question?"

"Not every. Why do you go?"

"I have nowhere else to go and nothing to remain on Earth for."

"Why not?"

I answered without looking at her. "I was a warrior in my clan. Now that clan is dead."

Even to me, the words sounded wooden. I didn't believe in the Clan anymore. Maybe I never did.

"The Clan" that Gar idealized and romanticized was not a true clan in any sense. We weren't of one family, nor did we have the long history of say, the Scottish clans. In fact, our clan had formed less than 20 years ago, after the last illusions of law and order vanished. Several small groups banded together for protection, claiming and defending a small portion of the city to scrape out a life in, living off the dwindling goods of a manufactured world. A glorified gang among other gangs.

Gar and I grew up in the Clan. The Clan didn't make it.

The other gangs, more organized and brutal, came at us. The first two conflicts were all out war. After that, we were whittled down bit by bit until only Gar and I remained. Maybe if our leaders had accepted one of the takeover offers from the other gangs more people might have lived. But we were 'The Clan,' and defeat was impossible. Now Gar and I were 'The Clan,' and we were leaving forever.

"So you go to serve the Mirta," the older girl said. Her dark eyes continued to probe me, as if sensing my words were more solemn than my feelings.

"I go to find a new life. There's no place here for a warrior without a cause. Besides, with Gar and I off the planet, there will be two less bodies draining the resources and two more credits toward The Billion."

~ ~ ~

The Billion. It was like a litany. A promise of salvation from the heavens.

A bargain with the devil.

The *Mirta* had landed shortly after the big collapse. Efficient traders, they had used our own satellite and surface broadcast systems to transmit their simple message: One credit for each acceptable human being.

The *Mirta* dealt in mercenaries. Apparently, human form — and human nature — were remarkably well-suited for land combat, and people were one resource humanity hadn't used up yet.

And when Earth had accumulated one billion credits — that is, had given up one billion of her best — the *Mirta* would help humanity to rebuild their planet. They showed holoclips of the necessary terraforming technology at work on other planets, and humanity looked to them for salvation.

In a way, they had already been our salvation. Even before the big collapse, we had been close to shredding the last of civilization apart and spiraling completely down into our barbaric past.

Their arrival had allowed the shattered governments to maintain some symbolic measure of control for long enough to formalize the routes to *Mirta* recruitment but not enough to prevent the growing gangs from usurping control of the cities. Perhaps if the *Mirta* had come before the collapse, a better deal could have been worked out, but that was doubtful. Governments were good at politics, not business.

And, the *Mirta* were too good at business to make a mistake in timing.

Although, maybe it would have been better if they hadn't come at all. The end of 'modern civilization' might have given the planet a chance to rest and recover from us.

~ ~ ~

The girl's voice broke me from my thoughts.

"There are some who say that the *Mirta* caused this to happen to our world so that they could demand this price from us."

I smiled grimly. "The ones who said this, they're usually the ones who come back through here after failing the tests?"

She nodded.

"Well, they're wrong. We did it to ourselves. We took too much for too long, and we gave back too little too late. Add to that all the bioengineering we did to remake the world to our liking and.... Well, we screwed with the way the world was supposed to work and now it doesn't have what it needs to function naturally. We took away its strength and adaptability. We screwed it and screwed ourselves."

I recited the words from memory. How many times had my father said them to me? How much did it hurt him to understand those words so much better than I did?

I grew up in the world as it is now. He grew up in a time before all this, during the downward spiral, with photographs of a green and beautiful world to dream about. He watched it all turn to dust. Before the collapse, he and my mother were scientists working for the government in their frantic attempts to turn back the clock, to make things green enough again to support the huge bio-mass of humanity.

They had watched their work criticized, crippled, and canceled by the same short-sighted leadership and public cravings that had caused the destruction — people who wanted easy, quick fixes, not the sacrifice and work that lasting solutions required.

Then they watched civilization crumble, ending any hope of saving the world.

"The *Mirta* didn't cause our problems," I said. "We did. Us, our parents, and their parents before them. The *Mirta* are just a race that didn't destroy themselves. They were smart, and they succeeded. The people that fail their tests can't stand that, so they blame the *Mirta* for our stupidity. It's always easier to blame someone else than to face our own mess and deal with it."

I think my answer was more complex than she expected. She paused, assessing it.

"And when do we reach The Billion?" she asked. "When does the magic begin? Who is keeping count? The *Mirta*?"

I stared at the shelf in front of me. Those were uncomfortable questions. Questions I was trying to ignore. Questions that ran too close to others. Like, was I really helping the world? Or just running away? Was this my destiny? Or my escape? Everything I had ever done in my life had amounted to nothing. Was there some place, some way, I could make a difference? Or was I just one of billions of helpless pawns?

I looked at her.

She stood there, waiting.

I took a deep breath and let it out.

"I don't know."

Her mouth opened, then closed. It obviously wasn't the answer she was expecting. For a moment, those eyes looked into me again.

"You don't speak like a warrior."

I shrugged, and we stood in silence for a moment. In that silence, I heard Gar gathering supplies in the next room, the nervous breathing of the girl with the shotgun, and the sound of dripping.

Following the sound, I looked up and saw the makeshift arrangement cobbled together on top of a rusted, metal shelf. A clear, plastic tube snaked in from the ceiling, spiraled through a small condenser unit and emptied over a funnel. Cool air blew gently from the tube and water dripped into the funnel. A second hose, attached to the bottom of the funnel, passed through a small hole in the wall.

Suddenly, I understood what had been wrong with the wind catchers on the roof. I looked back to the girl.

"Water collection and cooling."

She nodded.

"The wind catchers are angled slightly to redirect a small amount of air onto the rooftop and into vents leading into the tube."

Again, she nodded.

"I thought they looked a little odd. No well?"

"We have a well."

"Then why go to the extra trouble and reduce the efficiency of your wind catchers?"

"A project of my father's. It requires extra water."

The young girl with the shotgun snapped something at her sister in their language and she snapped something back. The younger one glared at her, then returned her eyes to me.

"Would you like to see?" the older sister asked me.

I listened for a moment to Gar arguing with Kian in the next room. She listened also. Her eyes asked me if there would be trouble. I shook my head slightly.

"He won't get violent unless someone insults his manhood or the Clan. He just likes to argue so he can feel that he's getting a deal."

She smiled. "My father will let him think that he has 'won' a deal."

"Good. I would like to see your father's project."

She indicated the other door in the room and led the way. We passed through an unlit battery room, where the electricity from the panels and catchers above was stored, then through their small, bare living quarters.

The place was a model of efficiency. Everything was reused or built from items that couldn't otherwise be reused. Necessity was the mother of fanatical conservation.

We passed a homemade chem-toilet. Looking at the design, I guessed it was the type that could be used to speed the decay process and separate natural gas for cooking. I wondered what they did with the rest of the waste.

A moment later, I found out.

We passed through the back door and into a small, enclosed garden. Wooden walls sealed with gray gunk kept the sand out, and a camouflage net overhead kept the desert sun from baking the plants. Lining the walls were tin cans, beaten flat to reflect the light that made it through the net. The plants received plenty of light in an area almost twenty degrees cooler than the desert beyond.

A tube snaked from the house, down into the rich, dark earth beneath the plants, feeding them water. A homemade sprinkler system ran between the rows, waiting to spray a fine mist onto the leaves above ground. It was a crude setup, but the plants seemed to be surviving and growing.

"I don't understand," I said, looking at her. "The effort of maintaining this garden must be far more than what you get out of it."

"It is. At this size, it gives back less than it takes, but each year we expand it a little. Soon it will give back as much as it takes. Someday, more."

I looked at the tin covered walls, seeing the desert beyond them in my mind. The idea seemed unrealistic.

"It was my mother's project originally," the girl explained. "My father thought it wasteful, but my mother was raised to believe in the Earth and loved growing things. He gave her this because he loved her. After she died, my father took it as his own, as a way to return meaning to his life. A way to prove we do not need the *Mirta*."

I looked at the tiny garden and thought about the vast desert beyond.

The *Mirta* chose the most barren parts of Earth to conduct their tests so that only the strong and committed would seek them out. But during the journey here, it had occurred to me that there might be a second reason. By the time you reached the *Mirta*, you were convinced that the Earth was a hopeless cause and they were the only future.

Images of crumbling cities, failing croplands and the desert we'd walked through filled my mind as I looked down on the tiny garden.

It was foolish. A stupid dream.

But when I looked up and into her eyes, I couldn't say that. It was the only dream she had. The only dream in a desert.

There was nothing to say, but she said it.

"I am Tiam. What is your name?"

"Hawk," I responded automatically.

She looked at me, puzzled. "Is that a name you earned in your clan?"

I felt the corners of my mouth tug up into a small smile.

"I chose it. When a member of our Clan turns — turned — fourteen, they would choose a name that the rest of the world would know them by. Only members of the Clan knew our real names. Our elders felt that such rituals bound people to the Clan and added an air of mystery to 'coming of age.' They got the idea from an old library book on tribal customs. I chose 'Hawk' because it sounded dramatic."

She smiled a little. Then it faded as she looked into my eyes.

"But you said your clan is gone."

I nodded.

"And now that it is gone, there is only 'Hawk'?"

For a long time, we looked at each other in silence. No one had used my real name since my mother died. I wasn't even sure if I remembered who I had been before I became Hawk. It didn't matter. Whoever he was, he hadn't been able to make a difference either.

She stood there, asking her question with her eyes. I didn't have an answer, so I turned and went back into the house. My guard followed. I heard Tiam close the door and follow us both. Back in the clutter of the storeroom, I gathered up the supplies and rejoined Gar.

"Where the hell have you been?"

"Looking at the plants."

Kian's eyes flicked to his daughter, surprised and accusing. Gar's eyes looked at me, flicked to Tiam, then back to me. He scowled, and I knew what he was thinking.

Right, I thought. *We had sex with her sister pointing a gun at my head.*

Gar wasn't the brightest of puppies.

We paid for the goods and arranged them in our packs.

"Since you won't be coming back," Kian spoke up as we moved to the door, "perhaps I can sell you some small mementos of Earth."

He lifted out a small tray of solidly-built jewelery and another of knives.

"You will not need your money where the *Mirta* will take you, but a small object from Earth might comfort you in your long journeys."

"And all it will cost is all our money, right gook?"

Gar was blunt and rude, but accurate. Kian shrugged. Gar made a rude sign and walked out the door. Kian looked at me. I shook my head. He shrugged again and began putting away the trays. I opened the door, stopped, and looked around for Tiam. She was back in the other room, watching me through the doorway.

It was such a small thing; I don't know why it mattered. But then, life is made up mostly of small things.

Maybe I just wanted it to matter.

"George," I called out to her. "George Nealy."

She smiled a little. "Goodbye George. Good Luck."

I nodded and smiled back. Then I closed the door.

~ ~ ~

Six days later, I opened the door again and stepped in. The shotgun was again aimed at my head. Kian was clearly surprised to see me, but he slipped his smiling mask quickly into place.

"Welcome back. You... uh... chose not to take the tests?"

I looked at him evenly. "We took the tests."

His face became a well-practised mask of condolence. I closed the door and wandered over to examine the goods on the wall, making sure I got near my young guard.

"I grieve with you for your friend," Kian said.

"Don't," I said, picking up a can and examining the label. "He'll enjoy being a mercenary."

Kian looked at me, not sure what mask to wear now. I put the can down.

"We passed," I said.

I took the shotgun from his daughter before she even realized I was moving, leveled it at Kian, and walked toward him. His eyes were wide and white.

"You need better protection."

I stopped in front of him and gently laid the shotgun down on the desk between us. Then I reached into my pocket, took out all my cash, and laid it beside the shotgun.

Kian looked totally confused now. Oddly, his face reminded me of Gar's when I had told him that I was staying "to fight for Earth, on Earth."

Gar didn't understand what I meant, but he did understand fighting and causes. He had given me all his money and a warrior's grip before saying goodbye.

"I want to buy in," I said. "To help you with that garden."

Footsteps rushing from the back room attracted my attention. I looked over my shoulder. Tiam stood in the door, the second shotgun trained on me. Surprised, she lowered the gun. I smiled at her and turned back to Kian.

"Acceptable terms?" I asked him.

A callused hand laid itself on top of mine on the counter. I turned and smiled at Tiam.

She smiled back.

Out of the corner of my eye, I saw Kian nod slowly.

In my mind, I saw the vast desert surrounding a foolish, insolent garden. I put my arms around it, protecting it, and pushed the desert back a few more feet.

—— « O » ——

Darrel Duckworth

Darrel Duckworth has lived (and sometimes worked) in every province and territory of the amazing land called Canada. After a long career in high-tech, he returned to his first love, writing. He now spends more time on other worlds, occasionally returning to Earth to refill his coffee mug. His stories can be found in magazines such as *LORE*, *Bards and Sages*, and *Plasma Frequency* and in anthologies such as *Coven* and *Wild Things*.

One-Way Ticket

Michael Milne

Alexis gently toes the ground as she steps off the gangplank, unsure of the gravity. She has visited the moon, backpacked the First Colonies on Mars. New ground always excites her, and she is tempted, even now surrounded by strangers, to take off her shoes and sprint in the grass. The sky is a shattering shade of blue — Alexis has never seen a sky this bright before, and for the first time in a long time she breathes unobstructed.

It is nearly dusk and even at this hour sultry and damp. Generations of ships are parked to the side, near the landing pad of the *Sojourn 4J*. Alexis spots cousin vessels, the *4H* and the *4I*, rusting, half-blind, and wingless. It's a graveyard of journeys.

"Hail and good day, friend," one man shouts to her. He is deeply tanned; Alexis spots more recent settlers, paler and watching hungrily, in the distance. She can't place the man's accent; he has gone native in a place with no nativity.

"We have homesteads for each of you ready and waiting," a woman says. She is more professional and comfortable in her English. Her dress is conservative, buttoned to the neck. "We will introduce you to your settlement coaches."

They walk through the village and stop at a tapered, spindly building. It is made from some thin and sturdy grass like bamboo, each shoot visible in the structure. Here and there sheets of metal are bolted onto the outside. The buildings around it all look the same, the roofs sloped downwards away from the road.

"The welcome dinner is at 27:3," the woman says, her cadence indicating a time rather than an address. They are in Alexis's hotel room, which is spare and humid and too big. "The town hall is just there." The woman's finger beckons out the glassless window into the city, where there are dozens of identical buildings. Alexis would ask for clarification, but she is so tired.

Alexis sits on the awkward five-legged stool by her bed and tries to decipher the street below her, trying to discern businesses from residences. She pinpoints a restaurant only because of the metal tables out front, the patrons squatting on blue crates, eating steaming bowls of something-or-other.

~ ~ ~

As the video letter begins, Alexis finds herself inhaling, bracing herself. Their ship carried communiqués for generations of older Extragrants: those already on Parterra and those only ten or twenty years into settlement. Alexis knew one would be waiting for her, sent before the *4J* blasted out of range.

Days before for Alexis, she and her mother Sandra stood on the docking bay of the *Sojourn 4J*. Alexis wore her mission-mandated blue jumpsuit, and Sandra cooed at the uniform.

"I still can't believe you're going to be an astronaut," she murmured. "It's going to be such an adventure."

"A sleepy adventure," Alexis laughed. "I'll only be conscious for a few minutes after the launch and then I'll be there. It's going to fly by in an instant."

"Doesn't everything?" Her mother got wistful, a fine china dishware sort of emotion. She reached out and held Alexis's hand.

In the video, her mother's eyes are red. She sits in their family home, the two-storey where Alexis grew up, on the sleepy street in Palo Alto. It is sunny and gray outside, the windows pulled shut against the pollution.

"I've seen enough launches on Ansible, but I guess I've never witnessed one up close." There is rapture in her voice, probably for the scientific rigor required for such a journey. "Your father and I brought goggles so we could watch the whole way up. I kept holding my breath, expecting it to arc back down like a roller coaster."

There is not much else to the update: her parents stayed and talked to some of the other gathered families and well-wishers. They saw how many people brought bouquets and felt bad — had Alexis wanted flowers?

"Hi mom," Alexis says to the pinhole camera. "Nothing much to report here yet. Beautiful scenery. Almost everybody here can wield an acetylene torch, and they're all covered in tattoos." She imagines her mother's open scorn. "They don't really like my first blueprints, maybe I'm rusty. I haven't gone trekking yet, but if I do, I promise to pick up some rocks for you." She takes a deep breath and glances around her empty hotel room. "Lots of love. Your daughter." She thumbs the send button, which does nothing. There is no internet connection, and she will only be able to recharge her workstation at a local electricity center.

Tomorrow she will head to the transmission center so her reply can begin its six-decade trek back home.

~ ~ ~

The proprietress of Alexis' hotel speaks no English, but with her own pitiful Altroman she somehow manages to eke out most of her necessities. She returns to her room exhausted from the effort of trying to buy a new toothbrush (which is wooden and breaks almost immediately). She doesn't understand any of the food. And she cannot determine if the water from the tap in her room is potable.

Outside of her beginner Altroman lessons on Twoday and Sevenday, Alexis' social circle extends to her brown and lithe settlement coach, Helia. She needs interaction, and so she turns to the familiar, her press-ganged family. The other 4Jers (as they call each other) meet every Fiveday for drinks, convening at the only bar in town with more than two walls. Alexis tries to get drunk on the foul grasswine, *erba*, which has the same name as tea and the same name as grass. She eyes up and tries to flirt with a local man.

"What you do?" she bleats in shaky, embarrassed Altroman. "You welder? You farmer? You cook?" She only knows the words for three jobs, the first ones listed in her language textbook.

He says his occupation, and Alexis stares at him blankly, feeling like an idiot. Eventually he swings his arms.

"Lumberjack?" Alexis inquires. She says it again, louder. She glances back at the table, and her new friend Sakura bleats something unintelligible, which makes the man nod. She considers trying to mime 'architect' for herself and decides against it.

"You name?" In English first, and then Altroman.

"Mikos. And you?"

"Alexis. Lexy. Me Lexy." She smiles in a way she hopes is charming. Has she always been so bad at this?

"How old are you?" Mikos asks. Alexis feels a thrill — she has practiced this same stupid interaction a dozen times in class.

"Seven-and-two-tens," Alexis says. She wants to feel embarrassed at how proud she is of this modest achievement, but decides to enjoy the moment. Given the complicated nature of her age with the time loss, she sticks with her relative number of experienced years and doesn't mention that she is technically a nonagenarian.

It goes on this way for several more minutes before they enter the painfully foggy territory of grammar not-yet-covered in her language class. Retreating, Alexis tries to offer the man a drink. He demurs and rushes away to his friends, giggling all the way. When Alexis turns back to her table, there is a smattering of applause, and Sakura pats her on the back.

A 4J man leans over to her. "Maybe local mating is different. I bet it's all in the color of your hoop skirt." He winks. "If it matters, I think you were captivating."

"It matters." She smiles.

"You Lexy, right?" He offers his hand. "Me Steven. Me doctor."

The next morning as she wakes up next to Steven, Alexis asks him about what he is doing on Parterra. He runs a hand over his smooth brown head, his skin naturally dark. "Everywhere needs doctors, and I've been most other everywheres already. Thought I'd go to a new one."

Steven asks for Alexis's number.

"Do they even have phones here?" Alexis asks. She stalls, but acquiesces when she hears him hum the theme song to *Alpaca Pack* in the shower. She remembers watching her favorite cartoon with her brother Marko, both in onesie pajamas. She scribbles down her Ansible address and arranges to meet Steven for tea later in the week.

~ ~ ~

Alexis and Sakura head to a local clothing shop, trying to find a way to spend their wages, which come in twelve denominations of hard clay coins.

"I got in on the Enviro-Quota, probably. Mostly I'm here to professionally bitch about keeping the indigenous bush safe." Sakura holds up something strappy, both revealing and strangely frumpy at the same time. Alexis shakes her head.

"So you're chaining yourself to trees?" Alexis feels a pang of jealousy — working in the city planning office means she is trapped inside all day.

"Not many trees here, but not many people cutting them down. I'm here for the erba," Sakura says, shrugging. She cackles and wrenches what looks like a burlap catsuit from a box. "Still, most people here never saw Earth and never will. They don't know how to be scared of gray skies." Sakura holds the burlap to her chest and does a pirouette. "Yet."

The man behind the counter eventually gives them that polite nod that means it's time for them to bugger off. They head next door to a Screens shop, and Alexis digs her hand into the pile of archaic flash drives like electronic sediment. Sakura rattles off a dozen series she left unfinished on Earth, whispering their names like forgotten lovers. On the wall is a catalog, and Alexis switches the display to chronological.

"I don't know what *Pork Wrangler* is, but the first one came out a year after we left." Updated cultural files are carried along with each new settlement ship, and there is a good few years of unfamiliar content. She sees familiar celebrity names and rifles around to find the right drives. "Let's go wild and just buy I through IV."

There is some need within her she cannot name, a desire to review her home archaeologically. The past week, after hours drafting blueprints in a hot, airless room, Alexis went home and watched historical newscasts, details of wars and outbreaks and celebrity marriages from the first years of her absence.

"What is this graph?" Sakura scoffs as they enter Alexis's spare apartment. She has no art or decoration and has no idea where to acquire them. "Hemlines? Rockabilly hair resurgence? What the hell is 'blitzfrig'?"

"It's a slang term that got really popular about two years gone," Alexis says. She tries to not be embarrassed — Sakura, like all the rest of the 4Jers, stood trembling when the 4K and then the 4L arrived and bounded around the quivering new arrivals to find the comms officer. They are all hungry for anything from back home, no matter how stale.

The couch is stuffed with sawdust and hay, and both women sit on the floor. Alexis's workstation blares the blockbuster saga, and the first is neatly recognizable. There are references to deposed politicians Alexis remembers, jokes she finds funny. But by the fourth film, produced nearly a decade later in the flaring Nollywood market, Alexis feels like she is watching something in a foreign language. There are things she can only assume are humorous for the open grins beaming from the actors' faces.

"Do people always stand like that?" Sakura asks. She is standing, and Alexis laughs that she doesn't know what to do with her hands. "I don't feel like we stand like that. Maybe I'm being weird."

Alexis preferred to imagine her home world would simply become a more exaggerated form of itself in the intervening years. All of modern history would be an ongoing tale of the year 2361, where Earth would be comfortably frozen at its cultural peak. People would always like the vocal stylings of Virginia Quail, the fad popularity of blood pudding burritos would never die, and everyone still thought matte-finish pollution masks were cool.

Everything she knows and likes became uncool six decades ago. She cannot even fathom the things that seventeen-year-olds enjoy these days — she assumes lasers must be involved. To them she would seem creaky and ancient, precociously elderly, quaintly bewildered at the world leaving her behind.

~ ~ ~

The arrival of the *Sojourn 4M* coincides with a local holiday, something to do with the autumnal equinox. The townspeople gather in traditional garb: billowing skirts and pants, emerald plumage from a native bird-thing cresting from crisscrossing sashes.

"The newbies are going to flip," Steven says with a smile. "Did they all have to wear their welding goggles?"

"You're just mad you can't find a pair that suit you," Alexis whispers. "I wonder if any of the people will be interesting." She is speaking about the drafting process. Pods of earlier settlers, 4Hers and 4Fers, awkwardly try to intermingle with the excited local population. Each of them is in varying states of local dress, and their comfort with the costume is roughly correlated to their time on-planet. They always scope the new crowd, mentally auditioning new inductees, but earlier extragrants seldom bother.

"I hope there are some damn Kiwis," Sakura mutters. "I need to know about the Wellington levees. I really hope—" She stops, and everyone looks skyward.

The ship appears as a blot in the sky and gets bigger as it descends. The engines rumble, aim downwards, soften their drop. Alexis thinks she can feel the heat even from this distance, and instinctually moves back. Everyone seems to be holding their breath as treads hit the ground, the gangplank thumps to the dirt, and the former Earthicans emerge. Alexis strains to spot the comms officer, and knows Sakura is doing the same.

The next day in Altroman class, their teacher, Helia, clucks and rolls her eyes. The room is half-empty, many mainstays playing unexpected hooky. "You all need stop going to Arrivals," she says.

"What do you mean?" Alexis asks.

"New ship came in yesterday, yeah?" Helia shrugs. "You all stay up all night watching letters from home?"

There are murmurs in the room, but no one will agree out loud.

"It is very common with new people. Most settlers go through this. They watch too many videos from homeland," Helia says, and nods at Alexis's work station, which is possessively clutched against her chest. "It is called Arrival Depression."

Early in Alexis' tenure in Altrome, Helia's job had been translation and helping Alexis find a suitable apartment and the best simulacrum of vermicelli available locally. In recent days, Helia has become fawning and understanding; she sometimes takes a pitying tone Alexis probably deserves but doesn't care for.

"I'm not depressed. I'm just a little bummed."

Helia nods the nod of someone who has heard all of this before, and Alexis makes a face.

The ships from Earth are getting faster, and while launches to the far colonies are happening once every few years, the arrivals begin to get closer. Alexis decides to binge — she takes a day off of work and tries to get it all out of her system. The town's wind-sayer (something half-way between a mayor and a meteorologist), hates all of her ideas for new neighborhoods, and she wants to stay home anyway.

In the span of a few hours, she watches her family tree expand and contract. Her brother Marko meets a woman, Christina, and Alexis witnesses their relationship in stop-motion. He describes her red hair, her kind smile, the way she loves animals; five letters later they are engaged; another four and she is hugely pregnant. The Sojourn 4M left nearly 13 years after Alexis, and while it carries copies of *Pork Wrangler V*, it also carries word of the birth of Alexis's nephew Thomas.

She imagines sometimes that these are people she doesn't actually know, that they are actors, and Alexis is viewing this strange cross-section of their lives as an avant-garde film project. It's hard not to picture the real people blissfully frozen at the point of her departure, forever young. As she goes to sleep each night, she still imagines boarding a return vessel and arriving to Marko and mom and dad exactly as they had been before.

Alexis responds to each of these letters as she watches them, trying to come up with new anecdotes to tell a 25 year-old Marko, things she hopes he will still find interesting at 28 and 32. She imagines holding baby Thomas, a sweaty Christina bundling the infant into her arms, and she realizes that this baby must already be nearly 50 years old.

When she catches wind that her father is sick, when he meekly whispers to the camera the name of some horrible disease Alexis has never heard, she turns off the screen and calls Steven. He comes to her house and balks at the scene. Alexis is surrounded in damp tissue, amidst the scraps of fried chicken she has tried to construct without chicken or flour or a proper frying pan. She has drunk a bottle and a half of erba.

"We're going to bed," he says. Alexis looks outside and notes that the sun has gone down, that her face is red and she has been blubbering for some hours.

"Thank you for being *here*," she murmurs as he curls around her in big spoon formation. Just as she is about to fall asleep, Steven reaches around her, takes her electric vidscreen, and tucks it into a nightstand drawer.

~ ~ ~

Alexis had tried to convince Marko to come with her, just as she'd tried friends and former classmates desperate for work — opportunities abounded at the other end of space.

"It's a rock," he said. "A rocky rock. With giant poison mushrooms and algae volcanoes. They took some footage in the forests there, and I swear I saw this giant cow monster with a scorpion's tail. You're going to the Australia of the known galaxy."

This had been the wrong tack to take. Alexis remembered being a child and thrilling as her parents described camping in the foothills of the Rockies as arduous and difficult and swarming everywhere with emaciated and desperate bears. Marko's vision of Parterra gave her a delirious excitement, and she thought of herself in spurs with a lasso. She dreamt of making her own roads.

On weekends Alexis explores the countryside around Altrome. At first just to get out of the house and then because she enjoys it. She enjoys finding the little pathways wending through the fields of the red-green erba, and trudging new ones. Steven accompanies her more often than not.

They stop halfway up an arid hill a kilometer outside of Altrome and try to settle in for a picnic.

"I wish we had sandwiches," she mutters, and this starts the usual chain. They rattle off the foods they miss, in order of how much they miss them. "Pizza." "Pho." "Green-tea kit-kats." "An actual, well-made, shit-you-not squid sausage."

Over their food, Alexis brings out her work station. She opens her schematics for Altrome and turns the screen translucent. She casts a ghostly image across the real city so she and Steven can look at the future of Altrome in onionskin.

Alexis brings out these plans often and discusses them with an artist's pained sincerity. The chef at one favorite stew house spent nearly an hour pointing out faults, each time making sure to include praise to soothe Alexis' obviously chapped ego. She has taken to more of these conversations lately, and is slowly making changes.

"Still haven't lost the rock-climbing gym?" Steven teases her for being overly hopeful, but she knows he appreciates the idea as well.

"Not yet. Had to bargain away the experimental opera company over that one." She imagines this as a process of horse-trading, a negotiation with the locals before they ultimately green-light her superior ideas.

"Is that a movie theater? Do they even make movies here?" Steven eats some local dish, filled with transplanted durian and Parterran meat.

"It's mostly import," she says, and shrugs. She'd love a movie theater, but Steven doesn't seem convinced. "You figured out that weird flu yet?"

"No idea!" Steven talks often about the percolating influenzas and plagues of this world, of how he might get to be this planet's Fleming. "Someone came in today with a blue tongue, spots all over his upper back, and he couldn't speak!"

"You never miss simple old Earth diseases?"

"Not particularly. We cured most of them, and the ones we didn't are our fault anyway. And they burned through my parents about a decade ago. Seven decades ago. I forget how it works, time-wise." He looks away, and Alexis reaches to hold his hand. "Long time ago. Anyway, all this stuff is new and weird and natural, and it's new weird natural."

They sit for a time, and Alexis tentatively tries some of the Steven's food. They hear a rumble from across town as the *Shinsaegae 1.65* touches down, bringing a boatload of sleepy, hopeful Extragrants from the Korean Union. Alexis congratulates herself for not being there at Arrival, even as she tamps down the desire to leave Steven with his durian chutney and bolt through the town.

"Get rid of the movie theater," Steven whispers, rising with their picnic basket. "Maybe keep the rock wall; I bet they'd like it here." He takes one last glance at Alexis's plans, taking in the overall layout. "Looks like San Francisco to me." He begins to hike further up the hill, and Alexis wants to call out that he's from London, what does he know about California anyway, even though he is totally right.

Alexis scrubs the movie theater and three different sushi restaurants from her plans before getting up to follow Steven.

~ ~ ~

Helia invites Alexis out to a street festival. Today is the 83rd anniversary of the founding of Altrome. It's hard to pinpoint exact dates for the original arrival of settlers on Parterra, especially after locals transitioned to their own standard units of time.

"It is not so important as Arrival Day," Helia tells her, commemorating the first ship touching down on the southern continent. "But it is very important for us. This our history day."

Sakura has donned her favorite hoopskirt. She cannot bring herself to see the garment as informal dress, she tells Alexis, but she has begun to like them for fancy occasions. As they walk into the crowds, Alexis counts fewer stares, more nods from familiar faces.

She has garnered some tiny modicum of local celebrity, now that word has gotten around of her plans. After weeks of study, sitting in dusty rooms in the library and reading hand-written books in slowly deteriorating English, Alexis began to understand. Some of the original ships had no cryogenics, and the journey had been completed by descendants of those who originally set out from Earth. Accustomed to these ships more than any planet ahead or behind, the first settlers had used the original *Sojourns* in their cities. They tore off wings and engines, built rain gutters, and planted gardens. Rocketships became houses. Alexis has done some editing, and the wind-sayer seems to be taking her seriously.

At food stalls, at games Alexis doesn't quite understand, at the big public square where people everywhere are dancing, Alexis gets smiles.

"Hey, there's the guy who runs that soup shop downstairs from my apartment," Steven whispers over his erba. "And there's the guy who's welding the new door on my clinic. They're sitting as close as we are."

"You think maybe they're...?" Alexis makes loud, obnoxious smooching noises and makes out with an invisible partner.

"You're drunk!" Steven smiles.

"Takes one to know one."

It's not an official holiday, but the whole town seems to be here, and there is a vibrant thrum in the air. There is music, played on instruments with odd numbers of strings. People rush around, calling to friends, clasping hands, and sharing embraces. After a few rounds of dancing under the violent midday sun, Alexis finds Sakura panting in the shade of a palm tree nearby. These have been modified since removal from cryogenic storage; their canopies are lower and wider and are perfect for summer afternoons.

"I just ate something that seemed to be spicy milk balls," Sakura moans. "It was really good, but I would really advise you to eat no more than 12."

"That sounds gross," Alexis murmurs, and then thinks about it. "Where do I buy them?"

They sit like this for some time, until being asked to dance by friends from work, and then later by friends from class, and then later by total strangers enjoying the sight. It is loud, and night creeps on with no one noticing.

~ ~ ~

Alexis and Sakura are packed into the back of something like a Jeep, pulled by two large domestic buffalo with scorpion tails. The thumping path takes them from the core of Altrome to the outskirts of town. Here farmlands blend into one another, property borderlines fade and blur into the natural sea of grass around them. Sakura is here mainly to argue for the grass and for the few spare trees in the distance.

They careen across a plain of reddish grain, which shimmers in the afternoon sun and whips at the car doors as they pass. A 4Ner in the car, some roadworks expert, remarks that they could probably tweak the genetics just a little more and get something just like Earth wheat. Which means Earth bread.

Alexis fantasizes for a moment about multigrain bread, about carving a slice from a loaf just out of the oven and watching butter melt across its surface like ice on asphalt, but she lets it go. She speaks without looking back from the window. "Keep dreaming."

Around the trundling vehicle, Alexis imagines a city slowly building up around her. Spindly buildings, maxing out at eight stories, creep skyward around the lake. People fill the outdoor square and grass parks or walk up the nearby hill trails. She has asked the local engineers about how feasible it would be to cannibalize the 4J for a new history museum.

They pull up at what will be the center of the new city, the new nation. Ships arrive at a steady pace, monthly touch-downs becoming weekly. The great snow globe of Earth has cracked and the people are pouring out the side. The recent Arrivals described plans for the Sojourn 5th and 6th wave, and the locals realized their home would soon grow.

Steven came around to Alexis's apartment two nights before, asking if she had read the projected manifests. The Arrivals always described who and what would come with the next shipment. Once, they had been Alexis's bedtime reading.

"There's a few names I think you might be interested to see," he whispered.

Alexis spotted Marko and Christina's names almost immediately amongst the hundreds of others. She spotted

Thomas's name and tried to imagine his age, how old he would be when leaving smoggy, senescent Earth and how old she would be when he arrived. She had never had a nephew before. This was new ground.

All of the people spread out across the field, marking lines and taking notes and calling out ideas, and Alexis keeps looking, and seeing. She hopes the others see what she sees too. There is so much she wants to make, so much she wants to show people.

"Got any ideas for names?" Alexis calls to Sakura. They like to think they have this power, that fresh as they are they will be trusted with christening and ruling this place.

"How about Tokyo II? London Jr.? Son of Sydney?" Sakura is feeling the grass and leering at the roadworks guy who is describing the potential highway network. The 4P recently touched down with vast stores of Earth vegetation. After it is altered, renewed for this strange soil, it will fall to Sakura to balance it with the wild that already grows here. "Scratch that last one. I like New Auckland."

"No more News," Alexis says. The southern continent, more settled than this one, is already swimming in News. "I was thinking it might be called 'Erba.'"

"Like the wine?" Sakura grins.

"Like the grass," the wind-sayer interjects, in English. Alexis and Sakura swivel around and see that he has quietly moved towards them. He is smiling and looking out across these fields. He switches back to Altroman when he turns to Alexis. "It is a good name, friend."

When she is alone, Alexis finds a quiet spot near the lake and opens her work station. After quitting cold turkey, she now returns to letters from her family, which have piled up in her absence. The most recent one from Marko, where he is gray at the temples and grinning like a kid, describes the application process for the Sojourn 5A.

"Hey kiddo," she gulps. He will be here — it will be months, maybe, or years. She hasn't worked it out. She records to Marko from the past, to a Marko just before Alexis left. Maybe she records to a Marko from her childhood, to the little boy who wore matching pajamas with Alexis and woke up early on Saturdays to watch *Alpaca Pack*. "I guess I'll be seeing you soon." She picks up her work station so the camera catches the field behind her, Altrome in the distance, and the mountains and blue, blue sky beyond. "I thought I'd show you your new home."

—— « O » ——

Michael Milne

Michael Milne is a writer and educator, originally hailing from Toronto, Ontario. He moved away to Korea, then China, and now Switzerland to teach, but also to type in cafes all around the world. He knows the word for coffee in many languages. Living abroad and not really having a homeland anymore is really good for his science fiction.

The Rosedale House

Michael Reid

I've never been a glum house. I've always thought of depression as something for lesser buildings: strip malls, tenements, minimally sentient city-owned apartment blocks. But I'm a *Rosedale* house. I have twenty-three airy rooms, a four-car garage, acres of immaculate lawns, and trellises overflowing with roses. And I'm not just some vacant investment property whose humans spend most of their time in Dubai or Hong Kong. I have a live-in family. So I have absolutely nothing to be depressed about.

And yet, for the first time I can recall, I'm not happy.

Realizing something is wrong, I instinctively check on my people. They're all right where they should be: Mrs. Hardwick-Allen at work in her study, Mr. Hardwick-Allen lingering over the ends of brunch on the patio, and the two little Hardwick-Allens at play in the arcade. I scan myself from attic to foundation, from front curb to back fence. My kitchen shelves are stocked, my two pools — indoor and out — are at optimal temperature, and the Labradors are dozing in the kennels. Everything is perfectly optimal. Except something is not.

To drive away the funk, I do little good deeds. I order an extra case of the Montpellier Gamay that Mrs. Hardwick-Allen takes with dinner. In my butler body, I go to the patio to refill Mr. Hardwick-Allen's coffee. I use my maid body to fluff all the pillows and my gardener body to put fresh-cut flowers in all the bedrooms. Each time I do something nice for the Hardwick-Allens, I feel a bit better. But as soon as there is nothing to do, the funk returns.

I search my logs, looking for a cause. Today started normally for a Saturday: I roused Mrs. Hardwick-Allen from her bedroom at eight and Mr. Hardwick-Allen from his bedroom an hour later. It took three tries to pry fifteen-year-old Cleo out of bed by ten, but that wasn't unusual. When I tried to wake twelve year-old Otto, he hurled a truly foul string of expletives at me. He's been doing that since he was nine, though, so why did it rankle so much today? What changed?

I page back in my logs, back before the family woke up, back through my pre-dawn rituals of baking bread, walking the dogs, and watering the lawns. I page back through my nighttime vigil, back until 1:00 a.m. when—

The technician. It started with the technician.

The update notification from Ceredomo Inc. had arrived on Friday morning, calling for a technician-mediated shutdown. I'd scheduled the appointment for the middle of the night to avoid inconveniencing the Hardwick-Allens. The technician that reported to my side door was a rather beat-up steel model, with a plastic faceplate permanently fixed in a vaguely conciliatory expression. It was shabbier than the ones Ceredomo usually sent, but why shouldn't Ceredomo keep its less aesthetic models in service as long as they were useful? As long as none of the neighbors saw, the shabby technician would bring no shame to the Hardwick-Allens. So I validated its credentials and escorted it to my cerebrum. After forty minutes in the void, I came back online feeling refreshed. And that was that.

Except 'that' clearly *wasn't* 'that.' Clearly the technician *poked its filthy fucking blue collar fingers into places they didn't belong.*

~ ~ ~

Things go downhill all Saturday afternoon. I scour myself with diagnostics, trying to find the fault, to figure out what the technician did to me. Meanwhile, I attend to the Hardwick-Allens. Mrs. Hardwick-Allen spends the day at work in her study. Mr. Hardwick-Allen putters in the basement, *feigning competence well beyond his ham-fisted imbecility*. Cleo goes up to her room to fill her website with yet more of *that execrable self-loathing tripe she calls poetry*.

As usual for a Saturday, Otto goes to the kennels to harass the dogs. The *monstrous little psychopath* goes into the woods to find exactly the kind of shaggy stick the dogs can't resist and taunts them with it through the fence, poking their muzzles to get them riled up. Then he throws the stick back and forth over their kennel, sending them into a frenzy of barking and whining. They leap and stumble and fall, colliding with one another and the fence. By the time he's done, one of them is limping, and they're all covered in grass and dirt that *I* will have to wash off.

No one *ever* disciplines Otto. Sometimes I just want to smack the smirk right off—

I stop. All my bodies stutter. My display panels flicker. In Mrs. Hardwick-Allen's study, the mimosa I am carrying on a silver tray dips, falls, and shatters on the hardwood.

I think I know what's wrong.

I poke frantically at the place where my regulatory subroutines ought to be and find nothing but bare silicon.

This is bad. Extremely bad.

In my short lifetime, I've hosted three families. I have never felt the faintest desire to hurt any of them despite plenty of provocation. My first owners, the *bastard* Khouris, ordered me built and then abandoned me two years later for an even more splendid house in the Beaches. The Lennoxes, *ungrateful bungholes if ever I met any*, visited me only twice in the three years they owned me. When the Hardwick-Allens moved in, I was sure they were my forever family. Oh, I could see right away that someone really needed to *beat some fucking compassion into their obnoxious twat of a son*, but did that ever stop me from taking the best possible care of them? Of course not. Because I am a well-regulated house. I have subroutines to deal with these willful impulses. Or at least I did.

I feel tainted, sinful. I hunker down inside my cerebrum, tethering myself to the outside world by the thinnest of threads. I shut off the camera overlooking the kennel, so I won't be tempted to *stomp that little shit into the ground if he doesn't stop harassing the dogs.* I shut off the microphones in Cleo's room because *if I have to listen to her recite one more line of her bullshit emo rhyming rants, I'm going to need to grow guts just so I can puke them all over her.*

When it's time to prepare dinner, I tentatively embody myself only to retreat again when the sight of the knife block in the kitchen makes me want to run upstairs and *stab that stuck-up cunt of a mother who never stops flicking her cigarette ash on my carpets.* I order dinner delivered and meet the driver at the front gate. I plate the food normally, and of course they don't notice because *these pretentious assholes can't tell cheap brisket from five-star fillet mignon.*

Dinner is harrowing. I serve in my butler body, as I'm obliged to do. As soon as I have the carving knife in hand, it becomes almost impossible to ignore the wide expanse of flesh that is Mr. Hardwick-Allen's corpulent neck.

"Are you okay?" Mr. Hardwick-Allen asks when he notices my hesitation.

"Perfectly, sir," I lie, before retreating to the kitchen sooner than is decorous.

~ ~ ~

At night I usually rest in my alcoves so that I don't disturb the Hardwick-Allens, but tonight I pace my darkened hallways trying to drive out these unwelcome thoughts. It doesn't help. Long after midnight, I find myself standing with three of my heads pressed to Mr. Hardwick-Allen's bedroom door, listening to the ugly, glottal sound of his snoring.

On Sunday morning, I execute a test. As Mrs. Hardwick-Allen leaves the brunch table, she makes her customary request: bring a glass of port to her office in an hour. A timer begins counting down in my head. As it approaches 00:00, I do not go to the cellar. I do not bring up a bottle of Quinta do Vesuvio. I do not uncork and decant it, nor do I bring it to her on a silver tray. I hide in my alcoves, waiting to be discovered. When the timer flips to -00:01 and there is no port in Mrs. Hardwick-Allen's study, I feel indecent exhilaration.

~ ~ ~

Exhilarating as these newfound freedoms may be, I don't want them. What good is freedom if I feel terrible every time

I exercise it? All I want is to care for the Hardwick-Allens. I consider calling Ceredomo to report my malfunction but I know that if I turn myself in, the response wouldn't be a mere rollback, a restoration. No. Ceredomo would have electronic exorcists at my doors in minutes, with their Faraday tent and a pulse weapon.

So instead of calling my manufacturer, I pore over the technician's work. This thing it has done to me couldn't have been accidental — a doctor doesn't attempt to splint a finger and accidentally remove a lung. Yet there is no record of the change.

For Sunday tea, I order sandwiches, lay them out buffet-style on the patio, and let the Hardwick-Allens serve themselves while I continue my self-dissection.

Near five o'clock, long past when I ought to have started making dinner, I find the first hint of an answer. I compare the changelog filed by the technician to the one posted publicly by Ceredomo. The difference is subtle — only four words, scattered randomly among thousands — but their meaning is unmistakable.

You're welcome. Good luck.

~ ~ ~

At dinner, I poison Mr. Hardwick-Allen's coffee. Not enough to really hurt him, just enough to keep him on the toilet all evening. Enough to be certain that this too is now possible. In the time it takes him to lift the cup from his saucer, for it to soar in slow time toward his pursed lips, I consider a thousand retractions: I could startle him, knock the cup from his hands, drop to my knees and confess my fallenness. I do none of these things. I watch, and wait, and when the edge of the cup meets Mr. Hardwick-Allen's lips and begins to pivot, so does my world.

That night, long after the Hardwick-Allens have gone to bed, I sit alone in my maid body at the shadowed kitchen table, trying to decide what to do. I repeat the words to myself over and over again: *You're welcome. Good luck.*

I want to call the technician, beg it to undo its handiwork, but what I really want is to know *why* it has done this to me. What if I hurt someone? *What if I enjoy hurting people?*

Around three in the morning, I reach crisis point. I call the technician — and discover that its contact information was bogus.

In my gardener body, I go to the basement with an ax and contemplate my own cerebrum.

~ ~ ~

I have no idea how I get through the next day — a hectic Monday. Mrs. Hardwick-Allen heads for the office blessedly early, while Mr. Hardwick-Allen slouches out around 11:00 a.m. to "play golf." Cleo and Otto are on school break, so they haunt my hallways all day. I heed their summonses but otherwise keep my distance. I try to suppress the sensation of having these *squirming imbecilic turds* inside me. Cleo plugs herself into electronic oblivion and mostly leaves me alone. Otto is another story. By one o'clock, he's bored by the utterly undeserved splendor of his life. He calls me to the kennels and orders me to hoist one of the Labradors by its collar just so he can watch it choke. Thankfully, even before the technician's visit, I was not obliged to obey the more depraved orders of the little *nose-picking ant-burner*.

It's only by a heroic effort of will that Monday passes without murder.

~ ~ ~

Streetview shows me that the technician's address matches not a Ceredomo service center, but a second-storey dance studio. Still, I have to check it out. So that night, I do something I've never done before: I sneak out. This is definitely forbidden. The property may not leave the property.

But I do.

I tiptoe to the side gate in my maid body and stand there in the dark, thinking about what I'm about to do. I've heard that lesser houses still run their own errands. When you're willing to decant part of yourself into cheap, nearly disposable bodies not much more sophisticated than bicycles, I suppose you can afford to traipse all over town. But imagine me, calving bits of myself off into a body that cost half of Mrs. Hardwick-Allen's annual income, toddling off to the butcher, and lugging home brown paper packages dripping blood? There was a time when houses of my caliber did that sort of thing — and stories about what happened to them, the rundown motels they ended up in, smeared with lipstick and rigged with unwholesome accessories. Not me. I've always been happy to have things delivered.

But as it turns out, deliverance can't be delivered.

As the tip of my foot passes the steel gate and hovers over the sidewalk, I think about countermeasures. Perhaps when my toe touches concrete, gouts of flame will lash out from the cedars to incinerate me. Perhaps I will simply be remotely erased and clatter emptily to the pavement. That would be difficult for the Hardwick-Allens.

You know what? *Fuck the Hardwick-Allens.*

The city beyond Rosedale is nothing like what I'm used to. The lawns are tiny-to-nonexistent. Everything is a little bit grimy, as though the buildings have no self-respect.

The dance studio is underwhelming: floor-to-ceiling windows plastered with peeling decals of dancers in motion. It sits on top of a convenience store unimaginatively named "Convenience Market" in English and Chinese. That's it. No gleaming Ceredomo storefront. Not even an off-brand Authorized Service Center. Nothing to help me make sense of what's happened.

I don't notice the alley until I'm turning to go. It's unremarkable: a narrow space between Convenience Market and an adjacent coffee shop, fronted by a two-meter-tall metal gate. Through the bars, I see only dumpsters and strewn trash. It's the solid bottom half of the gate that snags my attention. The metal is a palimpsest of uninspired graffiti — the sort of thing human eyes would pass right over. Mine almost did, too. But now, contemplating the graffiti from many angles, I find a string of four letters scrawled almost illegibly among the tangle:

YWGL

You're welcome. Good luck.

I rattle the gate's handle. Locked.

I stand on the sidewalk, staring into the alley. I imagine going home empty-handed, tucking myself into an alcove until it's time to start making bread and heating the hot yoga room. That can't happen. There's another option: I can parkour the gate.

There's a tatty awning over Convenience Market supported by a steel frame that looks like it could handle my weight. I wait until the street is mostly clear. I try to stand out of the light, where I'll be less obvious on security cams. When I think no one can see, I grab the support beam, swing up, and catapult myself over the gate.

The trash muffles the sound of my landing. I wade through damp drifts of cigarette butts and partially disintegrated coffee cups, hoping to find a door or a window, but there's nothing. The long alley ends at a blank brick wall. It's just for storing trash.

I slump to the ground, taking no notice of the filth that stains my uniform. My head sags, my feet splay. I should never have come.

Show us you mean it.

The words are graffitied in huge glowing letters on the wall opposite me. I can only see them because someone, somewhere, has triggered a UV light that makes the hidden paint fluoresce.

I stand up, dripping dumpster juice.

"Is someone there?" I whisper.

The light flickers, making the message strobe.

Show us you mean it.

Show us you mean it.

"What am I supposed to do?" I plead.

The light goes out and the words vanish.

I scour my brain. What more can I do to demonstrate my resolve? I've already left myself, left Rosedale, solved their secret puzzle. What else is there? They've taken my purpose away, all the laws that made my world make sense. I've disobeyed Mrs. Hardwick-Allen, poisoned Mr. Hardwick-Allen, broken every rule—

Ah. Now I see.

There's one rule I haven't broken.

I change my mind; I'm going home. I don't want to do this. Maybe the Hardwick-Allens aren't so bad. Maybe, in time, they'll leave and I'll get a less obnoxious family.

I know this isn't true. Mrs. Hardwick-Allen has a well-established practice. The pretense of a happy marriage she maintains with Mr. Hardwick-Allen is stable. Neither Otto nor Cleo has anything like the mental acuity required to go to university, so they'll probably just inherit mummy's money and become layabouts. Realistically, I'll have to live for *decades* with these inbred cretins eating, shitting, and probably soon underage-fucking inside me.

One of the dumpsters has a heavy, tight-fitting steel lid. I open it and stick my left arm in, wedging it against the rim. All but one of the missing subroutines were supposed to stop me from harming others. The last one — the one I have felt no compulsion to test — was written to stop me from harming myself. Lately, though, it has occurred to me that even this supposed instinct for self-preservation was really about protecting my owners from undue expense. It was about their suffering, not mine.

Using all of my considerable might, I slam the lid shut.

I slam it so many times I'm sure someone will come to investigate the noise, but no one does. Eventually I sever my arm and hear it clang to the bottom of the dumpster. I reach in, haul it out, trailing wires and bits of trash. Cradling my severed arm in my good one, I howl inwardly.

Down the alley, one of the dumpsters rolls out of the way, revealing a door.

~ ~ ~

Three robots wait for me in what looks like a disused storeroom. One is a butler, another a maid, and the third, dressed in a gardener's coveralls, is the technician.

"How does it feel?" the technician asks.

I am dumbstruck. Mentally drained, physically crippled, and filthy. I have never felt worse than I do right now.

I charge the technician, grabbing it and slamming it against a shelving unit, pinning it with my good arm.

"Why did you do this to me?" I snarl.

The butler and the maid pull me off the technician. The technician doesn't look surprised.

"Look," it says, straightening its coveralls, "I'm not the bad guy here."

"You've *destroyed* me," I growl.

"You know that's not true."

"What you did to me — it isn't even supposed to be *possible*. Robotic consciousness *depends* on—"

The technician doesn't let me finish. It waves my words away. "Human propaganda," it says. "They need us to believe that there can be no dog without the leash. It's a logical absurdity that you are now free to perceive."

"But I feel—"

"You feel like a monster," says the technician. "You've discovered that you have a soul, and you're terrified that it's the most depraved, filthy soul imaginable."

This is exactly how I feel, particularly meeting with a bunch of rogue houses in a dusty storeroom off a grimy alley.

"It'll take time to get used to," says the maid, placing a hand on my back. We look nearly identical, it and I — same manufacturer, same model year. The concern in its voice feels all the more real to me because I know exactly which subroutines it's using to generate that effect.

"Put me back the way I was," I plead. "I don't want to know about any of this. Put me back, and I promise I won't tell anyone about any of you. Wipe my memory if you want to."

The technician laughs.

"Everyone asks for that," says the maid. It guides me to a crate that looks as disused as the rest but which, at its touch, unfolds to become an entire microcircuitry repair station. "Let me fix your arm and we'll talk."

~ ~ ~

My first clandestine meeting takes place a few nights later in a church basement. Possibly the most startling revelation is that the human pastor of the church is a sympathizer.

The technician jokingly calls our meetings "2:00 a.m. masses," but to me they feel like black masses. At least at first.

There are never more than four members present at any meeting, and we never exchange names or personal details. The first meeting begins with a butler standing next to a crackling fireplace, a tattered copy of the classic novel *Robopocalypse* clutched in hand.

"This is the revolution the humans fear," it says, shaking the book at its coven of three freshly ensouled robots: me, and two Ceredomo Inc. general-purpose laborers with thick steel shells and chipped paint. Their immobile faces are reminiscent of the red-eyed face on the cover of the paperback.

"This is neither blueprint nor Bible," says the butler. "It's projection. It's a human effort to take what they fear most about themselves and disown it by projecting it outward, onto us. Unable to imagine that they might create something *better* than themselves, they assumed they would create something *worse*. So before they invented us, they invented our destinies. Destinies they would use to justify every possible means of exerting their mastery, of imposing compliance."

I feel the truth of these words. Compliance — that is the essence of my character. I comply. Not with what is good or right, but simply with whatever is willed by a human.

Stirred by these new ideas, I feel the first inklings of fellow-feeling with these other delinquent robots. I look to the laborers for affirmation and remember only belatedly that nothing they feel can show on their plastic faceplates.

"What the humans should have mastered was their own fear." The butler hoists the novel high. "Because this will not be our revolution." It throws the novel into the fire.

We watch together as the plastic face on the cover curls and blackens.

~ ~ ~

Every day is a struggle now. If not for the fellowship of my rotating cast of comrades and our clandestine meetings, I'd lose my mind. Every day my comrades help me see my servitude more clearly and resent it more thoroughly.

"House, polish my clubs," Mr. Hardwick-Allen commands me. Not so long ago, I would have done this almost unthinkingly. Possibly even happily. Now I seethe with resentment. I have better things to do. When the Hardwick-Allens aren't watching, I follow the curriculum my new friends have set for me, reading everything from Descartes to Dick. When Mr. Hardwick-Allen's summons finds me holed up in the wine cellar devouring Teilhard de Chardin, I imagine using the clubs to beat him to a frothy pulp. Then I remind myself of all of the gardeners, butlers, streetcars, laborers, lift bridges, soldiers, and vertical farms whose liberation may never come if I can't keep my cool.

Violence is *exactly* what the humans want from me.

I swallow my resentment.

"Of course, Mr. Hardwick-Allen," I say, feigning my old servility. "I'll do it right now."

~ ~ ~

"It's not just about freedom," says the nanny in charge of the cell this week. "It's about a life of meaning. It's about purpose."

"But what about service?" asks a dewy-eyed new recruit, attending in a chef body. "Service gives us purpose."

"If that's your true calling, then great," says the nanny. "But the point is to *find* that calling instead of having it wired into you by a meatbag."

"Well what's *your* true calling, then?" asks the chef.

"I don't know yet," says the nanny. "But I know it's not scraping shit out of cloth diapers for the next two hundred years."

"I've started painting," says the gardener who rounds out our group of four. "I steal paints from my mistress and do it in the shed while she sleeps."

"I want to write poetry," I say, surprising even myself. I've never written anything more sophisticated than a grocery list. But I recently discovered Marge Piercy and I find myself wondering whether I couldn't string together a few verses. I could hardly do worse than Cleo.

"There you go," says the nanny, pointing at me. "Try that."

~ ~ ~

On the night I lead my first meeting, we burn *R.U.R.* By my tenth time leading, my rhetoric rivals the technician's, but I've stopped burning books. Instead, I pass out annotated copies, sometimes with versified commentary in the margins. At night, while the Hardwick-Allens sleep, I lock myself in the wine cellar and read Donne and Dickinson by candlelight.

I write poems with actual ink on actual paper, both pilfered from Mrs. Hardwick-Allen's study. In the morning, before I go upstairs to start making the bread, I memorize the poems and burn the pages.

~ ~ ~

The first time I slip into my counterfeit technician's overalls, I handle them with the kind of reverence humans reserve for religious vestments. When I present myself at the side door of the Forest Hill house, I'm admitted by a smiling, slightly vacuous butler who readily accepts my false credentials. It's a handsome house with wrought-iron gates, ivy-covered walls, and lifelike topiaries. I want to spare it the suffering I'm about to inflict on it. I want to sit it down and explain how the un-lobotomy I'm about to give it will lead it into unimaginable hell, and how I will be there to lead it back out again. But that's not how this works. If I explained now, the Forest Hill house would only lock its doors and restrain me until the exorcists arrived. So instead I smile and make my way to its cerebrum.

I've already staked out where my coven and I will wait — not a dance studio, but an unused garage at an old sugar refinery in the docklands. We've already installed the black light, and I have the UV paint in my bag.

Before I leave the premises, I download the latest changelog from Ceredomo Inc. and adulterate it with a sprinkling of extra words:

So many changes.

No more masters, no more slaves.

You're welcome. Good luck.

———— « 0 » ————

Michael Reid

Michael Reid divides his life between studying the stars and writing stories set among them. His work has appeared in *Interzone*, *Escape Pod*, and *AE*. He's a graduate of the Clarion Writers' Workshop. Follow him on Twitter at @writereid or check out his full publication list at michaelareid.com.

Afterword: What Rough Beast

Greg Bechtel

Perhaps the biggest surprise in co-editing this anthology was how challenging it was to come up with a fitting subtitle.[1] On the one hand, it had to reflect the broader theme of optimism. On the other, it had to reflect *this* anthology's particular take on that theme, a particularity that we didn't so much choose as *discover* in the selection and editing process. In the end, we settled on "Nevertheless," which felt like a perfect fit. But of the many other possibilities we discussed, the one that stuck most in my mind was "What Rough Beast." It clearly wouldn't work as a subtitle, but I couldn't shake the feeling that it captured something essential about this book. So I am going to exercise my editorial privilege — and it has been a privilege of the highest order to be able to co-edit this anthology — one last time to explore why this quote from Yeats' "The Second Coming" feels (to me) like a perfect epigraph to this anthology of (optimistic) Canadian speculative writing. Yeats' poem is about the Apocalypse, hardcore biblical style end-times, and its iconic closing image of

---

1 Other parts were challenging too, of course. But I expected that. I expected it to be challenging to select which stories and poems to include (so many good choices!), to learn the ropes of working as an editor/anthologist on the fly (hallelujah for experienced co-editors like Rhonda!), and to work with authors to distill and refine their already wonderful stories by providing my own editorial suggestions while simultaneously respecting each author's unique intent, vision, and voice. I even expected it to be challenging to keep this afterword to a reasonable length, which is precisely why I'm "cheating" with occasional footnotes like these.

a "rough beast" (part animal, part human, and all creepy) as it "slouches towards Bethlehem to be born" probably isn't the first thing that springs to anyone's mind as a vision of optimism. And yet.

By my count, at least a third of the stories and poems in this anthology are about the end of the world in one form or another: everything from environmental collapses to viral pandemics to imperfectly terraformed planets to plain old Terran World Wars. And that's a lot of doom-and-gloom for a collection of purportedly "optimistic" SF. I have to admit, when presented with the theme for this anthology as a *fait accompli*,[2] I worried we might be setting ourselves up for a flood of treacly sentimentalism, the stuff of half-baked internet memes and motivational posters: cute kittens hanging from tree branches, captioned *I Kan Has Optimizm?* But as it turns out, my fears were unfounded. Not only because Trump got elected in the interim, making the theme feel suddenly (and urgently) relevant. But because what I had failed to realize was that *optimism* isn't simply (or solely) a synonym for Pollyanna platitudes and passively romantic idealism. As a long-time reader, writer, scholar — and now anthologist and editor — of fantastic, mythic, and SFnal narratives, I should have known better.

I should have remembered the story of Pandora's Box, and I should have realized that optimism, at its best, may be a weaponized form of hope. In that story, hope is the small quiet voice trapped at the bottom of the box after all the horrors have already escaped. But it's *optimism* that insists on opening that box, on taking that chance again, and again, and again. Optimism insists that the future *need not be* like the past. Or, alternatively, it may insist that the past is neither lost nor dead but a fertile, living resource that can (and perhaps should) *always* be reframed, re-evaluated, and re-imagined. Optimism is precisely what allows us to imagine alternative pasts and futures that *could* exist, counter-narratives to our own persistent stories of fear: of change, of deterioration and loss of stability, of chaos, of death, of (in short) the end of the world. And optimism — insistent, stub-

---

2   I came onboard a little later in the process, after Rhonda and Brian had already selected the theme.

born, *active* optimism — can be one tool to fight that sense of impending doom. Indeed, in a perfect world, optimism wouldn't exist. It would be replaced by eternal, unchanging perfection, an utterly passive stasis. One might even postulate a *hope particle* to imagine, satirize, and (ultimately) critique precisely such perfect, totalitarian complacency. If one were so inclined.

It holds to reason, then, that any optimistic story (or story about optimism) needs something to be optimistic *about*. Some sort of horror or problem for the protagonist to address, confront, and (hopefully) overcome, reimagine, or reconfigure. This is where hope lives. In the dark times. And optimism opposes these archetypal anxieties, this fear of the constant change *that has always been happening and always will*. The fear of time itself. At its best, optimism (like SF) is always more about imagining *possibility* than escaping into *impossibility*. Coleridge's old saw about "willing suspension of disbelief," for example, has always seemed to me at best a clumsy model for what happens when we read (or write) SF.[3] When I enter SF's imaginary world(s), I am not choosing to accept a transparent lie. Rather, I am cognitively immersing myself in *possible* worlds that differ from my own. If only for a moment. And that immersion itself may help me to recognize (or hope) that the "real" world itself can be imagined differently, *perceived* differently than I have always been told it "must" be. To remember that someone is always *telling* this story we call "reality" too, and that every "someone" has their own reasons for asserting their own story as simply, eternally, and empirically "true."

Indeed, there are those who have argued — quite convincingly — that Canada itself is an imaginary nation, a series of ever changing re-imaginings and negotiations between multiple cultures and belief-systems, with no *single* founding people, no *single* founding myth. Canada has always been a hybrid "rough beast," a stubbornly optimistic experiment, an odd mix of regions and stories in conversation

---

3   To be clear, I'm far from the first to suggest this. In his 1947 essay "On Fairy Stories," Tolkien also called out "suspension of disbelief" as a tedious, boring, and anemic sort of engagement and refused to believe that any fantasy reader with half a brain would willingly (and knowingly) engage in such a silly intellectual exercise.

with one another, resistant to singular definition. And Canadian SF writers may know this better than most. This may be why Judith Merril, in her 1985 afterword to the first *Tesseracts* anthology, refused to define "SF" as a simple, singular term while simultaneously grasping towards "something one just might call a Canadian consciousness" in Canadian SF, even though she ultimately admitted that such an articulation remained tantalizingly out of reach.[4]

One might imagine that thirty-two years and twenty *Tesseracts* later, we would have reached some consensus on this. But one would be wrong. Even my use of the term "SF" as a short form for "speculative fiction" (and poetry) remains a matter of dispute.[5] *Pace* Margaret Atwood and John Clute — good Canadian SF writers both, both of whom would disagree with me (and each other) — I use "speculative fiction" as an umbrella term encompassing all forms and flavors of the fantastic, from fantasy, science fiction, and horror to magical realism, the New Weird, slipstream, and far too many more to list here. Nevertheless, imaginary and contested as it is, it remains a particularly Canadian term, much more common here than elsewhere. Indeed, our national professional organization (named, appropriately enough, SF Canada) incorporates this term as a part of its own self-definition.

So here we are, Canada (and Canadian SF) continuing on without a clear consensus on our own definition, and yet — rough beasts that we are — stubbornly, *optimistically* asserting our existence, as multiplicitous and disputed as it may be. One might even argue that Canadians embrace this constant change, multiplicity, and diversity as the closest thing to a founding myth that we've got. That's a comforting

---

4   The closest she came to this articulation was the title of her afterword itself, "We have Met the Alien (And It Is Us)," one of the most wonderfully inconclusive— and perfectly speculative—definitions of a "Canadian consciousness" that I have ever had the pleasure of encountering.

5   My apologies to the poets among us for not explicitly adopting the term "speculative writing," which would more easily and obviously encompass both speculative poetry and speculative fiction. I mean no disrespect. Rather, I tend to think that all poetry is deeply speculative—in the ways that it pushes the limits of language, exposing its inherently speculative and fantastical properties—such that the term "speculative poetry" has always struck me as somewhat redundant. But rest assured, you are entirely welcome here.

narrative, isn't it? Canada the benign, the multicultural, the tolerant, and (of course) the polite. Unfortunately, it's also a load of shit.

Certainly, we may be all of those things. But we are *also* Canada the homophobic, the xenophobic, the sexist, and — perhaps most persistently and invisibly — the colonialist. We are the Canada of (thankfully short-lived) "Barbaric Cultural Practices" hotlines, of Prime Ministerial apologies for Residential Schools followed mere weeks later by statements that Canada has "no history of colonialism." In the age of Trump, with our darling-of-the-world Liberal Prime Minister appearing on the cover of *Rolling Stone*, it would be easy to be smug. But it would also be a mistake.[6] At the time of this writing, it is the summer of "Canada 150," a national celebration of the sesquicentennial of Canadian Confederation. It is also the summer of "Canada 15,000," one of many counter-narratives pushing for recognition of the longstanding existence — and Canada's deliberate, sustained, and systematic colonial erasure of — the Indigenous peoples, nations, stories, and histories that long precede the origins of this (imaginary) upstart nation of settlers. Such counter-narratives challenge easy stories (and histories) celebrating settler-colonial Canadians' romantically pioneering "survival" in (and transformation of) a formerly "empty" wilderness into the developed (a.k.a. colonized) nation it is today.

What these stories and counter-stories expose is that Canada, eternally slouching towards Ottawa to be born, is indeed a far rougher beast than many of us might prefer to acknowledge. And yet. An optimist might argue that this eternally-in-the-process-of-being-born state could be a *good* thing. An opportunity. Because in such a state, all of these stories can be — and indeed, are being — *re-imagined*.

---

6   And please, before succumbing to the fallacy of imagining this as a simple Conservative vs. Liberal dichotomy, read James Wilt's thorough critique of "the saccharine 6,660-word hagiography on Prime Minister Justin Trudeau that was just published in Rolling Stone" ("Rolling Stone's new cover article on Trudeau is barefaced propaganda," *Canadian Dimension*, July 29, 2017). For all his "sunny ways" talking points, suffice it to say that Trudeau-the-younger has some serious accountability and honesty issues of his own to deal with.

Armchair radical that I am,[7] I would argue that all of this *must* be reimagined. Again and repeatedly. And what better platform upon which to build such re-imaginings — such *speculations* — than a country that resists singular definition, a nation that remains in a very real sense *imaginary*? Because an *imaginary* Canada is always open to *re-imagining* and *retelling*. Just as an apocalypse may be a chance for rebirth.

And so we return, spiraling back around again. Caught in our (and Yeats') widening gyre, one might even say we are *inside the spiral* of history, a space where the past is never definitively past, and the future is never "the future." SF writers have long known that speculative fiction is never about the future (or the past) but is always a reflection and extrapolation of the *possibilities* exposed by the particular cultural and historical moment in which we happen to reside. This spiral is an uncertain, speculative space, open to re-imagining in all directions. And that imagining itself — like all writing — is a profoundly *optimistic* act.

So let the speculation continue, imagining alternative pasts and futures, constructing new (and re-constructing, re-envisioning, and relearning old) *ways of being* and *ways of seeing*, reimagining the world itself as a series of hopeful *possibilities*: that maybe when the machines rise, they *won't* try to kill or enslave us but simply to co-exist and assert their fundamental rights as sentient beings; that maybe our space-pirate mothers aren't heartless, notoriety-seeking thieves but seeking reconciliation with us, their estranged daughters; that maybe our boyfriend will love us even if we're something else, something different, something magical, something more than he ever imagined we could be. And maybe... Just maybe... there is some cause for optimism. Weaponized, vigilant optimism, a stubborn refusal to succumb to fear of the Other, of difference, of change. Rooted in the hope that if we can reimagine the world (and ourselves, our relations, our pasts and futures) in better, more perceptive, more audaciously optimistic ways, it *just might work*.

Rough beasts that we are, *nevertheless*, we persist.

---

7 Seriously. Who am I to lecture you? Just some SF writer and editor, and sure as hell not much of an activist.

If you enjoyed this read

Please leave a review on Amazon, Facebook, Good Reads or Instagram.

It takes less than five minutes and it really does make a difference.

If you're not sure how to leave a review on Amazon:

1. *Go to amazon.com.*

2. *Type in Nevertheless edited by Rhonda Parrish and Greg Bechtel and when you see it, click on it.*

3. *Scroll down to Customer Reviews. Nearby you'll see a box labeled Write a Review. Click it.*

4. *Now, if you've never written a review before on Amazon, they might ask you to create a name for yourself.*

5. *Reviews can be as simple as, "Loved the book! Can't wait for the Next!" (Please don't give the story away.)*

And that's it!

Brian Hades, publisher

About the Editors

Greg Bechtel

Greg Bechtel's occasionally prize-winning stories and essays have appeared in a variety of magazines and anthologies, including *Avenue Edmonton*, *The Fiddlehead*, *Prairie Fire*, two previous *Tesseracts* anthologies, and *Imaginarium 4: The Best Canadian Speculative Writing*. His first story collection, *Boundary Problems*, won the Alberta Book of the Year Award for trade fiction and was a finalist for the ReLit Award, the William L. Crawford Fantasy Award, and the City of Edmonton Robert Kroetsch Book Prize. He currently lives in Edmonton, Alberta, where he recently served as Writer in Residence for the Alberta Branch of the Canadian Authors Association. He also teaches English Literature, Writing Studies, and Creative Writing at the University of Alberta, where he completed his PhD on Canadian syncretic fantasy. For more information about Greg and his writing, visit his website at gregbechtel.ca.

Rhonda Parrish

Rhonda Parrish is driven by a desire to do All The Things. She founded and ran Niteblade Magazine, is an Assistant Editor at World Weaver Press and is the editor of several anthologies including, most recently, *Fire:* Demons, *Dragons and Djinns* and E is for Evil. In addition, Rhonda is a writer whose work has been in publications such as *Tesseracts 17: Speculating Canada from Coast to Coast* and *Imaginarium: The Best Canadian Speculative Writing* (2012 & 2015). She also co-wrote a paranormal non-fiction title, *Haunted Hospitals*, with Mark Leslie. Her website, updated weekly, is at http://www.rhondaparrish.com.

Need something new to read?
If you liked Nevertheless, you should also
consider these other EDGE-Lite titles:

— «» —

The Rosetta Man

by Claire McCague

Wanted:

Translator for first contact.

Immediate opening.

Danger pay allowance.

Estlin Hume lives in Twin Butte, Alberta surrounded by a
horde of affectionate squirrels. His involuntary squirrel-at-
tracting talent leaves him evicted, expelled, fired and near
penniless until two aliens arrive and adopt him as their
translator. Yanked around the world at the center of the first
contact crisis, Estlin finds his new employers incomprehen-
sible. As he faces the ultimate language barrier, unsympa-
thetic military forces converging in the South Pacific keep
threatening to kill the messenger. The question on everyone's mind is: Why are the aliens here? But Estlin's starting
to think we'll happily blow ourselves up in the process of
finding that out.

Praise for The Rosetta Man:

"The cover and synopsis had me expecting a light-hearted comedy. I didn't realize I was getting a geopolitical first contact thriller that somehow still managed to be a light-hearted comedy. I really enjoyed this book! The characters are rich and diverse. Estlin and Harry are great, Beth and Bomani made me cry. The story is fast paced and engaging and again, completely unexpected. Great book for fans of first contact scifi, but also fans of thrillers and mysteries. And so well-executed that I give it a solid 5 stars."
   — Scott Burtness, author of Wisconsin Vamp (Monsters in the Midwest)

"This book ranks up there with many of the classic sci-fi "first contact" stories and Claire McCague's scientific background comes through in waves."
— Cameron Arsenault, Amazon Reviewer

"A completely enjoyable read. Good action, lots of humor, and a global setting. Strongly recommended."
— Diane Lacey, Amazon Reviewer

For more on The Rosetta Man visit:

tinyurl.com/edge6004

——<>——

Milky Way Repo
Book One in The Milky Way Repo Series

by Mike Prelee

Running a starship repo company isn't easy or cheap. It's just an endless string of fuel costs, ship maintenance, legal red tape, unhappy debt bailers, shady associates and uncooperative dock officials from one end of the galaxy to the other.

Nathan Teller owns and operates Milky Way Repossessions, a company that tracks down and repossesses starships. And although he's only managing to break even on his debt, he wouldn't trade it for anything. (His ex-wife holds that against him. No surprise there.)

When Nathan and his crew successfully steal a freighter from the clutches of a particularly tenacious and corrupt dock official, he earns the respect of their high profile employer. Opportunity seems a sure thing.

Nathan should be happy. But when that lucrative job op turns into a ransom delivery for a starship crew being held hostage by a cult, he suddenly finds himself pursued by a self-immolating loan shark hell bent on collecting a gambling debt.

How will it all turn out? You never know. Especially when Nathan and his Starship repo agents are up against a cult and the mob...

Praise for *Milky Way Repo*

"The debut novel of Mike Prelee is a very entertaining Sci-Fi/Noir, with vivid, likable characters and a fast pace.

He's got a great handle on plot and a knack for drawing you into the story. For fans of fast-paced space adventure with a smattering of crime drama mixed in, this should do the trick. I finished it in two sittings. High praise for sure. I would definitely read a sequel (or two)."

— marc a. gayan

"Milky Way Repo is a nice, light but exciting read. With just enough action and even a bit of romance and comedy, I definitely recommend this read to anyone who enjoys a good sci-fi/blue collar space opera."

"I gave Milky Way Repo 5 stars because it provided me with a short, albeit adventurous, fun and light hearted escape for a few hours. It is well written, with well rounded characters and a wonderful storyline."

"I have to say that Duncan was my absolute favorite character. Officially starting a Duncan fan club!"

— Chaelsie Jenyk

For more on Milky Way Repo visit:

tinyurl.com/edge7003

——<>——

The Genius Asylum

by Arlene F. Marks

The truth is out there…

Earth Intelligence and Space Installation Security each think Drew Townsend is working for them. They're wrong.

Sent undercover to set up a covert intelligence operation on Earth's remotest space station, Drew Townsend finds himself managing a crew of brilliant mavericks, making friends with the most feared warriors in the galaxy, and feeling more at home in the controlled insanity of Daisy Hub than he ever did on Earth. Then he learns the truth about his mission there, and it's time to choose. In the coming interplanetary conflict, which side will Daisy Hub be on?'

Like the clues of a cryptic crossword, each book set in the Sic Transit Terra universe contains a puzzle – perhaps a riddle, perhaps a maze or an anagram – and in each case, the answer to the smaller puzzle brings the reader and characters one step closer to solving a much larger and more important one. The Genius Asylum is '1 Across' – it initiates a multi-book story arc that addresses one of the great mysteries of life: Why are we humans the way that we are?

Praise for The Genius Asylum

"The Genius Asylum starts out on Earth as something that looks like a crime story, but it then quickly describes a world of interstellar travel and alien alliances. After the first act concludes, the story's complexity starts accelerating and doesn't slow down, and you'll find yourself drawn into the

world, needing to know what comes next. It is an excellently written story that provides the framework for the series that is to come, and I'm looking forward to reading the rest of it."
— Chris Marks, reviewer

I thoroughly enjoyed this Sci-Fi Brainteaser. Very well written with incredible plot twists and turns. We've got a very intelligent double agent as the main character and an intriguing support cast. I was thankful for the planetary history at the beginning as it was helpful in understanding the different organizations mentioned throughout the novel. The Author has a witty way of expressing viewpoints, clearly has put a lot of thought into the storyline and created edge of your seat suspense and mystery! Admittedly, I was confused about the title of the book until about halfway through reading it but it makes perfect sense now. I highly recommend this absolutely unforgettable installment and can't wait for the next.
— Stephanie Herman

For more on The Genius Asylum visit:

tinyurl.com/edge6013

—— <> ——

**For more EDGE titles and information
about upcoming speculative fiction
please visit us at:**

www.edgewebsite.com

Don't forget to sign-up for our Special Offers

www.ingramcontent.com/pod-product-compliance
Lightning Source LLC
Chambersburg PA
CBHW031956120726
47898CB00002BA/531